Satan's Laugh

Peter Johnson

Published in the United States by:

Curious Minds Classroom, LLC.
PO Box 551, Paradise, UT 84328
https://www.curiousmindsclassroom.com

First Edition
ISBN 979-8-9853374-0-2

To my brothers in arms
And their families
Who have borne the burden
Of politicians' folly

Contents

Prologue

Hateful things in human thought
Twisted minds this sin have brought
Barking dogs pull at the chain
Howling shrieks and moans of pain
Mothers weep and infants cry
Above the gate - ARBEIT MACHT FREI
Shuffling feet of broken hearts
Pause for families torn apart
Wives and children stripped away
Screams and cries that cannot sway

One by one sent there and here
For some the end is very near
While others hear the orders barked
For brutal labor they were marked
The crack of whips and thud of fist
The whimpered hope you're on the list
Yet labor's toil halts not the end
It just delays the captive's friend
Released as smoke to float away
To rest in peace 'till judgment day

The aircraft's roar makes rain of steel
The rumbling tank with squeaking wheel
The cannon's bark and tongue of flame
Cackling guns no man can tame
Hateful shouts dehumanize
All morals lost to human eyes

Torture, torment, words of hate
Pain designed to grind and grate

Little children weaponized
With vacant stares and hollow eyes
Mothers, fathers, infants, kids
Thrashed and killed as leader bids
Allah's name they shout aloud
And purify by purge the town
They claim to be God's army true
Do horrid things no saint could do

Hate and malice, selfishness
Idols finely shaped and dressed
Lure, distract and lead away
Those who stumble on their way
To wanton riot, heinous deeds
Anything to feed their greed
Shattered lives and broken dreams
Whimpered cries and shouted screams
Calls for vengeance swift and sure
Find neither answer nor the cure

These horrid sounds assault the ears
Tender hearts sprout monstrous tears
But hardened souls cannot be moved
Though hell itself their deeds reprove
Rumbling, thundering waves of sound
O'er the earth reverb, rebound
Satan's laugh with mortal voice
Cackling glee at human's choice
"Oh what fools these mortal souls
who let me in to take control"

Chapter 1

Packing Up

He sat on the edge of his cot, rifling through the papers that had been collecting in the small corner of the hooch he used as an office. Reports, maps, dossiers, printed emails... worthless – all of it. As he worked through a drawer full of folders, only glancing at one after another before adding the contents to a growing pile, he paused on a rather thin one and pulled out the few papers that were inside. These he would keep, nothing else. Setting them aside, he grabbed the rest in single motion and threw them down on the disordered pile without inspecting the contents. He felt an intense desire to burn the few he'd held back, but they were necessary until he had processed out of country.

Having found what he needed, he glanced at the pile, contemplating the wasted work it represented. There, at the top of the stack, a particularly hated memo was peeking out of a plain manila folder. He held it up, staring at it briefly before violently tearing at it with his bare hands as if by doing so he could tear the soul out of the author. The sound of the shredding paper, however, was completely drowned out by a stream of profane curses pronounced against the system that could ruin someone with nothing more than a paragraph of bureaucratic bullshit. When the largest fragments of paper were too small to reduce further, he slowly regained his composure and proceeded to collect every individual piece that had scattered across the floor. One by one, he deliberately picked them up, added them to the remainder already held in his fist, and crushed them together into a wad until his forearm and fist trembled with the exertion. This paper, he resolved, would be the first to go in the burn barrel.

───────────────

"Major Harwood," SSgt[1] Meyers said, standing on her tiptoes so she could just peek over the cubical wall.

"Yeah?" Jim asked without looking away from the report he was desperately trying to finish before calling it a day. He had been staying late for the last week in order to wrap this project up. It was his first formal product since checking into the unit, and he wanted it to make a good impression. The thought of it hanging over his head for a three-day weekend was too much to bear, so it had to be done this afternoon. He had also promised Leslie that he was hers for the full three days, starting with dinner at her favorite restaurant later that night.

"The colonel needs to see you."

"Coming," he said, saving his work then standing and stretching his back. "I probably need to step away from this for a minute anyway."

He followed her to the colonel's office. The boss, standing in the doorway waiting, motioned for him to enter and gently pushed the door shut with his foot after they had both crossed the threshold. The grim look on the colonel's face didn't bode well, but racking his brain didn't result in any kind of explanation for the unusual behavior.

"I debated holding off until after the weekend," the colonel started, "but I think you'll need all the time you can get to make arrangements."

Jim stared blankly, trying to figure out what on earth he'd need the weekend for that could possibly involve the boss. All he could manage was a quizzical, "Sir?"

"You've been tapped for a short-notice deployment. Came down this afternoon."

Jim felt the weight of every book, plaque, trinket, piece of furniture, and other movable object in the office come crushing down on his heart and lungs. He'd been non-deployable for years due to the nature of his previous assignments, and knew that he was due. However, he had hoped for a bit more than the minimum 45 days on-station prescribed by policy. They'd only just found and moved into a rental that Friday and boxes were still stacked everywhere waiting to be unpacked.

"You've got two weeks until you need to report for training," the colonel said as he handed Jim a manila folder that apparently contained information about the deployment. "Don't bother with any more work here. Get going with outprocessing and spend the rest of the time with your family."

"Yes sir. I'll start making arrangements," was all the reply he could manage.

He turned and left the office, walked back to his desk, and flipped through the paperwork. Checklists, training requirements and dates, and a letter from the CENTCOM J3.[2] As was his custom, he glanced at the letter in its entirety looking for anything significant in the structure. Immediately a few features caught his eye. First, it was a scan of another document. The general had personally lined through the traditional introductory "Major Harwood" and written "Dear Jim" in ink above it. This kind of personal touch was usually reserved for congratulatory notes on birthdays and such. It was also wet-signed in blue ink and dated by hand with the same pen only the day prior. This was a rather marked deviation from the much more ubiquitous and impersonal digital signature the DoD[3] had been adopting for everything.

This whole thing felt funny. As far as he'd ever seen, deployment taskings didn't come in a manila folder, generally requested a generic capability instead of targeting any specific individual, and weren't lavished with personal attention from one of the busiest generals in the DoD. He turned back to the papers that described the scheduled training and started scanning the familiar format looking for the few bits of real information buried in bureaucratic formality. Defensive driving, two different urban combat and small-team tactics schools, three months at DLI[4] learning Arabic, SERE[5] training. This list was significant and disturbing given his background and the associated role guys like him typically played in a combat environment.

Having completed this exercise, he returned to the letter and read through its contents carefully. It described an experimental program designed to break down al-Qaida by embedding analysts like him with special operations teams. It was supposed to shorten the analysis timelines and get inside the enemy's OODA-loop – there was a term he hadn't heard in a while... "Observe, Orient, Decide, Act." Whoever wrote this had been around a while. Boyd's work hadn't been all that popular in military culture for years. In fact, the last time he'd seen that term he was still in ROTC.[6] This brain-child may actually have come from the general himself.

He had been individually selected for this assignment, the note said, because of his experience and demonstrated prowess at tracking and analyzing the clan structure and tribal alliances in the specific region where he was being assigned. That meant Iraq, almost certainly Al Anbar, and probably Ramadi. There weren't any worse places at the moment. If there was going to be a major firefight and significant casualties on any given day, the odds were pretty good it would be there.

He had spent the last five years since 9/11 becoming the Defense Intelligence Agency's top expert on the people of that region, and had made a name for himself almost by accident. He was supposed to be a Korea expert when he checked into his unit, but there wasn't much new to do on that front so he'd branched out to keep himself entertained. When the Pentagon began seriously prepping for the invasion he had been asked to present some of his analysis to a small group. One of those in the room at the time owned the signature on this letter. He'd been specifically tasked, by name, by someone almost nobody could refuse.

While this information explained why the Boss hadn't tried to reclama[7] and keep him home a little longer, it really didn't make him feel any better. He was going to leave his wife and daughter to fend for themselves for almost six months of training followed by another six months of deployment. The previous year had left them all fragile, and now, when things had finally begun to settle down, he would be leaving them alone in a new city far away from friends, family, and help. Why couldn't they have at least told him before they moved? He could have left them in Virginia where they had a functioning support network.

The extensive list of pre-deployment training was highly unusual too. Staff weenies working in Qatar or even Baghdad and Ramadi didn't need that kind of training. He briefly toyed with the idea of hiding the nature of the deployment from Leslie under the formalism offered him by the "data masked" location, but he quickly put that thought aside. He knew she needed to know the full truth, and would find out eventually regardless. However, knowing he had to tell her wasn't enough to guide him on how to do it. How could he break this kind of news to her given what they'd just been through? He dropped the folder on his desk and walked dejectedly out of the office.

He watched as the flames devoured the handful of paper scraps, feeling some of the anger float away with the ashes that rose on the hot air. When nothing recognizable remained but a few feathery pieces of glowing ash, he stepped back to his hooch and the pile waiting for him there. Looking at it – the product of nearly four months of hard work – he concluded again that it was utterly useless. Everything had been digitized, making paper superfluous. Even in digital form, he was convinced, it had no real value to anyone outside this God-forsaken environment. Yet white sheets bleeding with black and blue ink or printer toner had been piling up since he got here. These endless reams of paper were his business – what a waste. He grabbed the whole stack, walked it outside, threw it in the fire, and started to turn his back on it before the first sheets had caught. Out of the corner of his eye, though, he caught sight of one paper he hadn't intended to include. It was a simple sheet of copy paper, but instead of toner from the printer or ink from his pen it was decorated with crayon.

In a silent panic, he plunged his hand into the barrel and retrieved the errant page, dropped it on the ground, and quickly but carefully pushed sand over it with the toe of his boot to extinguish the flames that were curling the blackened edges. Even in the putrid air that seemed to fill this place, he could smell the acrid stench of singed hair, and looked briefly at his now bald hand and fore-arm. It would burn for a few days, but what did that matter? Retrieving the paper from the sand, he looked at the damaged artwork and raged within himself over his lack of attention and the near loss of so precious an artifact.

"Hey Boss, we're done unloading. Mail came in too."

"Anything interesting?" Leslie had told him she had sent a care package a few weeks ago, but he'd almost given up on ever getting it. Deliveries to these small outposts could be erratic at times.

"Not for me, but looks like yours is here," he said, tossing the package to Jim before ducking out to let him open it alone.

He paused for a few moments, looking closely at the curved and neat handwriting on the label. He sniffed the box, hoping without reason to smell something other than the world around him. Having completed these rituals, he pulled out a pocket knife and carefully sliced through the packing tape. He set the knife down and gently unfolded the cardboard flaps to expose the inside. On the top of the open box sat an envelope that was decorated with large hand-drawn and lop-sided hearts and addressed in purple crayon by an unmistakable and very young hand. He'd start there. He again picked up the knife and inserted its blade into the envelope, cutting a clean slice down its spine. As he lifted the enclosed paper free of its wrapper, a ridiculous amount of red, sliver, and pink glitter spilled out, covering both his uniform and the floor of his hooch.

Shrugging off the almost impossible to clean up mess, he turned to the letter. The team would never let him live down the glitter no matter how hard he tried to clean it off, so why bother? On the front of the paper was a highly embellished stick figure unicorn, what looked like a smiling dog – probably their German shepherd Lola – and several brightly colored butterflies framing a few words written in a rainbow mixture of crayons – "Dad, I love you. Please don't die."

He initially grinned at the simplicity of a six year old, then turned the paper over to read the few lines penned much more neatly on the back. "The magic of the unicorn is supposed to keep you safe, and Lola is there to protect you. The butterflies are just because they're pretty." Before looking at the rest of the package contents, he walked to the wall of his hooch and hung the paper proudly on the wall. Standing there looking at his new protectors, it sank in just how much was contained in that simple picture. Sammie was worried. She knew he was in danger, and didn't know how else to express it other than to call on the only magic she understood. How do you console a child who barely knows how to share their grief and anxiety? Plumbing his feelings and experiences, he came up dry; so he turned to Leslie's letter hoping for something else to brighten his day.

His hands trembling with a mixture of eagerness and fear,

he opened the envelope and began to read. In the opening passages, Leslie included the traditional declarations of love and longing. It always made Jim smile to read these. She was a marvelous woman, and he missed her intensely. She then addressed typical business items like doctors appointments, activities at church, and news from family members. His spirits started to droop as he realized what wasn't included. It didn't look like it would be included. He read on hoping he was wrong until coming to the end without satisfaction. She had said nothing about how she was doing. Nothing about how she was adapting. Nothing about how she felt beyond wanting him to return home safely. The nothing spoke volumes.

Jim looked at the pile of uniforms and other stuff now piled on his cot, contemplating just stuffing them randomly into the duffel bag instead of neatly folding and organizing them. They all would be trashed when he got home anyway, and he wasn't all that sure why it made sense to drag them that far. None of that mattered, though. After briefly stuffing a few items haphazardly into the bag, he reversed course and decided it would be easier to get everything in if it were neatly done. He then emptied the bag and mechanically folded and packed each item.

Fumbling blindly in the desk drawer near his cot, he pulled out his padlock, folded each of the grommets around bag's opening over the metal fastening loop, and latched the lock through the loop to keep it all together. That was the last of the packing. He stood slowly and stepped back to contemplate the result. The strip of duct tape inscribed with his last name in permanent marker was still there from the last time he had packed this particular bag months ago. In fact, if it weren't for wear and tear on the contents, he wasn't sure there would be a distinguishable difference between this bag and the one he carried when he left home.

"Welcome to COP[8] Nowhere!" CW2[9] Warwick shouted over the roar of the rotor wash and turbine noise as he picked up the decidedly new duffel Jim had kicked out of the helicopter. Jim had been able to see Warwick as they approached the landing zone right up to the point where the open door was filled with flying dust. Warwick had been standing with his M4 hanging vertically in the center of his chest from a sling, his bare arms folded across his chest and the palm of one gloved hand resting on the butt of his rifle. He was positioned just off to the side of the improvised helipad with goggles covering his eyes and the remainder of his face covered by a tan and black Keffiyeh. Jim wasn't sure how the pilot had any idea what was below or around him, even less idea how Warwick had been able to see enough to approach the helicopter. It made him nervous to ever get back into a helicopter in this barren desert. Somehow Warwick had navigated through that dust, and he was at the door by the time things settled enough to see more than a few inches.

"Mr. Warwick, good to be here," Jim lied.

"I go by Warlock. You'll find everyone here uses a call sign. You'll earn one too, soon enough. . ."

The two stepped to the side, silently acknowledging that any further conversation would be best suited for after the delivery bird left. Immediately, a crew of six men from the outpost rushed to the helicopter, forming a bucket brigade and quickly unloading the weekly supplies along with Jim's gear. Within five minutes, everything was piled up a few meters away and covered with a tarp.

"Sir, you might want to turn around before he powers up," Warwick shouted when the crew was done unloading. "You don't have the right kind of protection on, and it wouldn't do to evac you on your first day because you got sand in your eyes."

Jim turned around, and right on cue the pilot powered up. Sand with characteristics identical to materials ranging from talcum powder to pea gravel began to pelt him from every direction, completely filling every exposed bodily orifice almost instantly. He instinctively buried his head in his arms and took a knee with his back to the now quickly rising helicopter in an effort to protect himself. Then, as the rotor wash faded away, Jim stood and turned to watch the green shape climb to altitude and turn back to the main base, abandoning him in this hell-hole far from all comforts and most help.

He looked around the hooch, scanning for anything he had forgotten... anything he actually wanted or was required to return. His bags were packed and had already been loaded on one of the trucks, but he couldn't quite convince himself he wasn't leaving something behind. He looked under and behind the few pieces of furniture. Nothing. There wasn't really anywhere else to look, but he kept scanning back and forth trying to be sure.

"Sir," Killroy said, sticking his head in the door and grabbing the duffel, "let me take this to the truck."

"Oh... yeah," Jim said, "Thanks." He hadn't heard the normally boisterous hothead approach. Either he hadn't been listening or Killroy was being uncharacteristically quiet. He turned and followed the young Sergeant as he walked over to where the convoy trucks were staged.

As they crossed the compound, an explosion shook the area immediately outside the sand-filled barrier directly across from them. This was followed by a dull thud from off in the distance to their left. A mortar, apparently, fired from somewhere relatively close. Neither man reacted much, but continued what they were doing as if they were completely oblivious to the sound other than a sideways glance at each other and a slightly raised eyebrow from Killroy.

With a half-grin, Killroy silently counted backwards from five on his fingers. Before he had folded the last finger into a fist, there was a short whistle and a much louder thud – counter-battery fire from the artillery unit nearby. Five more followed in quick succession. For the life of him, Jim couldn't figure out why anyone would lob a mortar anywhere near the COP. The futility of doing something you knew was likely to result in your corpse being picked up with a vacuum or a spatula (if at all) didn't seem to register for the seemingly infinite supply of gullible young men who had been manipulated into believing it was Allah's will that they be liquefied by the US Marine Corps. What a waste.

"This round's only worth a chuckle," Killroy said matter-of-factly.

"Par for the course," Jim answered flatly. "Hopefully today's comedy doesn't make the old'un break out into a full laugh again until after we make it back inside the wire."

Killroy nodded agreement, then turned to head towards the trucks as Jim continued towards the ready room.

"Tell the drivers I'll be ready in a few," Jim said over his shoulder. He had a few things to do before they could depart. Killroy nodded, but didn't say anything.

"Dinner's ready," Mutt sang out as he walked through the ready room tossing MREs out of the case in his hands, each one landing expertly in front of whoever it was intended for.

One by one, the team slit open the heavy plastic envelope of food and started inspecting the contents. Jim's was a ham and egg omelet, his least favorite. In fact, that particular menu item was so despised that nobody even bothered asking for a trade when they got stuck with it. You just knew that whoever drew that particular honor was stuck with it. About the best you could hope for was that someone would be kind enough to donate an extra ration of Tabasco to cover the flavor. You couldn't do anything about the texture except warm it up, and that was rarely worth the work. Maybe he'd do without the entreé tonight and satisfy himself with the crackers and other random crap that came in the meal.

Suddenly a crashing, whizzing sound tore through the air, followed immediately by the bang of an explosion. A mortar had landed just outside and shrapnel had torn through one wall, shattered one of the fluorescent light fixtures, and stuck in an opposite wall. Jim dove to the ground and covered his head with his arms, waiting for further impacts. He heard additional thuds of distant explosions, then silence. Nothing else came near. After what felt like an eternity of quiet, he peeked out from under his arms to see the entire team still sitting or standing upright and watching him silently.

"If you hear it," Warlock said calmly, walking to the wall and using the pommel of his knife to knock a two inch piece of hot jagged metal loose, "it's nothing to worry about."

"They never lob more than one at a time," someone called Monkey added, "because that would take the odds of surviving the payback from bad to zero."

"Finish your food," Warlock directed to the room in general before turning back to concentrate on eating his own.

"Sir," K9 said with a light touch on his shoulder. Staff Sergeant Steven Kelnhoffer was a mountain of a man who could fill a room without saying anything, and when his physical presence combined with his voice, it tested any safety margins engineers may have put into the walls and ceiling. But here he was gentle in a way that might have stirred ideas of a giant silver-back gorilla caring for one its young. Might have, that is, if anyone had been aware enough to notice. Jim wasn't. He barely stirred at the touch while staring blankly at the doorway in the opposite wall. The doorway that opened up to the outside. The doorway through which he would walk for the last time in just a few minutes.

"Gear's on the truck except this," K9 continued, gesturing to the pile of battle rattle[10] belonging to Jim. "Convoy's all geared up and ready to roll. Killroy, Cooter, and I will be going with you as far as the green zone to set up logistics for the swap-out. We'll come back on the supply bird tomorrow if they can get airborne. Otherwise, another convoy is scheduled to COP Grant in a few days and the guys here can come pick us up there." All he got in acknowledgment was a nod.

"SPC Maples," Jim started to say, extending his hand for a handshake.

"Everyone here just calls me Mutt, sir," he interrupted. "It makes it easier."

"Alright, Mutt, got a minute to show me around?"

"Not much to show, sir," Mutt offered by way of explanation. "You seen pretty much everything already walking across the vehicle yard. We do pretty much everything here in the ready room and some of the hooches. Follow me, and I'll show you yours. Some of the team have already unloaded your gear into it. They built up the buildings about a month ago and took down the tents, so there's at least that... the tents were a real bitch. Didn't even try to keep the sand out, not to mention the scorpions."

Mutt turned to go out the door with his new boss in tow, but didn't make it far.

"Have a plan to kill everyone you meet," Jim said aloud as he read the hand-painted four inch tall blazing red letters above the door.

"We borrowed that one from Mad Dog Mattis," Mutt explained proudly. "Not sure who actually painted it though.

Used to have a sign when we were in tents, but pretty sure one of the Red Horse team building the palace here lifted it when we weren't lookin."

"Seems a little harsh," Jim said mostly to himself, but loudly enough Mutt felt the need to explain further.

"Nah," he said with a shrug as he shouldered through the door into the blistering heat and blinding sun, "we steal stuff from them all the time. I guess it was only fair."

Jim peeled his eyes away from the door. How many times had he crossed under those words, rifle in hand and weighed down with gear, on his way to pick through and analyze the shattered remnants of someone else's life? It's odd, he thought to himself, how quickly the people whose things he picked over became something less than human. They were objectives. One objective led to three or four more. Those objectives, dealt with according to custom, generally led to more. That's how the game was played. Played on a giant chess board that used to be a large province. Played only with pawns, and under control of kings and queens who were far from the action.

Jim stood and walked over to where a large laminated map was hanging from some nails driven into the plywood walls. This map had been pristine when he had first hung it here. Now it was almost completely covered in red or black Xs, many of them clustered closely together in a few hot-spots. It didn't look much like a chessboard, but then again, the rules they played by didn't look much like chess.

"You got a bunch of them, didn't you?" CW2 Lowry, Warlock's replacement, said quietly. He had come in unnoticed and was standing just behind and slightly to his right.

Lowry, who went by Cooter, had come in early when Warwick had been evacuated. He was originally scheduled to come in with a complete team to replace the COP's veterans in just under a month. The powers that be, noticing the high success rate of this small outpost, opted to use the excuse to enable a longer hand-off period and sent the new team lead in early.

"Doesn't matter, though, does it Cooter?"

"What do you mean? You took down all those bad guys. That matters," Cooter said trying to sound encouraging.

"Yes. I suppose it does," Jim said tiredly, "but I'm pretty sure we created almost as many as we got rid of. Maybe more. Such a waste."

"They keep makin 'em, we'll keep takin 'em," Cooter said, trying to be helpful. He had only arrived on station a month ago, and didn't seem to understand what Jim meant.

"I'm glad you understand it that way. The team needs that," Jim said with a sense of finality in is voice.

"They told me the other day that your replacement washed out of training. Got hurt."

"Hmph..."

"I was planning on having a few months at least for you to train me. Now I lose even that," Cooter said sorrowfully.

Jim struggled within himself to keep from telling the new guy how selfish and irrelevant that point was given the circumstances. It's not like things here had turned out like he'd planned. In fact, if he'd been given the choice of going home under the current conditions or staying here, he'd have stayed here until hell froze over. He made a conscious effort to unclench his fists and stretched out his arm, placing the tip of his index finger on a single red X piled on top of four black ones. "This was the first," he said, but didn't say more.

Warwick had the newly printed and laminated map spread on the table in front of them. On it were a series of grease pencil marks indicating both the objective and planned ingress and egress routes.

"Another team over in Ramadi ID'd this one a few hours ago. They called in saying it promised to be honey hole," Warwick said with a grin.

"Don't get too excited Warlock," Jim said, struggling to suppress a yawn. He'd only fallen asleep an hour ago, and the mission wasn't real enough yet for adrenaline to compensate. "Do we know anything else about it?"

"Not much, sir. The area has been pretty quiet. Word from Brigade is that patrols have only encountered the occasional pot-shot. Should be a pretty good place to get your feet wet."

"You worried about me?"

"Sir, no offense, sir," Warwick said bluntly, "but you've already got three strikes against you. First, you're not an operator. I've never seen one of your type who couldn't get into serious trouble when surrounded by a squad of my brothers."

"Your team is anything but ordinary from what I understand, and I know enough to not let my ego get in the way of you doing your job. I'm here to take advantage of what your team can provide... not to run your team."

"You might not actively try, but it'll take time for you to make good on that promise. Besides, you're still a Major," he said somewhat apologetically and with a hint of warning in his voice. "Second," Warlock continued, "you're intel. There ain't any desks or power point slides out where we go."

Jim grimaced, but didn't say anything.

"And third, you're Air Force. If the Army does a bad job training management for this kind of work, I have serious doubts about anyone else doing better. Three weeks of predeployment training ain't going to count for squat out here."

Jim wanted to be angry, but this was exactly the kind of open feedback he'd told Warwick he expected. Experienced operators like him tended to overlook many of the traditional customs and courtesies in favor of avoiding an untimely death, and it wouldn't really change anything to tell him the training had been more like six months when all was said and done. It didn't hurt his decision calculus that his survival depended pretty directly on Warwick. A flat, "Thanks for the vote of confidence," was all the reply Jim offered.

"Well, sir, keep your eyes open, mouth shut, and ears on when we're outside the wire, and you'll do fine. Should we call in the team and get 'em spun up?"

"Yeah. We need to get on this one before word gets out and the cleanup crew arrives."

Warwick stepped out of the ready room to rally everyone, leaving Jim alone with his thoughts. Warwick was crusty, had been here four months for this tour, and already had four other tours in this god-forsaken country under his belt. He knew what he was doing, and had long ago lost the ability to be political or polite when it came to getting a job done and coming out alive. There was no way to misinterpret anything that ever crossed his mind or lips. Jim knew Warwick meant what he said in the kindest possible way, but it stung a little to admit to himself that he was almost certainly the biggest liability on the mission.

Aside from the quick tour by Mutt, he hadn't had much time with any of the team other than Warwick who seemed somewhat irritated at having to relinquish his position – especially to an outsider. That said, Warwick had dutifully handed over the reigns and provided an exhaustive in-brief earlier in the day. He couldn't help but wonder how many of the anxious looks he had been intercepting from the team, especially the more experienced ones, were due to their distrust of how he would handle himself in a firefight. Moments later, Warwick returned with the full team, who all circled the map, focusing intensely on the objective and instantly beginning their individual analysis of the situation as Warwick briefed them on the details.

Jim shook himself, blinking his eyes hard to pull his focus free, and looked wearily at the pile of dirty body armor and other battle rattle on the table. He wasn't all that convinced it would be worth the work to button up. Would it be all that bad, he thought to himself, to just get it over with quickly if something went wrong?

He stopped himself. He'd told himself over and over again not to let those kinds of thoughts creep back into his mind, but his success rate seemed to strongly favor his unseen opponent. It was a tenacious beast that had been growing stronger for a while now, and had made a habit of rearing its unwelcome and ugly head more and more frequently.

He picked up the plate carrier[11] and held it out at arms-length from him. Its familiar smell made him nauseous. The stench of sweat, sand, dust, dirt, blood, and all the other contaminants endemic to a destroyed city in a war zone permeated everything in spite of vigorous attempts to clean it all off. No matter how hard he scrubbed, some of the stains were still there, visible or not. All the scrubbing had done was to wear the fabric covers threadbare. A few spots in particular seemed to have been indelibly marked against any means of removal.

"Wolfpack one, Wolfpack two," the radio crackled in his ear. It had felt like an eternity since they had gone in. Hearing Warlock call him without having heard gunfire was an inexpressible relief. It meant they had *been* a nasty surprise rather than encountering one.

"One," he answered tersely.

"Objective secure. Come work your magic."

"Copy. Headed in."

"All clear, sir," the gunner in the turret called down. "Entrance is three meters, right side. Can't miss it."

Jim grabbed his rifle and ducked out of the truck with two more of his team and an interpreter close behind, leaving the drivers and gunners in the four trucks behind in case the team needed to make a hasty egress. Somewhere just out of sight there were half a dozen of his men who had been the first out of the trucks when they had halted. He couldn't see any of them, but was infinitely glad they were there.

The door to the building, what was left of it at least, was leaning haphazardly against the shattered door jamb. Apparently the breaching team had opted for shaped charges on the hinges and latch instead of just kicking it in. As he looked at the splintered wood, he couldn't help but wonder if it had even been locked. This thought didn't last long, however. There was a mission to accomplish, and it had nothing to do with the door. He entered the small dark space, scanning it through the still uncomfortable green glow of night vision goggles. It was empty except for his two protectors. He stepped forward into the darkness, but a dull pain in his chest made him realize he had been holding his breath. He consciously started to take a slow, deep, breath, but the pungent residue of explosives hanging in the air seemed to sear his lungs and triggered an involuntary cough.

"Don't worry about that sir. You'll get used to it," the young soldier in front of him said as he deliberately worked his way forward into a long narrow hallway, checking each connected room as he went. "I kinda like it now. Smells like work."

"Don't listen to him, sir," countered the other soldier keeping watch behind them as they moved forward, "Monkey just likes blowing stuff up. I still hate that smell."

"I'll take your word for it," Jim grunted. He didn't like having to search through the labyrinth of rooms in this unusually large building; it was making him uncomfortable. He keyed the mic on his radio, "Wolfpack two, Wolfpack one."

"Two."

"We're in, but don't see you,"

"Last door, up the stairs. Building's clear."

"Copy."

The three moved swiftly to where the rest of the team was waiting. A dim light from an infra-red glow-stick cast grotesque shadows into the corners and over the faces of everyone there. The entry team was spread around the room with two watching out the windows, two watching the door, and two more towering over a collection of hooded and flex-cuffed people.

"Warlock, can we get some light here?" he asked. Watching the world through NVGs[12] was disorienting, and with the combination of anxiety and sleep deprivation he was near enough to puking without adding anything else. They needed to come off.

"Monkey, find a light," Warwick commanded.

A moment later the light from a single bare and dim light bulb completely washed out his NVGs. He flipped them up out of the way and scanned the room with his natural eyes. He wouldn't have believed it possible, but the green scene in his NVGs was less disturbing than the shadows and darkness he saw all around him. Against one wall was a low table stacked with a jumble of large plastic containers and seemingly random scientific equipment. Against the opposite wall were a number of sleeping mats with blankets randomly scattered around. Apparently the captives had been asleep prior to the team's arrival – just like planned. Other than these features, the room was barren.

There was nothing hanging from the bare mud brick walls. Nothing covering the rough planking of the floor. Nothing but the single light bulb hanging from the ceiling. For the life of him, he couldn't figure out what the place had originally been intended for. Perhaps some kind of apartment building, or maybe a feeble attempt at an office building back before the city had descended into chaos. Whatever it had been, it wasn't that anymore. Like everything else he had seen, it had first been stripped of anything useful, then co-opted into the fight directly.

Jim moved over to the chemistry set and poured over its contents. It was just a simple IED[13] factory. Nothing sexy. The intel must have been over-played. The smell of diesel and nitrate fertilizer hanging in the air was all the evidence he needed to know what this crew had been up to.

"Grab everything with wires that isn't already attached to a container. Leave those to Warlock," Jim commanded. "Keep your eyes peeled for shaped charges, or even plain copper discs. Anything paper goes too. Keep your gloves on, and bag everything so we don't lose any finger prints."

"What about all the chemicals?" Gomer asked.

"Just fuel and fertilizer. Nothing to worry about unless we get stupid, and not much we'll learn about them we can't get from the photos." Jim paused here and thought for a moment.

"Monkey," he continued, "this place needs to have an industrial accident when we leave. We can't haul all this crap with us, and we can't leave it here. Make sure the place is empty and torch it off."

Immediately, two of the team started photographing the workbench and methodically collecting the items he had asked for, while Monkey went down to the trucks to collect what he needed for the fireworks show.

"Alright, let's see who our little chemists are," Jim said to nobody in particular. He moved to the nearest one and pulled off the hood. A pair of terrified looking brown eyes looked back up at him. She couldn't have been more than twelve. Maybe fourteen.

The interpreter stepped to Jim's shoulder, ready to be of use.

"Ask her what clan," Jim commanded. The interpreter complied, and Jim stood silently watching while the translator worked.

"She says she was brought here from Yemen as a laborer, and that she doesn't know anyone locally. She says the ties binding her hands are hurting badly. Begs you to loosen them."

"Go ahead and loosen them," Jim said. The interpreter immediately moved to comply.

Warwick, who had been studying the workbench, stopped what he was doing, turned, and just managed to bark a loud "Sir!" when the girl leaped up with a knife in hand that she had apparently been hiding under her long black dress. She lunged at Jim, but Gomer, who had been down on one knee a few feet away inspecting what looked like a remote-control module, turned instinctively when Warlock shouted, raised his rifle, and released a three round burst. At least one of the rounds caught the girl in the back just below the last rib on her left side. It exploded out her right side just below the breast, leaving a gaping hole and splattering both the wall and Jim with bits of blood and lung. She dropped the knife and collapsed on the floor within a foot of Jim's feet. Bright pink foam was starting to leak from the corners of her mouth and from the exit wound as she tried to speak.

"She prays," the interpreter said matter-of-factly, wrinkling his nose at the smell of fresh blood that was beginning to mingle with the smell of burnt gunpowder. All Jim heard was the ringing in his ears and the beating of his heart, but he understood what the interpreter meant.

"What did you do that for?" Warwick screamed. It was loud enough that it pierced through the ringing. A stream of uninterrupted profanity and reprimands for being an incompetent desk pilot officer filled most of the next several minutes while the rest of the team methodically identified and photographed the rest of the prisoners and collected evidence. "The next time you even think about risking my team like that, Gomer'll let the little whore cut you! Nobody here is innocent! *You get that! NOBODY!* We find a six year old kid in a place like this, they're a killer no different than Haji

Abdulla, and we treat them accordingly."

"The old'un is laughing again," Gomer said to himself, but loud enough that Jim heard. It didn't make any sense. Neither he nor Warwick were laughing, and there weren't any men over twenty among the captives.

Jim looked down at those brown eyes as they rolled uncontrolled in the young woman's head. Most of her internal organs had been devastated by the tumbling bullet, but it still took several minutes before she stopped struggling to breathe. The metallic taste of blood filled his mouth and nose, and he could feel the progress of a drip of sticky hot liquid as gravity slowly pulled it down his forehead. The nausea got the better of him, and he involuntarily puked all over the dying girl.

Jim retched as he pulled on the vest. It had been an involuntary part of the routine for months, and he couldn't wait to turn the awful equipment back in to supply and be rid of it forever. Thankfully, nothing came up; a consequence of his not having eaten that morning or even the night before. He wasn't going to go back into the world of men covered in vomit.

He plopped the Kevlar bucket on his head and adjusted the magazine holders and other gear. All told, the load added up to almost sixty pounds, and it had felt oppressively heavy when he first arrived here. However, it was just a matter of course now, and felt about like a heavy blanket draped over him. About the only part of him that registered the weight were a few bulging discs in his back, and he had gotten good at ignoring them with the help of large doses of Ibuprofen. The doctors would probably give him a hard time at his next physical, and his kidneys might never work the same again, but at least he had been able to function.

As he finished the ritual buttoning up, he felt an irrational desire to burn every piece of clothing and equipment he had on. He wanted to watch the flames purify it of all that had been absorbed from this putrid place. But the rules were the rules. He had to wear it for the convoy and turn in everything but the uniforms at his home station. He would definitely burn the uniforms though.

Chapter 2

Convoy

Jim picked up his M9, loaded a round in the chamber, dropped the hammer, pulled the magazine, and added an extra round from a few loose ones he kept in one of the pouches on his vest, and reinserted the magazine. There were three more magazines in various locations across his gear, all of them full, none of them ever used. The handgun was a backup, and he'd never needed it. Without having to even look, he quickly secured the pistol in the holster attached to MOLLE straps on the left side of his chest.

He next picked up his rifle, verified that the chamber was empty, sent the bolt forward, rotated the safety selector to burst, inserted one of his seven magazines with a slap, and gave it a tug to ensure it was locked in securely. All it would take was a quick pull on the charging handle and he'd be in business. It was a motion he had become very comfortable with over the last year. He clipped the rifle to the single-point sling hanging across his chest starting at his left shoulder, then turned to walk through that door for the last time.

He paused briefly and looked up again at the familiar lettering, including the rough blot of white paint covering over what had been the first two words. The red of the original was starting to bleed through the white patch, and it was legible to anyone who looked at it more than casually. "Have a plan to kill. . . " Having a plan and planning to do something weren't quite the same thing. With a new crew coming in, maybe it was good that the original intent was showing through.

Jim sat, pouring over the four-foot wide by six foot long printout he had spread across the table in the ready room. He'd been feeding all the information they'd collected into an algorithm he'd developed during his time in graduate school. The result was supposed to be a neat breakdown of known linkages and interdependencies. It was also supposed to identify the most likely points of intersection that had yet to be positively identified. Find an unknown intersection, and the odds were very good that it contained a high-level facilitator or leader. That was the theory at least, and it had worked excellently on the test data he had culled from the al-Qaida of 2001 and 2002. In fact, he could claim credit – at least in classified settings – for several very high-level take-downs in Afghanistan.

It was one of those take-downs, he was sure, that was responsible for him being here now. Damn that briefing. He should have kept his mouth shut.

Things were different here. In theory he was supposed to do real-time analysis and use that to identify and roll-up the next target before the enemy could react. The fundamental goal, he'd been told, was to use his analysis to map out the local leadership hierarchy and figure out where the head of the beast was so the Army, Marines, or Air Force could decapitate it. The idea was simple. Someone was behind the persistent insurgency, and all he had to do was to work his way through the data to map out the clans, tribes, and other social structures that determined so much in this sixth-century culture. He was to use that data to find the head and cut it off (or at least a relatively small handful of heads). Do that, and the beast would die. That was the theory.

The reality was a little different. In fact, the more data he gathered the more fragmented and fractured the results became. As they rolled up one warlord or cell after another, the map began to disintegrate into small clusters of genuinely unimportant thugs. Had that disintegration come with a similar destabilization of the insurgency he would have called it a success, but it didn't. Something was eluding him. There was a missing connection somewhere. There had to be.

His eyes swept back and forth, but kept coming back to a cluster of people the team had taken a few nights back. They all seemed to have some connection in common, but he hadn't been able to get that information out of them. The people they'd found claimed to be simple shopkeepers and craftsmen who had been coerced by brutal threats. If that were true and he could convince them they had nothing to fear, and if he could convince them that his team could take out their controllers, they might be more willing to talk.

"Warlock," Jim said when he saw him enter the room, "I think we need to take a flight to Mercury. I want to talk to the guys we rolled up last week."

"I'll call in to see what we can work out," Warlock promised and then left the room.

Jim continued pouring over his diagram for several more minutes until Warlock came back in.

"Chopper'll be here in an hour. But it's headed to Bucca. Your guys got transferred there last night."

"Fine," Jim answered, "if that's what it takes. I'll probably be gone a few days."

Warlock nodded, then turned and left him alone with his thoughts. He spent the next hour formulating a strategy for convincing the four men that he already knew what it was he was after. He scanned the chart again, and again, making sure he understood the connections well enough that he could catch enough of their lies to corner them.

The helicopter arrived as expected, lifting off and banking away from the outpost before Jim had a chance to strap in. Once above the range of RPG[14] and small-arms fire, the pilot leveled off and delivered as smooth a ride as can be expected in a Blackhawk. By the time they had landed Warwick had called ahead and explained the purpose of the visit, so a small team had gathered to meet him as he stepped away from the aircraft.

"Jones, S3,[15]" said a tall, lankly looking major who seemed to be the head of delegation, "but I go by Lurch most of the time. Warlock tells me you go by Shepherd."

Jim grimaced. He'd been trying to avoid a call sign, but the team had recently branded him after asking what kind of rat-dog was next to the unicorn on the picture Sammie had sent. Immediately, a universal cry of Sheppard went up, and when he tried to protest they offered only one alternative... rainbow. Shepherd would have to do.

"Warlock and I go way back," Lurch said by way of explanation. "Anyway," he continued, "Grammar here will set you up with an interrogation room and will keep you company while you're in the compound. He's pretty new to the interrogation game, but from what I hear, you'll end up doing all the talking anyway."

Jim handed Sergeant Grammar a folder with info on the prisoners he wanted to talk to. "I'd like to see if we can talk to these guys today, then let them stew on what I tell them overnight and hit them again early in the morning."

"Yes sir," Grammar answered, handing the folder back to Jim. "Mister Warwick sent over the info electronically. Paper copies can be dangerous around here. Anyway, I'll round 'em up as they leave chow. You'll only get a few minutes each this round or else the other detainees will figure out that you're talking to them. We'll have to arrange medical appointments or the like tomorrow if you want more time."

"That'll have to do, I guess."

"In the mean time," Grammar continued, "I'll show you to a rack you can use tonight, then I'll take you to the chow hall for some hot food. It's about the only advantage to working here."

The thought of hot food brightened Jim's mood significantly, and within a few minutes he was sitting at a table eating hot beef stew, fresh local flatbread, and cold ice cream with real utensils. He'd forgotten how much he liked food given that all he'd eaten for quite a while now was MREs. He stood and walked over to the ice cream machine to refill, then sat back down and ate it as slowly as he could without it completely melting.

Just as he was finishing up, Sergeant Grammar walked up and informed him that the detainees were prepped and ready. He stood and followed him to a nearby room built from concrete block and plywood containing nothing but a small table and three chairs. Jim took one of the chairs, and the interpreter (who had appeared seemingly out of nowhere) took another. Grammar turned and went out to collect the first detainee for questioning. Less than a minute later, he returned with a handcuffed figure who was unceremoniously dumped into the third chair. Apparently, Grammar would be standing.

"Remember," Grammar cautioned, "if anybody finds out who you're talking to, they might as well be dead. We can't keep these guys out of the block for more than a few minutes today or their 'mates' will assume they've been talking."

These pleasantries over, the interrogation started and continued for roughly fifteen minutes before the detainee was returned to their cell. This processes continued three more times in rapid succession. It wasn't much time, but it was enough for Jim to make his case and plant the seeds of doubt he hoped would germinate overnight.

- - - - - - - - - - - - - - - - - - -

"Shephard," Lurch said, lightly shaking Jim by the shoulder, "wake up."

"Huh?"

"We've had an incident."

"What?"

"Your boys are all dead. Targeted in their sleep."

Jim sat up with a start, briefly believing the discussion had to do with his team back at the COP. "What happened?"

"Don't know for sure, but at least a dozen other detainees used bed sheets to hold them down and beat them to death. Best guess is someone figured they'd been talking."

Jim felt sick to his stomach. Still disoriented he asked, "What time is it?"

"0330. I know it's early, but I thought you ought to know."

"Damn. What next?"

"For now? Go back to sleep I guess. We'll figure out logistics tomorrow."

Lurch turned and quietly left the room. Jim rolled over and fell back into his customary restless sleep.

"What a waste," Jim said to himself as he stuffed the few things he had with him in his ruck. "All I have to show for it is a few half-decent meals and a few more bodies in my count."

As he moved to zip the bag shut, the contents of the folder that had contained dossiers were briefly exposed. The dossiers had been replaced. Almost hesitatingly, he pulled the folder from his bag and opened the cover. The pages that had been a picture and detailed description of low-level insurgent nobodies were indeed gone, replaced with copies of a flier advertising movies that played in the evenings when the chow hall doubled as a theater for off-duty staff. Someone must have switched them when he briefly left the table to refill his ice cream. Those men died because he decided to indulge in an extra helping of ice cream and had been careless with a piece of paper.

― ― ― ― ― ― ― ― ― ― ― ― ― ― ― ― ―

Warlock was waiting for him as he walked through the door into the ready room. Warlock wanted to talk, but Jim was in no mood. He waved Warlock off, went through the room to a small maintenance area, retrieved a can of paint he'd noticed a few weeks ago, and returned to the ready room. Pulling a chair over, he used a folded up wad of paper towels as a brush and painted over the first two words above the door.

"Plan to kill everyone you meet" was all it said now. Nothing about being polite, nothing about being professional, and now... nothing about having a plan. Each truncation of the original quote had brought the sentiment closer to the reality of this God-forsaken place.

―――――――――――――――――――――

"What's your call sign?" Jim asked the driver.

"Slider."

"Capstone, Slider," Jim called over the radio mounted just to his left.

"Go ahead Slider," came the answer.

"Loaded up and headed out."

"See you in a few hours. Safe travels."

Jim put the microphone back and turned to the driver, "Lets hit the road."

―――――――――――――――――――――

"I'm so lonely here," Leslie sobbed uncontrollably. It was the first video chat in over a month, and it didn't take long to confirm what he had suspected for a while. After the first admission, a string of confessions came out, each one piercing him, making him feel like he had abandoned his family. It wasn't what she had intended, but that didn't really matter. Her herculean efforts to hide her pain, depression, and worry from him had collapsed.

"I'm so sorry," was all Jim could say. He didn't know what to say. There was literally nothing he could do.

"Everyone just assumes you've left us."

It was too true, and it hurt to hear her say it. He had left, but not of his own free will.

"Let them assume what they want. You know they're wrong."

"I'm so tired too. Sammie cries herself to sleep almost every night, and she wakes me up over and over again having nightmares."

"I've been worried about you."

"And when I do manage to fall asleep, I have nightmares about what you're going through over there."

"Don't worry about me, I'm in the best hands possible."

"I need you. So does Sammie."

"I need you too."

The conversation continued like this for most of the next half an hour, during which time Jim felt more and more miserable and powerless every minute. Finally Leslie calmed down a bit, giving Jim a chance to think.

"Honey?"

"Yes?"

"Load the car up and go to your mom's for a while. You need some help, and I can't give it from here."

"I can't just leave the house empty," she protested emptily.

The convoy had come to the outpost to deliver supplies, so neither the trucks nor the drivers were his guys. The only people he knew were K9, Killroy, and Cooter who were each in a different vehicle. That was a mixed blessing, he decided. If something happened to one of them, it would only happen to *one* of them. On the other hand, he didn't know the crew of his truck, and so didn't trust them particularly.

They drove onward without a word among the crew for several miles before the driver broke the quiet.

"I heard you rolled up a bunch of the Sadr organization."

"Not so much Sadr, they seem to have stayed in their sandbox."

"But you got a lot of bad dudes, right?"

"Ba'athists, old-school al-Qaida, Iranians, Turks, Saudis, Brits, Pakistanis, Chechens, Uyghurs, Americans, Yemenis, Syrians, Canadians, Palestinians..." he trailed off as if to say there were plenty more.

"Roads have been pretty quiet. We should be in Ramadi in about 40, and have you in the Green Zone within another two hours after that. Maybe an hour and a half."

Jim just nodded in acknowledgment.

"You rotating home?"

Another nod.

"Gotta be nice. The rotator[16] leaves tomorrow, so you won't even have to stay in Baghdad longer than overnight."

"I'm not on the rotator," Jim admitted. "My flight leaves as soon as I make the plane."

"Sir," Warlock said as he approached from behind.

"Don't tell me," Jim said acidly, "another hot tip like the last one."

"About sums it up."

"When was the last time we had a hot tip from someone that actually panned out to be more than a small-scale IED factory? About the only good tips we've ever gotten we've developed on our own."

Warlock shook his head silently. Truth be told, almost all the hot tips turned out to be nothing at all except an excuse to survive another ride into the hostile unknown.

"Never mind. I don't suppose it really matters," Jim said, cutting himself off. "This one might be the final straw that breaks the insurgency, right?"

Warlock twisted the corners of his mouth into a doubtful lopsided grin. "Yeah, I suppose so."

They had both become jaded over the last several months. The hope they had of making a real difference had been trampled by hard experience. It was a sure sign that it was time to find someone else for the job, but unfortunately, that didn't agree with CENTCOM's calendar masters.

"Well, let's go fishin' I guess."

The team spent several minutes doing what by now was completely routine planning. Ingress and egress routes, locations for security pickets, identifying who would be on the entry team. It was all so familiar any of them could have done it in their sleep, and this particular neighborhood had become so frequent an objective that they really didn't need the map.

"Cookie cutter," Monkey observed.

"Wrap and pack," K9 agreed.

"Careful," Warlock warned, "don't get lazy. That's a good way to get killed."

They all silently agreed, and went back about their business. Within an hour, the entire team had assembled their gear, loaded the trucks, and were ready for departure. Now it was just a matter of waiting until the witching hour. Everyone except Warlock and Jim found a semi-comfortable position in the ready room and tried to sleep. There really wasn't any better way to pass the time, and they had all mastered the fine art of sleeping on command. They planned to be on-scene an hour before sunrise.

"You should try and get some sleep," Jim cautioned.

"And you shouldn't?"

"I snuck in a nap earlier today," Jim lied.

"Yeah, me too. While we were standing with our eyes open." Warlock was starting to look tired. Not sleepy, but tired in a much deeper sense of the word. Jim was pretty sure he looked even worse himself.

"What do you have to go back to?" Jim asked. They'd never talked about home before, but somehow it just seemed like the time to ask.

"Nothing."

"Nothing?"

"Nothing. Wife left me two deployments ago after selling off everything I owned. Blew all the cash on drugs before I got home, so there wasn't anything to argue over in the divorce. We never had kids. Parent's died a few years back while I was in Afghanistan. This is all I have left. I'll probably start angling for another deployment as soon as I get off the plane."

"Oh."

"What about you?"

"Wife and kid."

"I know that much," Warwick admitted. "They surviving okay?"

"Not really. Timing was really bad for my family."

Standing next to the colonel was a chaplain he'd never met before. An officer with a chaplain in tow was a bad thing that had only occurred once before when Warlock and Monkey died. Immediately, Jim began to steel himself for news that Mutt had succumbed to his injuries as well. The team didn't need this right now.

"We can send everyone out of the ready room if we need to, but there isn't really anywhere that will be private," Jim said. "Even if there were, there aren't any secrets with much of a lifespan around here."

Apparently the Boss didn't plan on staying long, otherwise the pilot would have started shutting down by now. As they turned to walk that direction and escape the noise of the still idling helicopter, the third man said something to Lowry who then directed several of the men to unload a few bags.

"I can't stay. A major dust storm is only a few clicks away and inbound. Once it hits, we'll be grounded for a while."

Jim nodded acknowledgment and glanced over to where the third passenger was talking with his team.

"Specialist Maples' replacement," the colonel said, answering the silent question. "Most of your team already know him from Bragg. He'll fit right in."

"Mutt will be hard to replace," Jim said. He was waiting for the bad news, and decided to push the point rather than wait for the boss to get around to it. "Have you heard how he's doing?"

"He made it alive to Landstuhl," the colonel said sadly, "but I don't know any more than that."

So this wasn't about Mutt... It left Jim wondering what else this could be about. The colonel didn't wait long to relieve him of his curiosity. As soon as the door to the ready room closed behind them, hushing the worst of the noise, the colonel half sat, half leaned against a table and asked Jim to sit down.

"Jim, we got word a little over an hour ago through the Red Cross. Leslie and Sammie were killed by a drunk driver last night outside Shiprock, New Mexico."

An explosion a few yards in front of the truck blew a large crater in the road and threw an enormous amount of dirt into the air. The driver, unsure how to get past the hole, slowed to a halt.

"Don't stop now!" Jim shouted, but the driver never had time to react.

Chapter 3

First Steps Home

His body was on fire – especially his right foot – but that was like saying a blow torch was hotter than a glowing red coal. He felt like he'd been under the treads of a tank, and wasn't sure how he ended up here. A weak attempt to open his eyes did no good. Something was blocking his vision. He was vaguely conscious of some background noise, but his mind was so clouded he couldn't quite make sense of it. The one noise he could make out was the distinctive whir a Blackhawk made when you were sitting inside.

He tried to speak, hoping the unintelligible voices nearby would hear him and be able to tell him what had happened. The only sound that came out was a bit of a grunt and some gurgling. He tried moving his arms. They were strapped down, and the effort was extremely painful. He twisted his head, and he heard a voice saying something indistinct. Then, everything faded back to black.

He felt sick. Everything around him was moving and shifting. Had he somehow ended up on a boat? And his throat and mouth were extremely dry. He wanted to swallow to move some spit around and make it better, but there was something in the way. He shifted his weight a bit, and fiery bolts of pain shot through his right leg. Involuntarily he screamed, but no sound came out. Slowly becoming more aware of his surroundings, he became conscious of a throbbing pain in his leg and a burning sensation on parts of his face.

He was supposed to be in a truck headed to the Baghdad airport. The funerals were in three days, and it would take two of those to get home even if everything went smoothly. He made a conscious effort to open his eyes, but nothing would focus. In fact, he couldn't see anything. Beginning to panic, he tried to get up, but felt like he was strapped down on something. Had he been captured and was he being tortured?

He heard a quiet beep, and a mild burning sensation radiated from the back of his hand and up his arm. The warmth spread across his body and the pain didn't bother him any more. As little as it was, his efforts exhausted him; so he closed his eyes and faded out again.

— — — — — — — — — — — — — — — — — —

"Major Harwood..." He heard the voice as though it were from a distance and through a dense fog.

"Major Harwood," the voice repeated, slightly more clearly and seemingly closer.

"Squeeze my fingers if you can hear me."

Squeeze their finger... Why would somebody say that? He tried to open his eyes and look, but he could see nothing.

"Squeeze my fingers. You can do that for me."

Jim was grasping for understanding, but it was eluding him. He could hear what she was saying, but was having difficulty figuring out what the words meant. He felt a squeeze on his right hand as the voice repeated, "It's right here. Give my fingers a squeeze if you're in there."

Jim returned the squeeze with what he thought was firm pressure, but the feedback provided by his nervous system told him it was a feeble and barely noticeable touch.

"Do you know where you are? Squeeze my fingers again if you do."

Wherever this was, it wasn't the convoy. He was confused. Why was it so exhausting just to listen, and why was it so hard to answer?

"You've been injured, and we're working to get you stable enough to transport back to the states."

Jim squeezed the speaker's fingers again, but that was all he could manage. He faded back into oblivion.

Over the course of several days, Jim was conscious more and more of the time. He was able to listen and focus for a few minutes at a time as doctors or nurses passed through his room, but they refrained from talking too much with him about his condition. Jim was still unsure what happened or how badly he had been injured. Even through the fog of whatever kind of pain medication they had him on, he understood that something was wrong with both his face and his right foot. Both of them hurt intensely.

He came to realize that his apparent blindness was a function of his head being wrapped in bandages. He also came to realize that they were heavily sedating him any time they changed the bandages. Someone would come in and quietly tell him they were going to change the dressings, and then he would fade out again – for how long, he couldn't have said. In fact, he couldn't have said how long he had been in the hospital. Time seemed ethereal. In his highly drugged state, *he* seemed ethereal.

Periodically, when he was particularly drugged but still conscious, he would have terrifying hallucinations. He saw hundreds of spiders climbing on the ceiling. He saw the walls changing colors and warping in fantastical ways as if he was inside a pop can being crushed. He saw little people dancing on the foot of his bed. He saw all this while his eyes were wrapped in bandages.

He saw other things too... He had nightmares – had them any time he was conscious of having been asleep. He saw the young girl who had been killed on his first raid standing over him with the knife in her hand hacking away at his leg and laughing with evil glee. He saw prisoners at Abu Ghraib and Camp Bucca mobbing him and tearing at his face with their bare hands. He saw the torture chamber his team had destroyed, only this time he was strapped to the crude table and Abu Dura al-Baghdadi was using a blow torch on his leg. Baghdadi was dead... Jim had shot him when he had tried to rush him during a field interrogation – had shot him twice in the head – but somehow that monster, with blood running down into his face from a little black hole above his left eye and another in his right cheek-bone, had returned and was torturing Jim.

There seemed to be an endless stream of horrifying dreams; all set during one of the many raids he had been on; all twisted just enough to be absolutely horrifying. These dreams never lasted long – they woke him up. They woke him up with his heart racing. They woke him up with his body twisting and trashing in his bed. They also woke up the nurses who would then come and try to calm him before adjusting his dose of narcotics to send him back into oblivion.

– – – – – – – – – – – – – – – – – –

"Jim," said a mildly familiar voice he had come to understand was the ranking physician in the part of the hospital where he was, "we're going to send you to Brooke Army Medical Center."

Jim nodded understanding. It was all he could manage since he still couldn't talk. The ventilator tube down his throat prevented him making any real vocalizations.

Other than the fact that he was in an Army hospital, he had no idea where he even was, or how long he'd been here. Sometimes he felt like he'd been sitting in this bed for weeks. Other times he wasn't sure whether he hadn't just arrived. The last actually clear idea he had was climbing into the truck and driving out of the compound up in Anbar.

"They have a team here to pick you and a few others up and take care of you on the flight. They're finishing crew rest in the next hour or so, and will start loading everyone as soon as they're cleared. You'll be back in the states tomorrow."

Jim nodded again. That meant he was either in Balad or Landstuhl. Probably Balad. If they had taken him to Landstuhl, he had been completely out for the duration of the transport.

"I don't know how much you've been able to gather while you've been here. You've been pretty out of your mind the whole time."

Jim nodded again.

"Your convoy was caught by a diversionary road-block just outside the city, and your truck took a direct hit from a shaped charge. The driver and gunner were both killed."

More dead people he could blame himself for. Had they not come to pick him up, the convoy would have been part of an earlier run that apparently had made it without incident.

"You have serious flash burns on most of your face. We won't know how your vision will be affected until we remove the bandages, and that has to wait a while yet. The swelling in your throat will need to come down before they can take the ventilator out. Even then, it may be a while before you can start breathing on your own and speaking again."

Jim nodded again. His face was about the only part of him that wasn't protected by flame-resistant stuff when he'd last geared up. During his more lucid times, he had assumed something of that sort was responsible for the breathing tube and face-wrap. However, it was still crushing to have it confirmed. Up to this point he had been able to hope for something less dramatic.

"Your foot was crushed by something inside the vehicle when it flipped over, and it had to be amputated just below the knee."

Amputated? How could his foot hurt so bad if it wasn't even there anymore? No, the doctor must have made a mistake, but there wasn't any way he could communicate how bad it hurt.

"Ft. Sam has the best burn unit in the DoD, and the Center for the Intrepid will be open soon. There's nowhere in the world better at taking care of injuries like yours."

Rehab. Why bother? Why couldn't they have just let him die? Why hadn't K9 just let him do it when he had the nerve? Was there really anything worth living for at this point?

"They also have an excellent center for traumatic brain injury. We don't know how hard you got hit, but given the descriptions of your vehicle the pararescueman gave when they dropped you off, we're pretty sure you'll be dealing with at least a moderate case."

Jim was crushed. He was clearly broken beyond repair. He would be marred the rest of his life, all because of this misadventure in the most God-forsaken region of hell. In spite of his best efforts to find some kind of redemption in this fight, all he had found was the worst and most evil dregs of humankind running unrestrained while raping and pillaging the little that remained of humanity. But he stopped there... it took too much energy to try and arrange his thoughts. Everything was foggy, and it took enormous amounts of energy to get coherent thoughts to form. He could process what people were saying, but that was about it.

"You have a visitor, if you're up to it. It'll only be for a few minutes though."

Who could possibly be here to visit him? He nodded his consent anyway.

"I'll send him in," he said, adding a pause before continuing, "You won't see me again, so I'll wish you good luck and a quick recovery."

Good luck... What the hell did the doctor know about luck? Luck had abandoned him before he had left home. Luck had taken away everything he cared about and left him scarred in more ways than one. Luck, if it were to do anything for him now, couldn't do more than end his misery in oblivion, but he didn't even have that much of the mysterious stuff. He wanted to spit in the face of that doctor, but that was out of the question.

Jim sat quietly angry, incapable of doing anything else, and contemplated what he could remember of the last year. It wasn't much, but what he could remember was all damning. The effort wore him out and he began fading away again.

"Shepherd," a voice said from seemingly far away, "are you in there?"

There was a short pause.

"Sir, can you hear me?" it asked, and this time it seemed to come from much closer by.

Jim, suddenly aware of a hand on his, gave a squeeze of acknowledgment. It was K9's voice, but K9 had never before used his call sign to his face. The formalism of rank had always gotten in the way of that kind of informal address. He had often heard the team using it among themselves, but only Warlock had ever used it to address him directly.

"I'm coming back with you. Looks like we're going to be in this together for a while longer."

Jim desperately wanted to ask what had happened to him and about Killroy and Cooter. K9 seemed to understand.

"I took a round to the thigh after we dismounted. Tore a big hole that the doc's say will slow me down for a while. One of the boys from the convoy got a tourniquet on me just in time. I'll be running 10Ks again soon though," K9 laughed to himself, "no way they're going to make a couch potato out of me. Cooter and Killroy are already back at the outpost. They didn't even get a scratch."

Jim tightened his grip on K9's hand, trying to ask for more details.

"Killroy's been put in for a sliver star. He's the one that pulled you out of the burning truck after I went down. Cooter took over command as soon as the blast went off, and rumor is that he'll be decorated too."

Jim relaxed, hoping K9 understood his thanks.

"Sir," K9 said somewhat uncertainly, "would you mind if I asked for the two of us to stay together once we get back to the states?"

Jim gave the hand as firm a squeeze as he could manage, and nodded. K9 was about the closest thing to family he had left.

"Do you know why we all decided to call you Shepherd?"

Jim shook his head. He had assumed it had something to do with the crayon-colored stick-figures of his dog that Sammie would include in every letter.

"It started with the dog drawings, but by the time it stuck we all felt like you cared about everyone on the team. You always did your best to protect anyone you came across. You're a natural shepherd. Can I call you that from now on? Can I treat you like a brother instead of a boss?"

Jim nodded, and he could feel tears well up in his bandaged eyes. He didn't feel like he'd earned that particular brand of respect, but it still made him feel good to know at least a few of the team believed it. He was getting tired, but would fight that off as long as needed in order to give K9 a chance to finish what he had to say.

"Shepherd, I've got other things to say, but they'll have to wait. I'm supposed to be getting my stuff together for the flight. I'll see you in San Antonio."

Jim gave the hand another squeeze, then faded away again.

The next time he was conscious, he could hear the distinct sound of the inside of a C17 transport plane. He was freezing, and there was pressure on his hip that was uncomfortable. He tried shifting his weight, only to realize he'd been strapped in. Immediately he heard the step of a nurse nearby.

"How bad is your pain? Squeeze once for mild, three for bad, and two for bearable."

With as high as he had been for days now, he was used to the room spinning around, but the added motion of the airplane was making him seriously nauseous. The last thing he wanted at this point was another dose. His face and foot hurt quite a lot, but not so bad he wanted to be drugged any more. He squeezed the hand once.

"Is there something you need? Once for yes, twice for no."

A single squeeze. How could he tell the attendant what was wrong? He couldn't talk.

"Are you cold?" the nurse guessed.

A single squeeze.

"I'll get you some more blankets. Anything else?"

A single squeeze.

"I know the litter's are pretty awful. Is there something I can do to make it more comfortable?"

A single squeeze. The nurse was clearly well practiced at this game.

"Above the waist?"

Two squeezes.

"Pressure on your hip?"

One squeeze.

"I'll get some extra blankets for padding."

He disappeared for a moment and came back with a stack of warm blankets, using one to pad the offending area and the remainder to warm Jim up. Now more comfortable, Jim fell back into oblivion.

- - - - - - - - - - - - - - - - - -

He'd been awake for several minutes, but couldn't make out where he was. It was almost silent except for the sounds of the ventilator. He could also tell through the bandages and his closed eyelids that wherever he was, it was dark. He sat still, trying to pick up clues. Was he at Fort Sam Houston already? How long had he been unconscious?

He heard a light knock on the door and the handle rattle. A few footsteps followed, and a gentle hand was placed on his shoulder.

"Major Harwood," she said just above a whisper, "are you awake?"

Jim nodded his head.

"Do you mind if I turn the lights on?"

He shrugged his shoulders. With his eyes bandaged over, he didn't see how it could matter. She turned on the lights.

"I'm Doctor Mohammad, and I'll be managing your care while you're here with us."

Jim didn't respond. What difference did it make who was taking care of him?

"Can I take off the bandage on your head?"

Jim nodded consent. At this point, he was ready to see anything other than the back of his eyelids.

"If this hurts too badly, let me know," she said as she began unwrapping his head. She didn't say anything as she peeled away layer after layer of gauze. As she reached the final layers against his skin it began to stick, so she wet a sponge and used it to try and soften and loosen where it was sticking. It hurt intensely, and he was grimacing accordingly.

"It's good that it hurts," she said as she peeled the final layer away from his eyes. "That means there isn't too much nerve damage. Can you open your eyes?"

Jim slowly blinked. The room was painfully bright as if he had just stepped out of a dimly lit room into full sunlight of a noon day. As his eyes adjusted he saw a diminutive woman who was apparently in her thirties with dark brown eyes, short dark brown hair, wearing a white lab coat and blue-green scrubs.

"Looks like they did an excellent job debriding this. Some of it will definitely scar pretty badly, but not as much as I had feared based on the notes in your chart. How's your vision? Can you see me clearly?"

Jim nodded.

"Excellent," she said, looking at his eyes through a scope. "Thank God for eye protection. You would have been blinded if your eyes had caught the same blast as the rest of your face. I think we can leave the bandages off for a while. And we don't need to cover your eyes when we bandage you up again."

Jim was grateful for that. Not being able to see had really impacted his perception of the world, and it was a relief to be able to see the faces of the people who were talking to him.

"It looks like the swelling in your airways may have started to go down," she said, peering up his nostrils through the scope. "We may be able to get you off of this ventilator in a few days. Tomorrow, we'll do a trial run for an hour and see how you do breathing on your own. If that goes well, we'll start weaning you off of it."

She then moved to the foot of the bed and peeled back the blankets to expose his legs. For the first time, Jim saw that his right foot was missing from a few inches below the knee. In its place was a carefully bandaged stump. Jim looked away as the Doctor peeled away the bandages. He didn't want to see the result.

"This is healing pretty well. I think they'll start the process of fitting you for a prosthesis as soon as you're off the ventilator and self-mobile, but I'm not the expert there. That's Doctor Franks, who will come see you in a few days."

Jim steeled himself, then turned to look at the stump that had previously been the lower half of his shin and foot. It wasn't nearly as gruesome as he had feared. The doctors had kept a large flap of skin and sown it over the stump with a long row of neat stitches.

"As for the burns, we'll make a special splint to keep pressure on the burned parts of your face as soon as the ventilator comes out. The pressure will help limit the formation of thick scar tissue and keep you from losing mobility in your mouth."

Great, Jim thought to himself, I'll look like the phantom of the opera.

"We'll start tapering down the sedation to improve your odds of going without the ventilator. If it gets too bad," she said, handing him a push-button attached to the IV pump nearby, "press this button and the pump will automatically give you a small dose of medicine. You can push it as often as you like, but there is a limit to how much the system will deliver. Try to use it as little as possible."

Jim nodded understanding, and reached for the controller. His hands were leaden, and it was all he could do to grasp the small object and set his hand down again. He was also beginning to have terrible difficulty following the conversation. The walls were moving, and the words periodically sounded like they were coming from inside a fish tank. Involuntarily, he closed his eyes and faded out once more.

The ventilator test had gone well, and by the following day the doctors had pulled the tube out of his throat. With the ventilator removed, they also were working to taper down the level of sedation. Jim was aware of his surroundings more and more.

As soon as the ventilator had come out, they had replaced the bandages around his head with a piece of molded plastic that looked an awful lot like a hockey mask with an articulated chin and gel cushions on the inside of it. The pressure on the burns hurt quite a bit at first, but quickly the touch of the mask became preferable to having the skin exposed.

Assessing what he could from where he lay, he decided he was likely in an intensive care unit where nurses or residents came and went constantly. Every few hours, a nursing student would come in and ask a series of questions, followed a few minutes later by the real nurse, then the medical students on rotations, then the resident, and finally the supervising physician. This never-ending string of questions really irritated him. First, his throat hurt and his voice was raspy from being intubated for so long. It hurt to talk, and that kind of hurt was about the only pain he could avoid by any means other than narcotics. Second, he honestly couldn't remember the answers to many of the questions they asked.

They kept asking what happened. They asked how long he'd been unconscious after the accident. They asked questions for which he wished he could remember the answers, but couldn't. They also asked questions like the last thing he could remember before the accident. Those were memories that were his, and his alone. He wasn't about to tell some dumb medical student what he'd been thinking of when the world went black. Third, the last thing in the world he wanted right now was to be around a bunch of people. Why couldn't they just record his damn answers the first time he gave them and replay them for the next group? That way they could bother him once, then leave him the hell alone. It wasn't like his story was going to change in the fifteen minutes between visitors.

One of these processions had just come to an end, and Jim was grumbling to himself about the interruption, when he heard another knock at the door.

"What?" Jim asked angrily, if somewhat tiredly.

"Staff Sergeant Kelnhoffer wants to visit with you if you are up to it," said a young Senior Airman who Jim knew worked in the ward.

"Sorry. I thought you were another doctor trainee," Jim apologized sheepishly. "Let him come in."

She pushed open the door and wheeled K9 into the room.

"They told me only family could come visit up here," K9 said as he got nearer to Jim's bed. "I told them we were brothers and Senior Airman Gomez here seemed to understand."

Jim pushed the button that raised the head of the bead so he could be mostly upright.

"Aside from my parents," Jim answered, "you're the only family I have within 1500 miles."

"Not quite. Mutt is here too somewhere. Haven't found him yet, but I will. You look like hell Shepherd."

"They tell me it looks like raw hamburger underneath this mask," Jim said as he turned to look at K9. He was in a wheelchair, and was missing his left leg with just a short stump extending below the hip. "I thought you said you would be running 10Ks?"

"Yeah. More likely I'll do marathons. You know, they've got these racing wheelchairs that can really move. Either that, or we work together... between the two of us, we have a complete set of legs."

Jim was almost shocked at how glib K9 was being. He couldn't help but wonder if it was a just a show put on for his benefit.

"How do you do it?"

"Do what?"

"Joke around like that? Marooned here on the island of broken toys, I'm having trouble finding anything humorous."

"Self defense strategy," K9 answered simply. Jim thought he understood.

"Have they talked to you about a prosthetic yet?" Jim asked. He was curious how long it would be before he could start that process, and was hopeful that K9 had already been down that road.

"Yeah. Basically, I have a choice between hanging a tree stump from my stump, using crutches, or riding in a wheel chair. There aren't many good options for anything much more than walking. They say they should have the first version of it built in a few weeks, and I'll start therapy with it as soon as it's ready. How about you?"

"Nothing yet," Jim answered downcast. "They just took me off the ventilator last night. Hopefully they'll release me from solitary into general population now that I can breathe on my own."

"Are your parents here?" K9 asked

"They arrived late yesterday. Staying at the Fisher House on Lackland. One here is full I guess," Jim said. He was starting to have trouble talking. The muscles in his face hurt, and the skin around his mouth seemed to be on fire. He pressed the pain button, and the now familiar sensation swept over him as his attention span narrowed tremendously.

"Have they held the funerals yet?"

"No."

"They going to hold off until you can make it?"

"Yeah."

"I'd like to be there with you."

"Okay."

"Hang in there with me Shepherd. We need to be in this for the long-haul."

"Find Mutt."

"Okay. I will. You look tired. I'll come see you again tomorrow."

"Thanks."

Chapter 4

Rehab

The nightmares had returned as the doctor's began dialing back the sedation. They had morphed too. Now it was Sammie and Leslie who were being tortured or killed. Worse yet, now that he wasn't the focus anymore he didn't wake up at the climax. It was usually something like the horrifying image of his wife or daughter's corpse that shook him awake. Sometimes the bad-guy took the shape of a rotund, drunk Navajo who cackled mercilessly over their dead bodies while smearing their blood on his own face like war pant.

Jim had come to fear sleep, and he was getting less and less of it. As the drugs wore off, his memory improved, and he would lie awake staring at the blank television screen in his room while continuously revisiting every decision he had made over the course of the last several years. He would pick apart every bit of information he could remember, critique every action, and always he came back to the same conclusion – he had failed everyone.

Leslie and Sammie were dead because of his decisions. Warlock and Monkey were dead because of his decisions. Many Iraqis were needlessly dead because of his decisions. Why had he been spared? Why were K9 and Mutt still alive to live a partial existence? These thoughts played over and over again in his mind any time he was conscious and not otherwise occupied. The nightmares were even worse, and there wasn't much other than mindless television to occupy his time awake.

"Lieutenant Colonel Harwood," someone said happily as they stepped through the door.

"Major," Jim corrected.

"The O5 selection board results will be published tomorrow, and your name will be on it," said a colonel who Jim didn't recognize. "The hospital director told me I could pass you the good news."

"Oh," Jim said without any enthusiasm.

"I'm Doctor Chelwood, from mental health."

"Oh," Jim said with even less enthusiasm.

"I'm supposed to run you through this screener questionnaire."

Great, a checklist.

"I hear you haven't been sleeping well," the doctor said, looking at his clipboard covered in paper instead of at Jim.

"Yeah."

"Is that a recent thing?" still looking down at his papers.

"Not really," Jim had been having trouble sleeping since he had arrived in Iraq, but things had been worse lately.

"How long has it been a problem."

"A while." Another scratch with the pen on his clipboard, but nothing more.

"Do you have trouble shutting down your mind at night?"

"Sometimes." What business was it of this guy what was on his mind before finally managing to fall asleep. "Besides," Jim thought to himself, "I'm probably nothing more than a fifteen minute block on the schedule, and I won't mean anything to him after he leaves."

"Tell me about your dreams."

"I try not to dream," was all the reply Jim could muster. The thought of reliving those dreams was more painful than he could contemplate.

"Do your dreams wake you up?"

"Sometimes." This was a lie. They always woke him up, but if all this guy was going to do was run down his list of pre-determined questions, Jim didn't really have much else to say.

"Have you had any thoughts of harming yourself or wishing you were dead?"

"Yes," Jim admitted against his will. The memory of K9 pinning his arm against the table floated into his consciousness. He felt a wave of tension grabbing hold of his chest and throat. His heart was racing.

"Recently?"

"Yes." Did this guy really care that he constantly wished he hadn't survived the attack? The single syllable eked out of his throat, almost stifled by the rising panic attack.

"Have you thought about how you would do it?"

Jim just nodded. He couldn't bring himself to admit verbally that those kinds of thoughts were still in his mind. It was a form of moral weakness to even entertain them. He was such a weak man.

"Do you have the means to do it?"

He shook his head. How could he? He was watched around the clock and still couldn't move out of bed without help. The doctor apparently didn't look up from his papers to see Jim's response.

"Didn't catch that. Do you have the means to do it?"

"No," Jim sobbed. It was the only sound he could make. He had lost control of his voice, and tears streamed down his slowly healing face while his chest heaved violently.

"I understand you lost your wife and daughter recently," Doctor Chelwood added, "would you like to talk with someone about that?"

Jim couldn't answer. The panic rose from his chest to his throat. His voice was completely paralyzed and he felt like his chest was going to burst open.

"They died in a car accident, right?"

The panic attack overwhelmed him, and he blacked out.

"Shepherd," he heard K9 say through a dense fog.

"Hey, Shepherd," K9 repeated, "snap out of it."

Jim blinked a few times, then turned and looked at his friend.

"They tell me you've been staring at that blank screen for over an hour."

Where had K9 come from? Wasn't the colonel here?

"You okay?"

"Are any of us here okay?" Jim answered, trying to regain his bearings.

"It's a sliding scale, but no, I don't think so."

"Last I remember, the head shrinker was going over a psych-eval checklist."

"Worthless docs and their forms. Like their magical checklists will cure us," K9 growled. Apparently, he'd already experienced that kind of care. No wonder the suicide rate among recently returned veterans was so high.

"He never even looked at me," Jim said, still staring at the blank television screen. "Just stood there staring down at his clipboard. Wasn't even really listening."

"He ask about your family?"

"I don't think I can talk about that yet," Jim admitted.

"He kept asking *me* about the convoy as if that were the only bad thing that ever happened." K9 paused for a long moment, leaving the weight of their shared past sitting heavily in the room. He started saying something, but stopped. Started again with the same result. Sat there silently for what felt like an eternity, then finally eked out a quiet and shaky, "Do you have to leave your lights on too?" Jim just nodded.

_ _ _ _ _ _ _ _ _ _ _ _ _ _ _ _ _ _

Jim had just been delivered back to his room from another long rehab session. That was the routine. Try to sleep, eat bad breakfast, live through the interminable rotation of students and residents, try to ignore the talk shows his roommate watched all day, eat a worse lunch, go to therapy, choke down dinner, go through the rotation again, and try to get at least a few hours of sleep before the dreams started. The monotony of it depleted what was left of his fragmented soul.

"Dad's at your house working on getting things packed up."

"My house. . . " It didn't feel like his house. He'd only lived there for a short while before he left. Why did his parents come here? There wasn't much they could do. For all he cared, the stuff at the house could all be thrown on the curb for the neighbors to pick through. He knew they were trying to help, but mostly he just wanted to be left alone.

"We're having everything moved into storage while you do rehab. The landlord has agreed to cancel the lease. Is there anything you want kept out?"

"Clothes would be nice," Jim offered. He was so tired of the tissue-thin hospital gowns, PT uniforms, and gray sweatclothes. It was all they gave him to wear. You'd think that with all the advances in modern medicine they could have at least come up with a better alternative for the gowns.

"Have you thought about where you want to go after they release you?"

"No." He couldn't tell his mom what he really wanted. She wouldn't understand.

"Your dad thinks they'll medically retire you. Do you think that's true?"

"Yeah." He was going to be pushed out of the only life he'd known as an adult. Between the loss of his family, loss of his career, and apparent loss of his future, he didn't feel like he had anything left to lose. "It won't be long before they unceremoniously dump me on the VA."

"You know you can always come home with us."

"Thanks Mom," Jim said tiredly. He doubted they'd let him go that far away any time soon though.

His mom stayed another hour before the procession of students and residents started up and she left to get out of the way. Around mid-day, Jim got up to use the bathroom. He hadn't been able to stand closing the door and being in that confined space, but life had taught him not to care about anyone watching him do just about anything.

"Close the door, would ya?" Jim's roommate growled. The new guy was an infantry major who had been struck by an IED in Afghanistan, and he was a first-class jerk. All the infantry Jim had ever been around hadn't cared in the slightest if someone else saw them taking a dump or performing any other necessary bodily functions, but this guy seemed to think he was special. Jim ignored him. He wasn't going to be closed into the small confines of the bathroom. If the new guy had a problem with seeing him on the pot, he could look away.

Jim heard the blast of shaped charges and flash-bangs, followed closely by gunfire. Something had gone wrong. Raids weren't supposed to go like this. It must be an ambush. He was a few yards behind point but couldn't tell who it was. More gunfire from seemingly nowhere but he saw the point-man fall to the ground. More gunfire and another explosion.

Jim startled awake with his heart racing and cold sweat on his neck and hands. It was dark. Where was his team? Why didn't he have his rifle? How many were injured? Did he lose another one? Inspecting the shadows of the darkened room lit only with the flickering of a television screen, he slowly realized it had been a dream. He was in the hospital room. His roommate was watching some kind of action movie that was in the middle of a gunfight scene. Jim jumped out of bed on his one good leg and stabbed the power button on the television.

"Who do you think you are?" the roommate shouted, turning his movie back on again.

"Turn that off!" Jim warned.

"Fuck off."

"I mean it. Turn it off!" Jim shouted. The roommate ignored him. "Turn it off, now!" Jim ordered at the top of his lungs.

The roommate answered with a raised middle finger. The sound of more explosions and flashes of light from the television were driving Jim mad. He couldn't take it anymore. He grabbed his roommate by the throat and started choking the life out of him, dodging the wildly flailing arms.

"Maybe you're okay with living in darkness while celebrating and wallowing in the scum, trash, and inhumanity of the world, but I'm not," Jim screamed, tightening his grip on the thick neck, "I'm not going to sit here and watch it."

The roommate was turning purple. Jim didn't care. He needed the noise to stop.

- - - - - - - - - - - - - - - - - - -

"I found Mutt," K9 said as he rolled himself awkwardly through the door, "it isn't good."

"Oh?"

"Dude's almost a vegetable."

"He was talking when they evac'd him."

"They said his brain swelled up and caused lots of damage."

"Does he know where he is or what happened?"

"Don't think so. Didn't seem to recognize me. Just sat there drooling on himself watching *Teletubbies* or something like that."

"Damn!" Another lost soul to lay to his charge. Mutt would live a half-life at best, and take his family down with him as they gave up all they had to care for the large baby that had formerly been their intelligent athlete of a son. That terrible laugh was going to follow Mutt into the lives of those who loved him. Why?

"I heard about your roommate," K9 started to say.

"I actually wanted to kill him," Jim said flatly, "I wanted to choke the life right out of him."

"Seems like overkill."

"He wouldn't turn off the movie, and I woke up in a nightmare," was all the explanation Jim could offer.

"What're they going to do about it?"

"Keep me in a single room, and make more time for me on the head-shrinker's schedule. I guess I convinced them I have issues."

- - - - - - - - - - - - - - - - - -

"Jim, I can't help you if you won't talk to me," said Colonel Chelwood.

"There's a difference between won't and can't. You keep asking me about things I don't have answers for. You've asked me a couple of times if I'm having a harder time coping with the loss of my wife and kid, or dealing with my deployment. What makes you think I can separate the two?"

"You blame the loss of your wife on your deployment?"

"I blame the Air Force. I blame the government. I blame the people who can't seem to see anything in a human beyond a number. I blame people who forget that soldiers, sailors, marines and airmen are human. I blame bureaucrats who refuse to look beyond the statistics and policy to see the human toll. I blame myself for not going AWOL,[18] for not resisting an order I knew was pointless. I blame myself for being a part of that system. Yes, I blame my deployment, but only as an ugly example of the inhumanity and evil that masquerades as heroism."

Colonel Chelwood nodded, but didn't interrupt. This was by far the most he had ever managed to get out of Jim.

"I can't tell you how angry I am, or even who I'm most angry at. There aren't words. I want to use my bare hands to slowly strangle the family members of every politician and bureaucrat that made the long list of infinitely stupid decisions that killed Leslie. I want them to helplessly watch while I do it. I want them to understand what it feels like. I want them to see how depraved humanity can be when manipulated and desperate. I want them to feel what desperation is... because that's what *I* saw every day over there. I want them to understand the utter futility of what they are trying to do and the costs that come with it!"

While Jim said this, he crushed something invisible, his hands and arms shaking with the effort. He also progressively spoke more quietly, more deliberately, and more slowly – to the point where words were little more than elongated half-voiced whispers escaping through tightly clenched teeth.

"I want to find that drunken son of a bitch who killed my wife and kid and tear his beating heart from his chest with my bare hands, then show it to him before he dies. I want to find the judge who let him off after his last four drunk driving convictions and send her to see the kind of justice meted out in places like Anbar."

The colonel had leaned in to listen, but sat up and drew a short breath as if he wanted to say something when Jim paused. However, he sat quiet for a moment to see if Jim had anything else to add.

"And when that's over," Jim continued, "I want to die. I want the world to forget me like I never existed. I want to never be angry again."

"Jim," the colonel started to say, but Jim didn't hear.

"They've taken away my family. They've taken away my faith. They've poisoned memories of my past to a point where they're too bitter to revisit. They've taken away my future. They've taken away my hope. They've taken away sleep and rest. They've taken away my ability to feel empathy, patience, joy, compassion or love. They've taken away everything but anger, hate, and despair. They've taken away almost everything that ever really mattered and replaced it with corruption and cancerous rot. Why couldn't they just take the last thing left to me and get it over with?"

As Jim finished saying this, he sank completely forward onto the desk and sobbed uncontrollably for several minutes while the doctor sat silent.

"Oh God! I want to die!" he whispered over and over again between sobs. The colonel said nothing, but put a hand on Jim's shoulder for a moment before stepping out of the room to call an orderly. A few minutes later, the orderly appeared and wheeled a now silent Jim back to his room.

"Shepherd, you in here?"

Jim didn't answer.

"I'm going to turn on the lights, okay?"

Still no answer. It was odd to have the lights off. Jim had kept it like the noon-day sun in here round the clock. K9 flipped on the lights and saw Jim sitting in his bed staring blankly at the wall again.

"Anything new with the shrink?"

"Does it ever get easier?" Jim asked in an exhausted tone.

K9 understood this to mean that Jim had finally managed to talk at least a little about what he was feeling. "First time is the hardest," he said sympathetically, "but not by much."

"Rehab hurts less."

"I'm pretty sure pain is part of the healing," K9 reminded him.

"Why did you stop me that night?"

"Because I couldn't be outlive another friend."

"I think you were too late to save me."

"No, not yet."

"Can you still hear it?" Jim asked, changing the subject. "I can, even from here..."

"The Laugh? Yeah..."

_ _ _ _ _ _ _ _ _ _ _ _ _ _ _ _ _ _

As his physical wounds healed and he became more proficient with the prosthetic he had been given, it became more and more clear that the physical injuries were only a small part of what kept him in the hospital. Colonel Chelwood, it seemed, would have the final vote for when Jim could leave the hospital and continue rehab on an out-patient basis. In fact, his face had healed enough that they weren't doing much active rehab for the burns, and his stump was almost completely healed up.

If the physical therapy got easier, his sessions with the colonel more than compensated. He was constantly exhausted. Each visit, the colonel would make Jim relive at least a portion of the last two years. They would talk about it, analyze it, try to unpack it. Just forming the words to discuss the undisputed facts seemed a bridge too far, but he crossed it over and over again. Each time, he would swear he'd crossed it for the last time. Each time, he would step forward when bidden and cross it again. It was a mechanical motion, but over time he began to hope that it might eventually take him somewhere better than where he was.

"Jim," Colonel Chelwood said to start their regular session, "your family needs some closure. It's time to bury your wife and daughter."

Jim had been avoiding even thinking about the prospect of rescheduling the funeral. He just didn't feel ready to deal with the finality of it. He wasn't prepared to face the reality either. As long as he didn't see the caskets, it could be abstract; it could be buried.

"I understand the plan was to hold it in Boise, is that right?"

Jim just nodded as he visibly sagged.

"We can arrange for a wound-care nurse to accompany you, but it'll only be for a few days. You need to come back here immediately afterwards."

"Can Staff Sergeant Kelnhoffer come with me? Please?"

"We don't normally use another patient as a medical escort. . . "

Jim sank further.

"I'll see what I can do."

Chapter 5

Saying Goodbye

The airline had arranged for wheelchairs, but both had refused. They were still capable of moving under their own power, and they were determined to do so. Instead, they sat patiently on the plane waiting for everyone else to get off before carefully picking their way down the isle on crutches. Emerging from the jetway, Jim first and K9 right behind him, the small crowd parted silently to reveal a small formation of veterans who rendered a salute. Jim balanced his weight on his remaining foot and returned the salute without saying anything. He hadn't expected this.

"Daddy!" Sammie squealed as she broke free of Leslie's hand and ran towards him.

He had just deplaned after flying in from Fort Bragg. The training had been six weeks long, and had taken a significant toll on both is body and mind. The joy of his wife and daughter was the best medicine he could imagine right about now.

"Key kiddo!" Jim said as he dropped his bag and scooped her up in his arms. "I missed you so much!"

Leslie had closed the gap between them and embraced him, sandwiching Sammie between them.

"Oh. . . It's so good to have you back," she whispered in his ear while squeezing him very tightly.

"Hey beautiful," Jim answered, "you smell amazing."

"It's just shampoo and conditioner."

"Yeah, but it's the stuff you use. You could wash your hair with vinegar and I'd learn to love the smell."

"Well, I'll admit I go in the closet sometimes and smell your shirts when I get really lonely."

"Let's get my bags and get out of here."

"Gentlemen," the apparent head of the veteran delegation said addressing both Jim and K9, "we are here to honor you and your sacrifices. While we cannot know your individual struggles, we want you to know that you are not alone. Please allow us to escort you on this leg of your journey."

It was a stiff and clearly carefully prepared introduction. Jim would have been happier if nobody had been in the terminal, but he recognized that this was at least partly about the people here trying to feel like they could do something. . . anything.

Jim silently nodded and shook the hand extended towards him. With a veteran on either side of both Jim and K9, the group started to walk down the terminal towards the baggage claim. A wave of silence followed them. As soon as they approached any area, everyone stopped what they were doing and turned silently to offer their respect. A mixture of crusty veterans and guardsmen in uniform lined the pathway every fifteen or so feet to render a salute as they passed.

When they reached the baggage claim, one of the veterans had already retrieved their bags and was waiting to follow them to the curb. Outside, a small motorcade of cars with a police escort was waiting. The two climbed clumsily into a limousine while others loaded the baggage into the trunk. Then the motorcade pulled slowly away, directly to the funeral at a chapel only a few miles away. All along the route, people had gathered, placing their hands over their hearts as the cars passed. Jim had seen this kind of procession before, but only for soldiers being brought home in a box. It would have been easier if he'd been in a box.

"Wonder who set this up?" Jim asked without directing it at anyone in particular.

"Your brother-in-law, sort of," one of Jim's escorts answered. The speaker had on an expensive suit and had an air of importance about him. "He told a friend of his what had happened, at least what he knew of it. That spread, and the local VFW, American Legion, and a few of us others took it from there. He didn't mean for it to be this big a deal, but I couldn't let you come home without letting you know you weren't alone."

"Is it going to be like this at the funeral?" K9 asked uncomfortably.

"No. We made it very clear that the funeral was for family and close friends only. We'll deliver you to the chapel and leave you in your family's care."

The whole team was here. Everyone was silent, waiting, knew their place, and knew what they were supposed to do. The door opened, and someone nodded. That was their cue, and with a single motion they stood and filed out the door behind their guide and into two vans that made their way down the parking ramp. Nobody spoke during the short drive. The vans stopped just short of a C-17 transport and everyone filed out and formed up.

Another vehicle approached and backed up close to the assembled team. Eight men stepped forward and carefully lifted the two flag-draped aluminum coffins onto their shoulders. They turned and began marching in slow unison towards the airplane's open cargo door, stopping just short of the loading ramp.

Jim rendered a final salute to his fallen friends, and on cue the remainder of the team raised their rifles and fired three successive volleys. Somewhere nearby taps began playing as the coffins were carried up the ramp and into the airplane.

The public viewing wasn't supposed to start for another hour, and the funeral wasn't going to start for two. Consequently, the chapel was mostly empty when they arrived. Jim's mother, father, and in-laws met him at the door and took turns embracing him. Nothing was said. Nothing needed to be said. Nothing could be said. They then took turns introducing themselves to K9, shaking his hand.

"Jim," his step-father said, "why don't you go in and say goodbye. When you're done, we've got your clothes in one of the rooms here so you can change and have some privacy until the services start."

Jim nodded and followed as they all headed towards the room where the caskets stood open. As Jim crossed the threshold of the room, everyone else stopped, then pulled the door closed, leaving Jim alone. He hobbled forward to Leslie's casket. She was dressed in the same simple white dress she had worn for their wedding. Now she wore it laying in a simple wooden casket – she had always said she didn't want an expensive or ornate funeral. That had always been her way.

There she was, at the altar smiling at him. A small group of close friends and family occupied the few seats available and looked on as the officiator spoke words of counsel. Jim didn't hear a word of what was said. All he heard was his heart beating in his chest, and he didn't see anything other than Leslie's smile.

He leaned heavily on his crutches and reached out to touch her hair, then he gingerly touched her face. It was cold and waxy. It didn't feel like her. She was gone, and had only left this empty, lifeless shell behind. Tears streamed down his face as he moved backwards and sat down on a nearby chair, hanging his head between his hands. He sat there for several minutes before pushing himself upright again and moving to Sammie's casket. Running his fingers through her hair, he began to talk to his daughter through heavy tears.

"Kiddo. . . I miss you so much. I don't know if I'll ever understand why you had to go instead of me. I don't understand any of this. If you're really on the other side, and can hear me, help me to learn to be simple again and to know that you're okay where you are."

Jim reached into his pocket and pulled out a charred piece of paper, gingerly unfolding it, looking at it one last time, then refolding it and placing it under Sammie's hand.

"Grandma's taking care of the real Lola until I'm a little better, and the unicorn magic seems to be done for me, so I'll give this back to you so they can protect you on your journey."

"Daddy, I'm scared."

"What are you afraid of kiddo?"

"The witches."

"You mean the ones in the story I've been reading to you? The ones who turned the boy into a mouse?"

"I don't want to be a mouse."

"You think there are witches around here?"

"Uh huh."

He knew there was no point in trying to convince her they were all imaginary. "Give me just a second, and I'll be right back with some witch spray."

"Witch spray?"

"Yep. I can make up some witch repellent. Two squirts around the window and two around the door, and no witch in the world will make it anywhere near you."

"What if a witch comes while you're getting it ready?"

"Lola," Jim called, "come here girl." Lola obediently came into the room with a quizzical look on her face. Jim motioned for her to lay down near Sammie's bed. "Lola will protect you while I'm gone. Witches don't like German shepherds."

"But what if that doesn't work?"

Jim walked over to the dresser and picked up the unicorn music box she had gotten from her grandma for Christmas. He wound it up, and it began playing a lullaby. "Witches don't like happy music either, and I'll be back before the music stops."

He stepped out of the room and started rummaging in the bathroom cupboard.

"What are you up to now?" Leslie asked.

"Witch spray."

"Witch spray?"

"Yep. I need some witch spray to keep the witches out of Sammie's room," Jim said as he found a mostly empty squirt bottle and filled it with water. "Two squirts by the door, and two by the window."

"That'd better work. We need some quiet time," Leslie said with a wink.

Jim stepped backward and fell back into the same chair. It took several more minutes before he had the strength to stand again and approach Leslie's casket.

"Hey gorgeous," Jim started, "I really screwed this one up, didn't I? This isn't how our story was supposed to go. Why didn't I walk away from the Air Force when I had a chance? None of this would have happened if I hadn't stayed. I'm so sorry..."

Jim reached into his pocket and pulled out his wallet. Opening it up, he removed a small picture that was well-worn from years of abuse. It was one of their engagement photos that he had carried everywhere with him since it was taken. He placed the photo under her hand.

"I kept this with me to always reminded me of the commitment we made to each other. It was a symbol for me of your unconditional love and support. I never doubted you. Keep it with you until we meet again. I wish I were with you now, but that doesn't seem to be the way things are going to work out."

Jim stood there for what seemed like an eternity, caressing the hair that framed her face and bathing her face with tears. Her hair, at least, felt like he remembered. How many times had he caressed those loose curls?

"I cut my hair," Leslie said rather sheepishly as he walked into the small apartment they shared. It wasn't as if she could have hidden the fact. She had always kept her hair at least shoulder-length since they met, and now it was only a few inches longer than his.

"Do *you* like it?" Jim asked, turning the unspoken question back on her. He knew he was standing in the middle of a mine field. If he said he liked it but she didn't, he would be in trouble. If he said he liked it better longer, he'd be wrong. The only way he could come out of this ahead was if he said he liked it, and she agreed. There was no right answer until she had spilled the beans first.

"It's so light," she said beaming, making Jim's path suddenly clear.

"I love it," he agreed. Anything that brought that kind of smile to her face had his seal of approval. For all he cared, she could shave her head if it made her feel beautiful. Anytime she felt beautiful, she *was* beautiful. The fact that she would spend the next ten years oscillating between short and long hair had very little impact on him. Long, short, or in between, he loved it all.

"Her fight's over now," K9 said quietly as he hobbled to Jim's side. Jim hadn't heard him come in.

"How is it that she could win ugly and prolonged battles only to get taken out by something as random as being on the wrong road at the wrong time?"

"What do you mean?"

"Some of what she went through makes Ramadi look easy. She was only just getting back on her feet and feeling close to normal when I got orders."

"And just like Iraq, it's not always the hot fights that end up getting you in the end," K9 countered. He didn't quite understand what Jim meant, but this wasn't the time or place to probe further. There would be time for that later.

Jim nodded his assent, then the two friends stood silently for several minutes until they were disturbed by the sound of someone clearing his throat.

"Mr. Harwood?" The funeral director said timidly.

Jim turned and faced him.

"Guests will start arriving shortly. You should probably get changed now."

Both his and K9's dress uniforms were waiting for them in a small room just off the chapel, and the two turned and moved that direction. A health aide who had been sent as a medical escort for both of them was patiently waiting there to help them get dressed and adjust the uniforms for the missing limbs.

"Last time I wore this, I was meeting my new boss for the first time," Jim said, looking at his neatly pressed service uniform. Someone had already added the bronze star and purple heart to his ribbon rack and replaced the rank. "I wasn't sure I'd ever put it back on."

"Me either. Then again, it wasn't all that long ago when I wasn't sure either of us would ever put anything on again."

The aide alternated between the two of them, helping them pull their pants up and pin the unused legs out of the way. Shirts, ties, socks, a shoe a piece, and finally the service coat. They were ready.

"Sir, there's a mirror in the bathroom next door if you want to look yourself over."

Jim just shook his head. He couldn't stand the sight of his face – whether covered in the splint or not. K9 asked the aide how he looked, and was satisfied with the answer. The two sat down in the chairs that had been placed for them and waited.

Jim's parents and in-laws were in the foyer greeting people as they came in. Jim felt like he should be there, but he just couldn't face the family right now. He couldn't take any more pity, and he didn't want to have to explain anything. He didn't want to have to tell people he was doing all right. He didn't want to have to lie. Instead, he sat in that small room hidden from scrutiny.

"Where do you think you'll go when the doc's are done with you?" Jim asked.

"I don't know. There's a crazy part of me that wants to go back to Iraq."

"You too? I hated that place, but I can't think of anywhere else I'd rather be."

"The team's long gone by now," K9 said flatly. "I think that's what I actually miss."

"Sure don't miss the desert or getting shot at," Jim agreed.

"My cousin's invited me to come live with her, but Jersey isn't my kind of place anymore. Too crowded."

"Jersey... long way from your life in the Army."

"I've got another cousin in DC, but that isn't any better. What about you?"

"Lots of family here, but I don't think I'm ready to be around them. Is that wrong?"

"Probably, but that doesn't really change anything."

"They talk to you yet about the rest of your treatment plan?" Jim asked.

"About another four weeks of therapy, then I'll be in and out on a routine follow-up basis. They've already started the medical retirement proceedings. I'm supposed to move into a sort of halfway house in town for the time being."

"Looks like they're going to retire me too. I have no idea how long that will take though."

"What do we do next?" K9 asked uncertainly. Jim didn't have an answer, so they just sat quietly waiting for the funeral to start.

A few minutes later the chapel was full and the service was about to begin. Jim and K9 mounted their crutches and began making their way to their seats on the front pew. An organist was playing a quiet hymn, but it wasn't loud enough to mask the rhythmic click-squeak of the two pairs of crutches as they moved down the isle.

The service proceeded without interruption as one speaker after another shared memories of Leslie and Sammie. Many laughed, all cried. Leslie's lifetime of service and caring for others was on bright display. Jim's mind repeatedly left the confines of the funeral and followed one of the anecdotes further, looking for reprieve in the solitude of his own mind. He was lost in memories when the service ended and everyone moved to leave the chapel for the cemetery across town.

The burial plot was in a small cemetery near Leslie's parents' house. Both caskets were to be interred in the same grave, and Jim watched as the grave was dedicated and flowers were placed on the caskets. That was the extent of the graveside service. The caskets would be lowered into the gaping hole in the earth once everyone left. One after another, family and friends filed past Jim, laying a sympathetic hand on his shoulder or kissing him on the cheek as they went by. Within minutes Jim was left alone to offer his last goodbye.

"God, if you're out there," Jim muttered almost silently, "watch over them. Even if you've abandoned me, take them home and make them happy."

K9 had withdrawn to the car, but was standing outside looking at the blue sky and leaning against the door to take pressure off his crutches. A short, round-faced woman with wrinkled brown skin and gray hair approached him timidly.

"You're very close to Colonel Harwood?" she asked.

"We've chewed up a lot of dirt together..."

"My name is Maggie Tso. My son caused the accident that did this," she said, gesturing towards the grave site. "When the time is right, please let him know that I would like to help him heal. Tell him I will help him visit the scene of the accident, and that my heart and home are always open to him."

She handed him a small envelope, and turned to leave without saying anything further. She had driven all the way from

Shiprock the day prior and waited patiently through the funeral just for this short conversation. It would be a long drive home, but she couldn't afford to stay longer.

K9 watched her walk to an old beat-up Chevy truck and climb in. She was tilted and hunched, and the impact of arthritis was clear in her shuffling gait. With effort, she climbed into the cab and pulled the heavy door shut. The creaky old truck started in a cloud of blue-white smoke and rattled slowly out of the cemetery. As she drove out of sight, K9 worked his way back towards the grave and sat down next to Jim.

"I need a wheelchair. I don't think I can walk," Jim said after a few moments of silence. K9 nodded and waived to the health aid who was waiting just out of earshot.

Chapter 6

Transition

"Colonel Harwood," the technician said, smiling and standing up as Jim entered the small room, "I've got the final one here."

Jim limped towards a chair stuck in the corner and dropped himself into it before taking off the temporary prosthetic he'd been using. It was getting more comfortable as the stump hardened up and he got used to using it, but it was still unpleasant. The phantom pain was getting to be less of an issue as well, so long as he was busy doing something.

"I'm getting better with these things," Jim said as cheerfully as he'd said anything lately. "It's better than crutches."

"Give it a few weeks with this one, and you'll be walking like you never lost your real one."

"What about running?" Jim was hoping to get back to distance running, but he hadn't brought the subject up. The thought of getting into the zone and just focusing on the run for an hour or two at a time seemed really appealing to him.

"I wouldn't try running with this one, but the doc's already ordered one that will work for that. You'll just have to swap them out before chasing down any purse snatchers. It should be ready in a week or two."

"Do you do that for everyone?"

"Doc Stephens does. He's a runner himself, and he likes to encourage folks who can to try getting back to it."

"How does the fit change as I gain or lose weight?" Jim asked as he put the new limb on. He'd been sitting still so long he'd gained fifteen pounds, but he had every intention of getting back to his fighting weight once he was out of this place.

"Depends," the technician answered. "If you chunk up, it'll get tight, but unless you lose a whole lot from where you are now you shouldn't have too much of a problem going down. Now," he said, reaching out with his hand to help Jim to his feet, "let's see how it works."

Jim stood up and reached for the double handrails that were by now very familiar. He walked almost effortlessly to the other end and turned to come back. "Seems a little lighter than the last one, and it moves better."

"We'll work over stairs and level ground today, and probably get you on the exercise bikes tomorrow to try something different."

The next several hours consisted of repeatedly stepping up, stepping down; stepping forward, stepping back; walking down the hall, then turning and walking back. It was mind-numbingly boring, but so was everything about spending endless days in a hospital and rehab center. It was getting easier to just switch off and let the time go by, but that had its downsides. He couldn't switch off just the bad or boring stuff. When he switched off, he switched off almost everything and moved through the motions of his daily routine mechanically doing what he knew needed doing and nothing more.

As Jim sat down to rest for a few minutes before making his way back to the shuttle that would take him to his apartment, Colonel Chelwood walked into the large room scanning it for someone. Seeing Jim, he walked directly over.

"Jim," the doctor started to say. Jim began to stand up to greet him, but Colonel Chelwood waived for him to sit back down as he took a seat on a nearby stool. "I came down to let you know the medical review board will be looking at your case in the next few weeks. I'll be sitting on the board."

"Do you think they'll retire me?" Jim asked.

"It depends a lot on what you want to do."

"How do you mean?"

"If you don't do anything, they'll almost certainly retire you. However, if you want to stay on active duty I can fight for you. There are plenty of active duty soldiers, sailors, marines, and airmen who are missing one body part or another. With what you do, you could probably function just fine."

Jim expected this conversation, and he had spent considerable time pondering how he would respond. For months, he was certain there was nothing that would convince him to stay on active duty. That was true even before the accident, and losing his family and then his leg seemed to cement that resolution into an impermeable mass of granite. But now that he was facing that prospect for real, he was having second thoughts. Looking around the room he realized that the Air Force was about all he had left, and leaving it, no matter how much he hated it, would be difficult.

"What do you think doc?" Jim had developed a good deal of respect for the psychologist. Next to K9, Doc Chelwood was the closest thing Jim had to a friend in this place.

"I can't make that decision for you, but if it were me, I'd take the retirement. Any way you cut it, all going back to regular duty would do is postpone the next phase of your life by a few years."

"Can I spend a few days thinking about it?"

"Sure."

Do four years then get out... that was always the plan. But the job prospects weren't all that good when the time came, and an assignment to the gulf-coast of Florida sounded like a good time. He and Leslie had agreed he would continue on active duty at least until they got another assignment, then decide from there. That was four years ago, and time was up on his current assignment. This round, there hadn't been much discussion about whether to stay or not. Inertia had mostly taken over.

Jim opened the email and began reading – Bolling. DC. This hadn't been on his wish-list, but then again, that didn't surprise him. The bean-counters at the personnel center didn't seem to care even a little bit about what you wanted when it came time to match people against the available jobs. At least it was just Leslie and him... it'd be a lot harder to do DC if they had kids. He picked up the phone and called Leslie.

"Hey gorgeous," Jim started.

"Are you inviting me out to lunch?"

"No. I've got a meeting in a few minutes I can't get out of. I just wanted to let you know I've got our next assignment."

"Where to?"

"Bolling Air Force Base."

"Where's that?" Leslie asked.

"Just across the river from DC on the Maryland side."

"Oh..." She didn't sound particularly enthusiastic.

"Something wrong?"

"No. It's just kind of a shock."

"I've gotta run. See you tonight."

"All right. Love you."

-- -- -- -- -- -- -- -- -- --

Jim walked into the house almost an hour later than usual, which wasn't in itself particularly unusual. Leslie was waiting for him with a candle-light dinner all prepared.

"Wow," Jim exhaled, "I didn't think you'd be this excited about moving to Washington."

"I'm not. This is for something else."

"Then what are we celebrating tonight?"

"We're going to have a baby!" Leslie beamed.

After years of trying, Jim had given up and resigned himself to being a rent-a-dad to other kids at church whose parents were divorced. This was awesome news!

The revelation did come with other implications though. Jim had spent a fair portion of the afternoon thinking about leaving the Air Force rather than accepting this assignment, but with Leslie's medical history it would be a very bad idea to drop or change medical coverage until after the baby came. It looked like it would be at least another two years.

Jim shook himself back to the present. Life was less complicated here. All he had to worry about was the daily grind of rehab. But that sense of ease faded just as quickly as it had come to mind. The status quo was about to change, like it or not. He had picked up hints that they were coming to the end of his rehab and that it wouldn't be long before he had to move on with life.

Jim got up, thanked the therapist, and began down the hall, leaning heavily on his cane as he went. He was tired from the session, but that was only a part of it. He was replaying the conversation he'd just had with the doctor in his mind, and couldn't believe what he heard there. Was he really having second thoughts about letting them quietly retire him? A year ago he would have given almost anything to be a civilian.

"K9, you in there?" Jim shouted as he banged on the door. His apartment was too quiet at the moment and he didn't want to be alone. Jim heard a bump and a crash, but no other answer.

"Hey, open up, would ya?"

"Just a sec," came the very slurred reply. A few minutes later Jim heard the click of the lock as K9 unlocked it, but the door didn't open. Jim turned the handle and let himself in.

The apartment was trashed. Much of the cheap furniture in the room was scattered and overturned, several dishes had been shattered with the shards covering the floor, and there was a large pile of empty beer bottles on the coffee table.

"You do all this?" Jim asked.

"Yeah..." K9 said sadly.

"Come over to my place. We'll clean this up later."

K9 nodded, then started struggling to get up onto his wheelchair. His prosthetic was nowhere to be seen. Jim moved in and tried to help prop K9 up, but he was far too unsteady himself to be much use. The best he could do was hold onto the chair to keep it from rolling away as a severely inebriated K9 hauled himself into it. After several failed attempts resulted in very loud strings of profanity, K9 finally succeeded in hoisting himself into a seated position.

"Where's your key?"

"Coffee table."

Jim scattered the empty bottles and found the key right where it was supposed to be. A fact that amazed him.

"I'm not done..." K9 started to say. Jim didn't need him to finish. He knew what was wanted, and gingerly made his way through the mess to the fridge and found a full case of the cheap high-gravity stuff. It was going to be one of those nights.

Getting the beer out of the kitchen turned out to be an ordeal though. He couldn't quite navigate the broken glass on the floor, scattered chairs, and overturned table with the heavy box in his hands. To avoid falling over, he settled for progressively leaning forward as far as he could without losing his balance to set down his load, stepping forward using his hands against the wall to stabilize himself, then repeating the process until he reached the door and K9. Setting the beer on the wheelchair where K9's leg should have been, Jim made four more trips to the kitchen to retrieve a half-empty bottle of whiskey, another of vodka, a case of Coke, and a large bottle of orange juice. All these he set down by the door so he could come back and get them after delivering K9.

Jim wheeled the chair out the door, using it as much to steady himself as to move K9, pulled the door shut behind them, and made the short trip to his apartment. After pushing K9 in the door and propping him in a chair, Jim rolled the wheelchair back to retrieve the rest of the booze.

"Shepherd..." K9 said after Jim had pulled the door shut behind him.

"Yeah?" Jim said, handing K9 a beer.

"Don't you ever want to drink your troubles away?"

"Every day."

"Give in tonight. Let's be oblivious for a while."

Jim hadn't been drunk since college. It hadn't worked then, and he didn't honestly think it was working for K9 now.

"Does it really help?" Jim asked, mostly trying to convince his friend he'd had enough.

"No. You have to sober up eventually. But tonight is special."

"Why's that?"

"Sixteen years ago today my life ended. I'm celebrating my death."

"Selection?" Jim asked. K9 had said a few times that making it through Special Forces selection was the biggest mistake of his life, followed closely by surviving the Allegheny mountains.

"Enlistment. That's where it all started."

The two of them sat in silence for a while staring at a blank television.

"Doc told me they were going to board me soon," Jim said, still staring at the television. "Asked if I wanted to stay."

K9 looked at the beer in his hand. He hadn't touched it yet, so he held it out to Jim. "You need this more than I do."

Jim mechanically took the bottle and took a long pull on it. The bitter taste was as bad as he'd remembered, but he didn't care at the moment. A few minutes later K9 handed him another. Jim drank it quickly without saying anything more, then reached for another. And another.

"My board made their decision today," K9 said sadly. "I'm medically retired effective immediately." He broke down sobbing and started beating his head against the back of the couch. It was the only life he'd known, and now what remained of it was over.

An hour passed in silence, the two friends sitting side-by-side staring at nothing. The only sound was the occasional hiss of a beer being opened.

"What next?" Jim asked.

"Well," K9 said thoughtfully, "I can't keep doing this."

The floor was moving every time Jim moved his head, and the walls seemed completely unstable. He was thoroughly drunk, but didn't feel any better. Maybe it would change with another beer, but first he needed to pee.

"C'mon" Jim announced unexpectedly, "we both need a pit-stop. I don't want to have to replace the couch."

K9 nodded and started crawling on his three good limbs towards the bathroom a few yards away. Jim followed in the same manner, unsure he was stable enough to use his crutches.

"What a sad lot," Jim said as he came out of the toilet, "crawling our way to the crapper."

They both rolled on the floor laughing for several seconds, but the laughing turned into tears and self-loathing before they made it back to the couch and sank down sullenly.

"How much do you have to drink to make it go away?" Jim asked in tears. As stupid as he'd been in college, he'd never blacked out, and he hoped there was a threshold somewhere nearby that he just needed to cross.

"More than your liver can process, and then you wake up and nothing's changed except for how you feel about yourself."

Jim grabbed another beer. K9 poured a stout shot of whiskey in a glass and topped it off with Coke.

"What next?" Jim asked again.

"What about a road-trip. You're about where you can drive again, right?"

"Where to?"

"Anywhere... just away from here."

They sat in silence again. It was getting late, but neither moved other than to crawl to the toilet or get another drink.

"I've hated the Air Force for the last two years," Jim said suddenly, "why on earth would I want to stay now."

"What else do we have left?"

"Would *you* stay if they let you?"

"Hell no, but I don't want to leave either," K9 answered emphatically. "It's like the kind of relationships you see on Jerry Springer. You love it and need it, but you can't stand to live with it. I don't know anything else anymore."

"A road trip..." Jim mused, then opened the last beer he'd drink that night. "Here's to being screwed-up civilians," he said, raising his bottle and almost falling over in the process.

Chapter 7

The Letter

It had taken the two of them three days to sober up and clean up the mess in both apartments. Aside from a few broken dishes there wasn't really any damage. Just a lot of mess.

"Why didn't you ever get married?" Jim asked as he came out of the bathroom he had just finished cleaning – the final requirement before the aides would start helping them again.

"I did," K9 replied flatly.

"Huh?" Jim was surprised. In all the time they'd been together, he'd never heard K9 mention an ex-wife.

"Yeah, high school sweetheart. We married the day after I graduated basic. She divorced me before I finished AIT. Wasn't really much of a marriage, but it left a bitter taste in my mouth. All the guys I saw getting dear-John letters on deployment didn't help. With our ops-tempo in the unit and all, I just decided it was easier to stay single."

There were times when Jim almost wished he didn't have to deal with the memories. But overall, he still would rather have once had and then lost it than never known what he was missing.

"You ever regret that?" Jim asked.

"Not until recently," K9 said thoughtfully. "There was always another deployment to keep me occupied until this. . ." He gestured towards his missing leg.

"I've been thinking about the other night. . ." Jim started to say.

"You remember any of that?" K9 asked in disbelief. "You were putting them away like a champ."

"Wish I could forget. That's why I quit in the first place. . . I couldn't drink enough to forget whatever it was I didn't want to remember. All I ever did was wake up feeling like I was a failure even at being a failure."

"Yeah. . ." K9 looked at the floor, clearly sharing some of the sentiment. "You thinking about taking that road trip with me?"

"Where would we go? We're not really fit company for too many tourist hot-spots."

"I've thought about trying to find my old man and patch things up. But I'm not sure that's a great idea. He's more screwed up than us. For all I know, he's living on the streets of San Diego again."

"How'd he end up like that?"

"Schizophrenia. My mom left him when I was a baby, but he'd float through every so often looking for a handout until I was a teenager. I'm pretty sure he ended up in jail about then, but I never went out of my way to find out."

Jim had always wanted to tour the National Parks, but neither of them were in much of a condition for hiking trails in the Grand Canyon, Zion, or Yellowstone. He thought for a moment about going to New York to see Broadway, but that lasted only a split second – that had been Leslie's dream.

"Everything I've always wanted to go see seems out of reach for a while yet. Either too inaccessible or too many people," Jim concluded. "But I definitely want to get out of here for a while."

"Did I ever tell you about Maggie?" K9 asked suddenly.

"Who?"

"The lady who came to the grave-side at your wife's funeral. She came up to me and handed me a letter, said a few words, then drove off."

"No, you never did."

K9 then told the whole story, except for the fact that it was Maggie's son who had caused the crash. Shortly after the funeral, K9 had written to Maggie while he was drunk and angry to tell her that Jim wasn't interested. Undeterred, Maggie had replied with another letter, and the two had been pen-pals ever since.

"She's kind of a Navajo social worker, near as I can tell. Maybe she's just a good listener, but I really like getting her letters. Sometimes she even makes me feel human for a minute. I'd kinda like to go see her."

Navajo... why did it have to be that? Jim just shook his head and walked back to his apartment.

- - - - - - - - - - - - - - - - - -

Jim jerked awake, knocking over the lamp on the nightstand by his bed as he flailed. Would these nightmares ever let him sleep? Though he didn't want to admit it, he knew they were worse when he was drunk. But that didn't seem to matter when the bottle held out the promise of temporary relief. It also didn't seem to matter that the promise was never kept.

Some nights the nightmares were a replay of a raid gone wrong. Others were tied to the funerals or the car crash. Some were just nonsense. But this one was different. This one went further back. He sat up in bed, trying desperately to find the lamp that was now laying on the floor. He needed to get some light in the room and reassure himself where he was.

"Captain Harwood?" the nurse called out into the waiting room.

Jim stood up from where he was seated in the waiting room and walked over to the door where the nurse was waiting.

"The doctor asked me to let you know things were taking longer than planned, that he needs to consult with you briefly, and that it'd probably be another hour or two before she'll be out of surgery."

Jim nodded and walked back to the chair he'd occupied for the last four hours and dropped heavily back into it. This was supposed to be a routine procedure, but he'd heard nothing from the surgeon. It was just a cyst, the plan was to open her up, cut it out, and be done. That was the plan.

The fertility doc had noticed it on an ultrasound and had referred her to the oncological surgeon to get it removed. They had told him it was almost certainly benign, but that they needed to take care of it before it cut off it's own blood supply and went necrotic. No big deal. The longer it took the more Jim started to worry that things weren't what they had appeared.

As Jim finished his hundredth lap around the waiting room the doctor stepped out into the waiting area scanning for Jim. Spotting him, the doctor waived Jim over, led him to a private consulting room, and motioned for him to sit down.

"Jim. . ." The Doctor paused for a moment waiting for Jim to sit down. "Things didn't go like planned."

Jim sat frozen in his chair, dreading the rest of this interview.

"We removed the cyst with no problems. The trouble is what we found under it. There was another growth that doesn't look good."

Jim slumped over, and his head drooped into his hands. He couldn't speak.

"We've consulted with the oncology team at Walter Reed, and we all agree the best thing we can do at this point is remove the ovary and some of the surrounding tissues now so we don't have to do another surgery."

Jim nodded without looking up. "Okay."

Why was he having nightmares about that? He knew that story ended fine. He hadn't even thought about that day since before Sammy was born. Chemo was bad, but in the end she was fine. He reminded himself of this fact over and over again.

He reached over, grabbed the crutches propped against the wall near his nightstand, pulled on a pair of shorts and a t-shirt, then hobbled out into his kitchen/living room. Automatically, he opened the fridge looking for a beer where one had never been. It was getting easier and easier to talk himself into drinking with K9, and every time he felt more and more worthless when he sobered up the next morning. Rather than make it easy to fall further down that hole and start drinking alone, he deliberately never brought any alcohol into his own apartment. Unfortunately, that knowledge didn't generally stop him looking for it anyway.

He closed the fridge empty handed and moved across the room to the couch with the intention of turning on whatever was playing on late-late-night television. Anything to crowd out some of the thoughts in his head. Reaching for the remote on the end table to his right, he noticed a sealed envelope with his name neatly printed in close handwriting. K9 must have left it there. He was the only other person who had been in the place all day, and it definitely wasn't there yesterday.

Jim picked it up and looked at it, turning it over in his hands. It wasn't K9's handwriting. It wasn't anyone's handwriting he recognized. However, he didn't feel like exploring further at the moment. He stuck it in his pocket, meaning to take it back to K9 in the morning, and turned on the television. Infomercials. Nothing but infomercials. Giving up on television, Jim stumped out his door and began pacing the long corridor connecting the ten or so apartments. Just moving, even if it was in tight circles or up and down the hallway, was better than sitting still in the dark alone with his demons.

How many times had he paced these corridors over the last few months. He knew every nursing station and most of the nurses. They would smile at him, but for the most part they just ignored him and went on about their business. The chemotherapy was aggressive, and Leslie had to stay in the hospital for several days after each round. Jim felt fortunate that he was able to take the time off and be with her in the hospital, but when Leslie finally succumbed to exhaustion and fell asleep, Jim was left alone with his thoughts. This was when he walked the halls – for hours at a time. Eventually, exhaustion would take over for him as well and he would crash on the terribly uncomfortable chair next to Leslie's bed for a few hours only to repeat the process a few hours later. But, until he was overcome with fatigue, he walked.

This place looked too much like a hospital, Jim thought to himself as he began another lap up and down the hallway. Smelled like a hospital too thanks to the industrial cleaning chemicals the aids used. Jim moved faster and concentrated on the click-thump of his crutches and good foot, trying to drown out the remnants of his nightmare. The smell seemed to get stronger. The impression he was at the hospital intensified and started to overpower him. In his mind, he could hear the sounds of the hospital. He moved faster, and panic began to set in.

With intense tightness in his chest, he began almost running on his crutches, racing toward the door at the end of the hallway. He needed to get out of here. Get away from the memories. A few feet short of the door, one of his crutches slipped and he crashed headlong into the door of the last apartment. The world went black.

"Colonel Harwood," a familiar voice said, penetrating the blackness, "I need you to try and focus."

It was Dr. Mohammad. He could also hear the sound of nurses and medical equipment in the distance. Another nightmare. Jim squeezed his eyes tightly shut and shook his head to try and clear it.

"Jim, it's okay. You hit your head; you're back at the hospital."

The panic started to return even as Jim realized this wasn't a dream. Hyperventilating and rocking back and forth uncontrollably, Jim struggled to make sense of the world around him. The tightness in his chest seemed like it would break his ribs. At some level, he knew what he was feeling was irrational, but that didn't change the situation any.

"It's okay," the doctor said, placing a hand gently on Jim's scarred face to try and calm him down. "Focus on me. Focus on my voice. You're going to be okay." She continued to work on calming him for several more minutes until the worst had passed and Jim was able to regain some self control.

"You hit your head. One of your neighbors found you and called the ambulance. Do you remember what happened?"

"My crutch slipped and I fell over. I think I hit the door, but don't remember for sure."

"What were you doing walking the halls that late at night?"

"Nightmares," was Jim's only reply.

"Does Dr. Chelwood know about the nightmares?"

"Not these ones. They're kinda new," Jim admitted.

"How did your crutch slip?"

"It just did," Jim said flatly, trying to deflect the question.

"It's important for us to rule out something like a seizure. It could be a sign of more significant issues."

"I had a panic attack and tried to run out the door," Jim admitted, "I guess crutches weren't meant for running."

She seemed relieved. "I'll have the ER doc send you up for a CT-scan to make sure there isn't any bleeding. If that comes back clean, we'll go ahead and admit you for a few days of observation. Repeat head injuries, especially in cases like yours, can be tricky."

"I didn't think you worked in the ER," Jim said.

"I don't. They called me down when you came in. I'll come see you again after the CT-scan."

Hospital gowns... damn he hated hospital gowns... Why couldn't they have let him stay in the clothes he had been wearing? After a few minutes of wishing he had something warmer on, a nurse came into the small room.

"Is there any reason I can't put my clothes back on?" Jim asked.

"They cut them off when you were brought in," he said matter-of-factly. "Chart says you were unresponsive and came in as an unknown trauma. Standard practice is to get all the clothes off so they can be sure there aren't any injuries hiding under them. Only way to do that without risking further injury is to cut 'em off."

The realization that his clothes were destroyed hit him like a ton of bricks. It wasn't that he particularly cherished the clothes, but he had really hoped to get out of the gown. There was a special place in hell reserved for whoever designed the damn things.

"This was in one of the pockets," the nurse said lifting a small letter from the table near the bed and handing it to Jim, "nothing else."

Jim took the letter and laid it on the tray in front of him as the nurse checked his blood pressure monitor. Realizing he had nothing better to do, he picked the letter back up and decided to go ahead and read it.

Dear Mr. Harwood,

My name is Maggie Tso. You don't know me, and I wish for your sake it could have stayed that way forever. Unfortunately, my son Raymond was responsible for the accident that killed your wife and daughter. I want you to know how terribly sorry I am for your loss, even though my sorrow can't ease your burden.

I also want you to know that my home will always be open to you, and that I will do everything I can to help you find peace. I know how the accident happened, and I can take you there. Please let me help you find a path that will help you heal.

The letter ended with a mailing address. Nothing more. Jim was dumbstruck. What was he supposed to say in response? How was he supposed to feel? Grateful? The woman who raised the man responsible for the greatest tragedy in his life had just invited him over to dinner.

"Jim," Dr. Chelwood said as he stepped into the room after a perfunctory and obligatory knock.

"Hey doc. . . " Jim said tiredly.

"So what were you doing pacing the hallway in the middle of the night?"

"Couldn't sleep."

"Had you fallen asleep and woken back up, or had you been up all night?"

"It was a nightmare."

"Iraq still?"

"No. Nothing that simple."

The Doctor raised a curious eyebrow and waited for Jim to continue. Jim hadn't told Dr. Chelwood about his wife's illness before, but it seemed like this was the time to change that. Jim related the dream and the context behind it while the Doctor sat quietly listening. It was the first time in several years he'd talked about it with anyone, and when the story was done he felt completely drained.

"I'm curious why you didn't tell me about this before," the doctor said kindly.

"I've tried hard to forget about it. It was mostly working until recently."

"You know that's not a winning strategy, right?"

Jim nodded, looking defeated.

"How many times have you had panic attacks since the last time I saw you?"

"Not many. Maybe half a dozen," Jim said, trying to sound nonchalant. It didn't work.

"What do you think is triggering them?"

"Last night the hallway smelled like the hospital, and that combined with the nightmare. . . "

"The others?"

"A kid playing with a remote-control car at the park. Once just being in a dark room alone triggered a flashback. I had one standing in line at McDonald's – it was too crowded, I felt trapped. Some of the others... I can't give you a reason."

The doctor motioned to the letter laying open on the table, "is that from family?"

"No."

"You had that on you when you came in, right?"

"Yeah."

"Tell me about it."

"It's from the mother of the guy who killed my wife and kid."

"What does she have to say?"

"You read it."

The Doctor picked up the letter and read it quickly, then turned his attention back to Jim.

"You know, Jim," the Doctor said after some thought, "it might give you some closure to go out there. Some people find it helpful."

"I'm almost having a panic attack just sitting here thinking about it," Jim forced himself to say through tightening vocal cords and chest.

"About the nightmares... You know what I'm going to ask you to do, don't you?"

"Write it down," Jim said sadly, "and then we'll talk about it."

"You've kept this one buried for a while, it may take some extra work. And... it's got the more recent stuff piled on top of it."

The doc paused for a moment, then asked, "You still spend a lot of time with Kelnhoffer, right?"

"Yeah."

"How's his drinking?"

"We've both been on a bender."

"You too?" the doctor said with obvious surprise.

"Yeah. . ." Jim sank in his bed at the admission. He didn't want anyone to know about that, but he learned a while ago that there wasn't any point in trying to hide anything from the doc.

"Has he made it over to the VA yet?"

Both Jim and K9 were supposed to be seeing the doctors at the VA now that they were medically retired, but neither of them had been able to navigate the maze of paperwork and bureaucratic bull. K9 hadn't been with a therapist in several months, and the results weren't good. It didn't help that he had given up on trying to get space-available care at Brooke. Jim was pretty sure that was significantly contributing to the alcohol, but he didn't know what to do about it.

"That place is a black hole. The odds look pretty good that we'll drink ourselves to death before we can get an appointment there. Then again, we'll probably run out of money and starve to death before we can even do that," Jim said bitterly.

"Is he seeing anyone?"

"Jim, Jack, and Jose."

The doctor thought quietly for a moment. Jim had learned not to interrupt that process. The results of these quiet reflections were generally worth the wait.

"I'll see what I can do to pull the two of you back into my clinic. . . at least until the VA clears the backlog. Let me head back to my office, and I'll find times when we can wedge the two of you into the schedule. I'll come back and let you know what I work out."

Chapter 8

Pen Pals

"You still writing to that medicine woman?" Jim asked, looking at K9 over his glass. They had agreed this would be the last time. Drink what was left and be done with it.

"Yeah. You still angry about it?"

"No. Not about that."

"Why?" K9 asked.

"I read her letter you left me."

"I know."

"Maybe we could go see her."

"Okay."

They sat quiet for a while. With anyone else the quiet would have been uncomfortable, but not here. To some extent, it was a matter of drinking alone while in the company of others. Then there was a lot that was unspoken between them that filled the gaps. Both were content to just sit and listen to the silence for quite some time.

"What went through your mind when you found out I was joining your team?" Jim asked, breaking the silence rather abruptly.

"I thought you'd get us all killed," was K9's blunt reply.

"Me too."

"Everyone thought it was a bad idea. You can't make an operator out of a desk weenie like that – at least, that's what we all thought."

"That was my fault," Jim admitted. "I made the mistake of sparking a GOBI."

"Gobi?" K9 asked. Jim looked at him puzzled. He'd been using the term for years, and had heard it used frequently during his years of service. It seemed implausible that K9 hadn't heard it, but then again, they ran in different circles before Iraq.

"General Officer Big Idea."

K9 nodded understandingly. Apparently he'd been the victim of GOBIs before without having had a name for them. No further explanation was needed on this front.

"I'd made a name for myself analyzing and breaking down the clan structures in the area," Jim continued. "I showed them how that could be used to find connections and roll up the key players. That's where this all started. I should have kept my stupid mouth shut."

"You sure about that?"

"Yeah... I could see it in everyone's faces that first night."

"We were worried, that's true," K9 admitted, "but we trusted Warlock to keep you in line, and we had plans to keep you from getting into too much trouble."

"How's the saying go? The best laid plans never survive first contact..." Jim trailed off, not willing to talk about that first raid any more.

"You made it out of that one, didn't you?"

"Yeah, but the girl didn't," Jim countered, forgetting his resolution to leave that one alone.

"She made her choices and dealt with the consequences. You didn't make her do what she did. You can't blame yourself for that."

"Seems like I screwed it all up. You guys would've been better off without me."

K9 thought for a few minutes, trying to focus through the booze. After a few seconds of silence, he started up again. "You remember the night we found the spider hole?"

Jim wasn't sure which event K9 was referring to. His memories of all but a few of the raids were hazy at best. He shook his head.

"Yeah, the one in Ramadi?" K9 pressed.

Jim didn't remember.

"We pulled a bunch of guys out of a cellar without firing a shot or even kicking in a door..." K9 was still trying to get Jim to remember, but it wasn't working.

"Anyway, I remember the looks on their faces. They were terrified. A bunch of grown men who had killed who knows how many people acting like terrified little cowards. I remember the lady too... beating them with her shoe while screaming and spitting on them. I've never seen a woman that angry. You've gotta remember the bread she sent us afterward, don't you?"

Suddenly, Jim remembered.

Warlock leaned against the door, and it gave way without forcing it. He entered, and the entry team followed. Silently they moved into the small and sparsely furnished house only to find a single occupant. A middle-aged woman sitting upright on a sleeping mat.

"Get the interpreter," Warlock ordered, "and bring the boss in."

Moments later, Jim and the interpreter came into the room.

"Ask her why she's awake this time of the night," Warlock commanded the interpreter, who relayed the message in

Arabic. She wouldn't speak, and stayed seated and nearly motionless with Warlock's gun pointed at her. She kept her hands palm down and plainly visible on her upper-legs, not moving except to breathe.

"Something's funny," Kilroy said under his breath while he watched the street from the building's single window.

The occupant looked at the interpreter pleadingly, but still didn't speak or move. Jim looked around the room, scanning for anything that would tell him why he had been wrong. All the intel they had said there should be at least a few targets here. He cracked an infra-red glow-stick to brighten the room and began sweeping over the small space looking for anything unusual.

"Ask her where her husband is."

She answered this time, and the interpreter translated. "She says he's buried. That she's a widow who lives here alone."

As Jim's scan came to where the woman was sitting, he noticed what looked like scuffs in the floorboard under the edge of the mat. Jim motioned to Warlock to look down, and the two of them closely inspected the floor. Simultaneously, they both stood silently and motioned to the woman to ask if there was something under her. She nodded very slightly, but didn't otherwise move.

Jim looked again at the mat and the floor, looking for signs of a pressure switch or any other indications of an IED. He looked up and answered Warlock's questioning eyes with a shake of his head. Nothing visible.

Jim stood up and moved directly in front of the woman. Gesturing for her to watch him, he told the interpreter to ask her if she had any other relatives in the area. As he did so, he pointed at the floor and made a motion to simulate an explosion. She seemed to understand, and answered with a shake of the head.

"Ask her if the house has a cellar," Warlock directed the interpreter. She answered no again, but nodded slightly in the process. Jim looked at the floorboards again, and became convinced she was sitting on top of a trap door. Jim pointed to the floor and held up five fingers – the number of targets he had expected to find here. She shook her head and pointed upward slightly with her right index finger. Jim added more fingers progressively until reaching nine and she nodded yes.

Warlock started directing the team to clean up and get ready to head out, declaring the raid a bust, but all the while using hand signals to get more support in the room and position the team where he wanted them. He pointed downwards and silently asked how big the cellar was by holding his arms up wide like he was explaining how large the fish was he caught last year. She shook her head. It was a small space. One flash-bang would be plenty.

Silently, the team choreographed their next move. K9 would grab the woman and pull her out of the way, Kilroy would lift the hatch and drop in a flash-bang, and Warlock would go down the hole ready for anything.

"Nine bad dudes in a single action. You gotta admit that made a dent," K9 pressed. "We'd have never found that house without you."

Jim nodded. More than the impact of taking those men out of circulation, Jim thought about the look of relief on the woman's face when all nine of the men were dragged out of the cellar in flex-cuffs. She told the interpreter how they had tortured her husband for not joining them, and had eventually killed him after cutting off his fingers one at a time and castrating him in front of her.

"Heartless bastards," Jim replied. "You know, some of those guys were the ones that got it in Bucca..." he said,

connecting dots he hadn't before. Somehow, he hadn't consciously realized the men he'd gotten killed at the prison had
anything to do with this woman. Why was it that so many of
the memories were blurred? Or were they just that far buried?

"Deserved what they got," K9 concluded forcefully. "All
I'm saying is that we made a difference. Even if it didn't
change a thing in the big picture, there are lots of guys still
alive because of the work we did. That lady thinks you made
a difference. You've gotta believe that."

Jim reached for the remote and turned up the volume on
the movie playing in the background – some Pollyanna-ish
Disney movie from the '60s. These kinds of movies were safe,
if boring. Besides, being drunk made them slightly funnier.

– – – – – – – – – – – – – – – – – –

When he sobered up, Jim wrote to answer Maggie. He told
her he had received her letter, but couldn't commit to going
out to visit yet. He admitted to struggling with how to feel
about her letter and being uncertain about how ready he was
to see where the accident happened. As an afterthought, and
in an effort to take up more than two sentences, he asked what
she found to write about with K9 and signed the letter with a
simple "Jim." Within a week, she had written back.

Dear Jim,

I was so happy to get your letter. I understand
your hesitation. For now, maybe we can just write
a few words back-and-forth just to break the ice.

I went outside last week to water my animals
just before sunrise. It was very cool, and I could
see my breath in the air. But everything was so
still and quiet, I couldn't help but stop and watch
the sunrise. I sat down on my back porch, and
Maki, my dog, came over to sit by me while the

gray sky turned red and then orange. It only took a few minutes, but it was enough to brighten my whole day.

Write soon and tell me about your favorite sunrise.

Maggie

She had included a picture of one of her goats with its upper lip pulled back in a strange sort of smile. He couldn't help but chuckle at the ridiculous image. Goats were ugly critters, that much was certain.

When his dad had brought home the goats, Jim had been mortified. The thought of getting out of bed early every day to milk them for most of the year didn't sound like his idea of fun. But over time he had come to appreciate the morning quiet. It was a few minutes to almost meditate to the background noise of the rooster and rhythmic sound of milk squirting into the pail.

It had been a rather cool night, and a thin fog hung over the pasture. With the sunlight just beginning to creep up over the mountain to touch the world around him, this small patch of land just outside a small town looked almost magical. He couldn't imagine leaving it. Why would anyone want to live in a big city?

Heavy drops of dew covered the grass and dripped onto his rubber muck-boots as he walked through it, leaving a clear trail where he had stepped. The rustling of him walking through the grass was enough to let the goats know that he was coming, and they came out to meet him at the gate. They were always so excited to see him.

Sticking the picture to the cork-board next to his refrigerator, he sat down at the kitchen table to write a reply. It
seemed odd to be using a pen, paper, stamps, and envelope,
but he didn't have any other contact information. Staring at
the blank sheet of paper, he thought for several minutes, trying to figure out how to answer her question. In the end he
drew a complete blank, pushed the paper away from him, and
decided to take a walk outside. He'd have to think about it a
little longer.

Dear Maggie,

I don't often get to see sunrises. Most of my
adult life I've been up before the sun and inside an
office without windows by the time it came over
the horizon. Sunsets aren't much different for a
good part of the year, with the sun setting and the
sky going dark before I make my way home for the
evening. Lately, I don't really see the sunrise even
if I'm up – it's hidden behind the building next
door.

It took me quite a while to come up with a
sunrise that I can call my favorite – even the best
ones are tinged with bittersweet memories. But
I think I can say that a quiet spring morning in
Virginia Beach seven or eight years ago is in the
top ten. Leslie and I had gone to visit friends in
Norfolk who had a timeshare a few blocks from the
beach. For no particular reason, we both woke up
early that morning and decided to take a walk to
the beach so we wouldn't wake our friends.

The beach was empty, except for a few joggers
and one or two people fishing. We took our shoes
off and walked barefoot on the cool damp sand
near the water as the gray sky turned a bright pink

and the few clouds glowed orange. It was the last vacation Leslie and I took without Sammie.

Jim

Jim had just finished another cognitive processing session with Dr. Chelwood. They had been working through one traumatic memory after another, spending multiple sessions on each one, but there were still many more to go. Jim found the process exhausting, and putting a voice to his history was among the more difficult things he'd done. Reliving the memories made his emotions raw, but little by little each one hurt less and less. He doubted he'd ever be normal again, but he was starting to hope that he'd at least be able to function in some kind of job again. Sitting unemployed at home was slowly killing him from the inside-out.

"Doc," Jim said as Dr. Chelwood typed a few notes from this session into the computer, "I wrote back to that Navajo lady."

The doctor stopped and looked at Jim, "And?"

"She wrote back almost immediately to tell me about a sunrise. She's been writing me every few days ever since. She'll tell me about something insignificant that happened to her, then ask me if I've seen or done something similar. I don't get it."

"She's probably hurting pretty bad too... she lost her son in that crash, and I'm pretty sure she asks herself every day where she went wrong."

"He lived," Jim said almost angrily.

"Yes and no. He'll probably be in jail for the rest of her life. Anyway, how do you feel when you get her letters?"

"It doesn't bother me anymore. She doesn't talk about the crash or her son."

"Well, for next time I want you to write a letter to her telling her how you feel about the accident. You don't need to send it to her – just bring it here and we can talk about it."

Dear Jim,

I know your last letter must have been terribly hard to write. It is so hard to talk about what happened that day.

Have I told you I work for the Indian Health Service? I spend a lot of time in emergency rooms. Some days we get so busy, and weekends are the worst. There are never enough people on staff to deal with all the bumps, bruises, and other stuff that comes through the door, but I love the work. I get to help people who are having a bad day.

Sometimes the repeat offenders who come in time after time with the same kind of problems or who are just looking for pills can be hard to cope with, but then I get to help a young child who fell off a horse or crashed their bike. We help them get bandaged up, feel better, and get ready to climb back on. Those kinds of patients keep me going – the ones where I get to help make someone better.

One of the hardest days I've had at work was the day your Leslie and Sammie died. I was in the emergency room when they brought my son in. He was bloody, broken, and so drunk I could smell him from across the room. It was the third time in a year that he had been in an accident while drinking. I prayed he had run off the road and not hurt anyone else, but within a few minutes I found out that your family had died at the scene.

I often wonder what I could have done differently... how I failed as a parent in order to produce a son like mine? He started drinking as a teenager, and when I confronted him and tried to get him to quit, he left home and disowned me. He would only ever come back when he was in trouble, then he would disappear again as soon as he was back on his feet. It didn't seem to matter what I did.

That was the last time I saw him. Once he was stabilized, he was transferred to a hospital in Albuquerque and then to jail. He refuses to see me.

On a happier note, one of my goats kidded last night. When I went out to feed the animals this morning I found two little kids (a boy and a girl) jumping around in the stall. One of the best parts is that in a few days I can start milking her again. I love the fresh milk, and there is something peaceful about spending twenty minutes early in the morning milking.

Maggie

_ _ _ _ _ _ _ _ _ _ _ _ _ _ _ _ _ _ _

Jim picked up his ringing phone and answered it with a brief, "Yeah?"

"Shepherd..."

"What's up?"

"I want to get drunk."

They had both been sober for two months. K9 had been through serious withdrawal, and was finally starting to feel better. Jim wasn't about to let him fall off the wagon now.

"Let's go for a drive," Jim suggested without really knowing where they would go other than drive around town.

"Where?"

"Shiprock," Jim said, surprising himself. However, as soon as the words came out of his mouth he was determined to go.

"When?"

"Now. Pack a bag and let's get out of here."

"Now?"

"We're not getting drunk again. We've been talking about going out there for months, I'm tired of talking about it. Let's just go."

"Not today. We have to get stuff ready."

"When?" This time it was Jim who asked the question.

"After we hear back from Maggie. We can't just show up. Besides we need to reschedule appointments and let the facility here know so they don't send people looking for us." It seemed odd that K9 was being the rational one when just a few moments ago he was ready to get drunk again.

"Fine. I'll write to her, then we'll go."

"So what are we going to do tonight then? I've got to go somewhere."

What do you do when you need to get out but can't stand being in social situations? Jim racked his brain for somewhere that wouldn't result in a panic attack or a hangover. Bars were out of the question. So were noisy restaurants. Jim thought for a few minutes then offered up a suggestion.

"There's a café in Castroville my grandpa used to go to. It's the kind of small-town place that's pretty quiet, but it's only about a 30 minute drive."

"Okay. I'll meet you outside in ten minutes."

Chapter 9

On the Road

It took three more months before everything could be arranged for the trip. Doc Chelwood was the worst of the hurdles, and wouldn't consent to them going until they had managed to stay sober. The last thing he wanted was to have to answer questions about why two of his patients ended up dead on the side of the road after a drunk-driving accident.

Sobriety wasn't easy though. At least twice a week either K9 would call Jim, or Jim would call K9, needing support and something to do to overcome the temptation. A small altercation over something as simple as a parking spot would send either of them into a spiral and the panic attacks and anger would begin to claw their way to the surface. When that happened, alcohol seemed like the easiest answer, but they had promised each other to stay sober.

For now, at least, Sammy's Diner had come to expect them and always made a place for them in a quiet corner where they could eat in peace and quiet, then sit and drink coffee or water and talk as long as they wanted. When they had first come here there was a somewhat steady stream of local farmers who would come by and shake their hands, but one of the waitresses noticed that it made them uncomfortable. After that, the farmers would just nod or waive in acknowledgment before going on about their business.

"I'm glad you knew about this place," K9 said as he cradled his coffee cup in both hands. "I think we both needed somewhere like this to escape to."

"Yeah. Grandpa used to have a place a few miles west of here. He was always the kind of guy who loved a little hole in the wall. My dad told me he kept coming out here for breakfast even after he moved back closer to the city."

"I thought your family was in Idaho?"

"Grandpa was a wanderer. Moved all the time until after I was born. Dad just happened to be in Idaho when he got married and stayed there. My dad was born here, and this is where Grandpa was when he finally decided to quit moving. Most of my dad's family lived around here until a few years ago. I've still got a few cousins in the area, but I was never close to them."

They sat quietly for a few minutes just listening to the low din of the restaurant until the waitress came over to ask if they needed refills.

"No thanks Amy. We'd better be going," K9 said, declining more coffee.

"See you next week then?"

"No, it'll be a while before we make it back."

The waitress looked slightly concerned.

"We're taking a road trip. No big deal. We'll be back."

She smiled. "Y'all be safe. Where ya goin?"

"Going to visit an old Navajo woman and see what it's like to milk goats."

"You know," she said with a sideways smile, "if you want to milk goats, there are plenty of folks around here that wouldn't mind some help. You don't have to drive that far. On the other hand, I don't know any local Navajo women... Anyway, I guess I'll see you when you get back."

"So run me through your plans," Doc Chelwood said as he entered some notes in the computer.

"We're stopping for the night on-base at Cannon in Clovis, then on to Farmington the next morning. We're planning on staying there for two weeks, and taking it from there."

"What's your plan if either of you backslide?"

"We've been keeping each other honest."

"You need a backup plan."

"I've got the emergency number here I can call if something happens."

"Who else?"

Jim stared blankly at the doctor. He couldn't think of an answer.

"What about your parents?"

He hadn't spoken to them directly since he had developed an alcohol problem. He wasn't ready to tell them that part of the story.

"They're still in Idaho, right?"

Jim nodded.

"Would they come get you if you needed it?"

"Yeah," Jim sighed.

"You need to be ready to call them. You might need it. There needs to be someone who can come get you if things go bad, no matter how far away they are."

"Okay."

"You can go to any emergency room or call 911 too. Do you know where the hospitals are along your route?"

Jim gave the doctor a look that said it all – something along the lines of, "Do you even have to ask that question?"

"All right, all right. Give me a call when you are back in town. In fact," the Doctor said, "give me a call when you get there, and any other time you need to talk."

"Will do Doc."

"Well, safe travels then."

Jim stood, shook the doctor's hand, and walked out of the office. This time tomorrow he'd be on the road.

"Hey Dad."

"Jim!"

"Don't lecture me, please."

"No, I'm just excited to hear from you. That's all."

"I had some things I needed to work through..." That was all the explanation Jim could offer. He still couldn't admit to his parents how bad things had gotten.

"Can we help?"

"Maybe. I'm going to take a road trip to visit the crash site and meet someone there."

"When are you leaving? Mom and I could meet you there, or fly down and drive with you."

"No, I'd rather do this mostly on my own."

"Tell me about your plans."

"K9 and I are going together. He's been writing to a Navajo lady, and we're going to go meet her. We'll be driving out tomorrow, stopping for the night in Clovis, then finishing the trip to Shiprock the next day."

Jim's dad tried not to sound surprised or troubled. It had been so long since he had heard from his son that he feared doing anything that would send Jim back into a self-imposed exile. He listened intently while choking off multiple urges to press further.

"How long will you be there?"

"At least two weeks. Maybe longer, depending on how things go." To be honest, Jim had no idea how long they would stay. They didn't have any firm plans in that regard.

"Any chance I can convince you to let me check in with you every few days while you're out there?"

Jim sighed audibly. The last thing he wanted at the moment was another obligation to keep track of, but he felt guilty for keeping his parents at such a distance for so long.

"Yeah. I'll answer. In fact, that's part of why I called."

"Oh?"

"One of the conditions the doc gave for letting me go... I need someone who can come get me or K9 if things go bad."

"You know we'll be there if you need us. What about Leslie's parents? They're missing you too."

"I'll call them. I promise."

"What the hell?" K9 grumbled to himself as he looked at the pile of stuff they needed to cram into Jim's van. "I used to be able to walk into the house, grab two bags, and be ready for anything, anywhere – and for as long as it took."

"I used to give Leslie crap abut how much stuff she would pack for her and Sammie every time she went on a road trip. I guess I can't talk anymore," Jim grunted as he lifted a bag into the back of the van.

"The sad part is, one of those bags was full of my plate carrier and other battle-rattle. Now we're taking everything *and* the kitchen sink, and we're not even bivouacing in the field," K9 said shaking his head.

The two wheelchairs, crutches, and prosthetics were a decent pile on their own, and then there were clothes, food, and other random stuff they had agreed they might need. It did feel excessive, but neither of them felt like wearing the same two or three sets of clothes over and over again. They'd both had enough of that experience. Aside from the usual road-trip junk food, they also had enough MREs for a week, a large trauma kit, road-flairs, a ruggedized GPS, a waterproof map, several gallons of water, and a collection of other emergency gear. The last thing to go in the van were two large backpacks – what K9 referred to as the "oh-shit" bags – which were hidden underneath other gear but left easily accessible.

Jim paused for a second, contemplating the carefully selected collection of gear. Packing the van was always like a big game of tetris, but this time the pieces were very differently shaped than what he had been used to. He'd never had to figure out how to pack wheelchairs before.

Shades of Green... not much of a name for a resort, but it was significantly cheaper than staying at one of the better known hotels within earshot of Disney World. Why the military had chosen to open a resort here where there were plenty of civilian alternatives was something of a mystery to him, but he was grateful for the discounted rate none the less. There were advantages to being in the military, Jim thought to himself.

"Do we really need all this stuff?" he hollered towards the house where Leslie was checking to make sure all the curtains were closed, lights were off, and doors were locked.

"Quit complaining," she said as she came outside, pulling the door shut behind her and turning the deadbolt. "We might need it. We'll be in the park all day."

"I'm not carrying that enormous bag around the park. Sammie's been potty trained for a while now." Leslie had packed a backpack full of everything she had ever included in a diaper bag. It was like she hadn't learned anything about the difference between essentials and overburden in the almost five years she'd been a mother.

"Daddy, you know Mom's right," Sammie added with emphasis.

"All right grumpy-butt. I'll carry it. But the first magician I find, I'm making him shrink it."

Jim pushed the back door of the van closed and buckled Sammie into her seat. "You ready to go see some princesses?"

"I suppose so," Sammie said in her best adult imitation. She had been looking forward to this trip for months. Three days in Disney World and dinner with Cinderella.

"Really?" Jim laughed as Sammie strutted out of the bathroom in her blue Cinderella dress.

"Apparently this is the approved dress code for the under six crowd," Leslie said with a smile as Sammie twirled the blue dress.

"Well, let's head for the park I guess."

A short ride over on the monorail and they were in the Magic Kingdom. Then, almost perfectly on-cue, Cinderella and Mickey Mouse walked over and knelt down to take a picture with Sammie. She was smiling ear to ear. That alone was worth the ridiculous cost of the trip.

Jim smiled at the memory. That little girl was so thrilled with everything there. The stupid little rides, the puppets on "It's a Small World," the actors dressed up like Disney characters. All of it. It had been a while since a memory like that had surfaced voluntarily. He replayed that whole trip in his mind as he finished packing and slammed the door closed on the now fully loaded van.

K9 was fidgeting with and checking the gear they wanted within reach from the front seats, testing to make sure certain things were readily accessible.

"I'm not really comfortable leaving my leg off while we travel. I'll be helpless if something happens."

K9 had developed a pressure sore where his prosthetic attached, and it wasn't quite healed yet. The doctors had threatened to cancel their trip if it didn't start to heal up and K9 didn't spend more time off of his "feet." It irritated him that he was just sitting and watching while Jim did the work of loading the van, but without his leg he couldn't be much help at the moment, and the last thing he wanted to do now was cancel the trip because the sore opened up again.

"It's behind my seat. You can reach it from where you sit."

"Yeah, like I'll have the time to do that if something goes wrong."

"It's the best we can do for now. Once we get out of San Antonio, it's all small towns until Lubbock, and we can avoid the busy stops like Junction by just blowing through them."

They'd talked through this before, but K9 still hadn't figured out how to accept the fact that he would be helpless in a fight. Even with his prosthetic he wouldn't be particularly fast, but without it he was almost helpless. That bothered him deeply. Jim, on the other hand, had his running leg on and had spent the last few months getting good at using it.

"And if we end up off the road?" K9 said, running down the contingency list he had in his mind.

"There's cell coverage almost the whole way, and the radios are programmed for the local amateur repeaters along the whole route."

"Trauma kits..."

"Left and right map pockets, and the big one's behind my seat."

"Go bags?"

"One layer down from the top in the back."

"I don't like that I can't reach it from here..."

They'd been through this before, and neither of them were happy with the compromise, but there simply wasn't any way to make them accessible without drawing unwanted attention.

"They can't be visible... We don't want to give any cops or the base gate-guards an excuse to search them. I doubt they'll dig deeper into the pile once they see my walking leg on top. Besides, you've got a pea-shooter under the seat-cover flap in front of you."

Jim had the seat covers for the van custom made by a small independent upholsterer, so each of the seats had a concealed holster under a Velcro flap on the front of the seat. To the casual eye, they looked completely normal, even with a full-sized handgun and two spare magazines tucked away in them. To Jim's surprise, the shop had already made several similar designs and had some excellent ideas for how to make it work even better. The result was worth the work.

"I-10 to Junction, north on 83 to Ballinger, 153 to Sweet-water, 84 through Lubbock, and on to Clovis. Cannon is a couple clicks east of town, and impossible to miss. We RON[19] there."

K9 repeated the same information verbatim, confirming the route both with what was programmed in the GPS and the highlighted route on the road atlas. They then went through the same procedure for the leg from Clovis to Shiprock.

"Bandage?" Warlock quizzed the group.

Jim had been through this routine with Warlock and the rest of the team every time they'd left the compound since he'd gotten here. He checked his right cargo pocket and gave a thumbs up. Warlock simultaneously checked his pocket for the same device, as did the rest of the team.

"Tourniquet?"

Left cargo pocket and another thumbs up.

"Quick clot?"

With the bandage.

"Airway?"

With the tourniquet.

"Who's got chest catheters?"

Six of the team raised their hands.

"Radios and backup batteries?"

Everyone checked the radios for the correct primary and alternate channels, but didn't do a radio check. It was too easy for the bad-guys to hear that kind of activity and give away the fact that they were headed out. The fact that these radios were difficult to detect didn't alter the team's use of radio discipline.

"Magazines?"

All across the room the sounds of Velcro and the metallic tapping sound of the magazines being checked could be heard.

"Rifles?"

Sounds of weapons being rechecked for the hundredth time were the only response.

"NVGs and spare batteries?"

More thumbs up.

"Flex-cuffs? Glow Sticks?"

The process continued as Warlock worked down the general gear then continued on to the specialized teams. Drivers had fueled and ops-checked the vehicles. Both drivers and spotters had memorized and double-checked the ingress, egress, and divert routes for the objective. The breaching team had the required shaped-charges and other tools of the trade. The entry team knew who was going in first and the order for everyone following. Flash-bangs were in the right places and on the right people, those with fragmentation grenades didn't have flash-bangs, and everyone knew who had which.

The quick reaction force was on standby and ready to roll if something went wrong. The COMPASS CALL was overhead and would begin jamming as soon as the team was en-route. Intel had confirmed that the targets had been seen entering the objective and appeared to still be there. Everything had been checked and re-checked.

The whole process took less than ten minutes, but it had felt much longer the first several times Jim went through it.

"Over to you boss."

Jim looked at the team. They had lost that look of concern he'd recognized the first night out with them. He had earned his place. Grateful for the trust, Jim reviewed the objective and specific people and materials they were looking for. None of this was new, except for the trust.

"Any last minute concerns?" Jim asked the team in general.

The team stood stoically silent.

"Are we ready Warlock?"

A simple nod was the only answer.

"Everyone makes it back in tonight." Everyone nodded agreement. "All right, let's go shake some people out of bed. Saddle up."

They filed silently into the trucks – Warlock in the lead truck and Jim in the middle. Jim picked up the mic and called in.

"Canebrake, Wolfpack."

"Canebrake."

"Moving out."

"Copy. Good hunting."

"What are you thinking about?" K9 asked, noticing that Jim had a far-away look on his face as he climbed into the driver's seat.

"The first time the team didn't look worried about me before we went out."

"You'd earned it."

Jim half-smiled. It was quite a thing to know that a team of the most highly trained warriors and athletes in the world had felt like he was one of them. Two smiles in one day. That was a success to remember.

"Call it in," Jim said as he started the car. K9 grabbed his phone and texted Jim's parents to let them know they were on the road.

Chapter 10

Detoured

As Jim made his way through the early morning traffic, K9 was scanning the radio looking for traffic reports. It didn't take long to find one, and it wasn't good. According the to the report, a semi loaded with gravel had overturned and completely closed I10 northbound just beyond Boerne. Reportedly it would take hours to clean up and re-open the road, and travelers were advised to avoid that area at all costs.

"Which divert do you want to take?" Jim asked as K9 pulled out the road atlas and considered the alternate routes they had mapped. "173 will be a mess with the regular detour traffic. What's the best alternative?"

"Looks like 16 through Pipe Creek all the way to Kerrville. It'll be busy through to Bandera, but 173 will take most the traffic from there."

Jim shifted lanes and set his course for the north-west corner of town. The house he'd rented when they first came here was in that area, and he knew it well. He would be on autopilot for a while now.

"Only catch," K9 said as he considered the map, "is that there's a significant hole in cell coverage on that stretch." He flipped on one of the radios and set it for the pre-programmed frequencies in that region. "Hopefully we don't have an excuse to test how well maintained the radio networks are..."

Within a few minutes they had left the city behind and were winding their way up into the hill country. There were a lot of cars on the road, but traffic was flowing at a decent pace. Apparently, there weren't really too many people who were headed out of town early on a Thursday morning.

"Wolfpack, Overwatch."

Overwatch never called them, and this was a guarded channel that wasn't supposed to be used except in emergencies. Normally, Overwatch's information was funneled through Brigade and came to them in the form of confirmation that a given target was at the objective within a reasonable time window. It had never been anything else. Concerned, Jim picked up the microphone and answered.

"Wolfpack."

"Divert to an alternate route immediately."

"Roger."

Jim glanced at his map, but knew the alternate routes as well as any other man on the team at this point.

"We're monitoring, and will provide further instruction once you have established the alternate route."

Jim stabbed a button on the radio so he could talk to Warlock in the lead vehicle. The whole team would be listening as well. "2, 1."

"Go for 2," came the reply.

"Get off this route immediately. Divert to ingress 3 and standby for further guidance."

Jim looked around the truck, catching the puzzled looks on everyone's faces. Everyone, that is, except for the new translator. He looked terrified. But then again, he'd looked that way himself on his first mission. The lead truck made a hard right-turn and the remaining trucks turned to follow.

"What is happening?" the interpreter asked nervously.

"Just taking a different route," Jim said calmly. Jim's forced calmness didn't seem to help the interpreter, who was becoming increasingly agitated and nervous.

"Wolfpack, Overwatch, Lumberjack. Repeat Lumberjack."

Lumberjack? Did he really just hear his own duress word? *He* was supposed to use that word if he was compromised, not Overwatch. That must mean they had information that his team was compromised. What's more, Overwatch knew that only his vehicle would be monitoring their channel. They must think there was a high probability the problem was right next to him.

"Copy, Lumberjack," Jim answered.

"What is Lumberjack?" The interpreter asked with a wild look in his eye and near panic in his voice.

One of the other team members shrugged to say "who knows" then shushed the agitated man with a finger to his lips. When the interpreter turned again to look at Jim, he found a handgun leveled at his forehead.

"Smitty," Jim said to the soldier next to the interpreter, "give our friend here a set of bracelets and a hood, then check him for extra stuff. Lumberjack is MY duress word."

The interpreter's eyes grew wide and he started to speak very rapidly though unintelligibly. The only word Jim understood was "Major."

"Show me your hands and stop talking." Jim ordered. "You move even a little bit, and it'll take a week to clean your brains off of the walls."

While the soldier followed his orders, Jim keyed the radio again, "abort, abort, abort." He provided no further explanation, and none was needed.

The lead truck in the convoy made an abrupt turn down a wide street, then a series of further erratic turns as they made their way back to the compound by a circuitous route. However, other than the roundabout course they took, the remainder of the drive back was uneventful. The interpreter had gone silent and appeared to have accepted his current condition, but Jim never took his gun off of the now hooded and flex-cuffed man. As the convoy pulled through the gates, Jim directed the team members in his truck to treat the interpreter as a direct threat until he could get confirmation over secure channels what this was all about. He then ran directly into the building without a word to anyone else.

"Mac, what the hell is going on?" Jim asked over the encrypted phone.

"Overwatch intercepted kill-chain comms. Can't tell you what over this line, but your team's been compromised."

"From the inside?"

"Looks like it."

"New guy?"

"Yes."

"I've already wrapped and packed him."

"I figured you'd understand. Anyway, we'll get a bird out there ASAP to pick him up. I'll send someone to back-brief you on the details. They should be on-site within the hour."

"All right Mike, what's this all about?" Jim asked as the brigade S2^{20} closed the door to Jim's hooch. It seemed odd that the head intel guy in the brigade had come out instead of some lieutenant, but the major was the one who had come in on the helicopter none the less.

"It was a setup."

"I gathered that much," Jim said impatiently. At this point, he was in no mood to play guessing games.

"Your interpreter's buddies were going to disable the lead truck not far from where you were when you diverted, then set off several more IEDs to try and take out the rest of the team."

"Overwatch caught all that?" Jim said doubtfully.

"No, not exactly. You've been at the top of the hit-list for a while now. We've known generally what their plans were, but didn't have enough to go on. That intercept was the final piece in the puzzle."

"So what you're saying is that you've been using my team as bait?" Jim asked angrily.

"No," the major backpedaled, "it's not like that. We just didn't know enough to do anything."

"You could have warned us," Jim growled threateningly.

"Would it have changed anything? Would you have quit going out? Were there precautions you weren't already taking?"

"No," Jim conceded reluctantly. It wouldn't have changed the way they had been doing business.

"Anyway, Overwatch heard someone passing your route info to the placement team. As soon as they confirmed that you were the target, they called you. The pause before the next radio call was while we were working with them on a way to let you know discretely what the problem was."

"Did anyone roll up the placement team?"

"QRF rolled as soon as Overwatch found them. The bastards got a bit of a nasty surprise."

"Cowboy town... looks more like a tourist trap to me," K9 grumbled as they came into Bandera.

"Wasn't like this when I was a kid. My uncle had a place out here, and it was no-kidding country back then. Still quite a few old-fashioned cowboys out here somewhere, I expect."

Traffic had been heavy, but it had been moving along well. As they came to the intersection with Highway 173, all the traffic turned north, leaving the road ahead of them completely clear. It was what they had hoped for. Within a few minutes they were well outside the small town and winding through the hill country.

"Did I just see a zebra?" K9 asked, looking out the window at a game ranch. Jim just nodded.

"What the hell?"

"If you've got the money, you can come and shoot it. There's all kinds of exotic game on these places, and if you're willing to pay a premium, they'll put you up in a luxury hunting cabin, feed you filet mignon, sit you up in a hide over the feeder, and let you pretend to hunt the dumb animals. Not really my kind of hunting," Jim explained, "but it's better than letting the land go to developers."

K9 nodded, and the two sat quietly for several more minutes until they rounded a corner and Jim let out an involuntary "That's weird..." He had noticed what looked like a pair of tail-lights up in a tree just off the road.

"Stop the car!" K9 almost shouted as he reached behind Jim's seat for his leg. He had seen the skid-marks and broken tree limbs Jim had missed. Apparently someone had run off the road, flipped their truck over, and landed in the canopy of a large live oak down the embankment. The lights were on, and the vehicle was smoking. "This looks bad."

Before Jim could stop the car and circle back to the accident, K9 had his leg on and had grabbed the trauma kit. He was on the ground and moving towards the wreck the moment their car came to a halt. "See if your phone works or get on the radio and get some help on the way," he shouted at over his shoulder at Jim.

K9's limp was quite pronounced, but it didn't seem to slow him down any as he approached the truck and peered inside. The cab was empty and the driver's door was open and folded back unnaturally. "Tell them to send the helicopter when you get hold of them. Whoever it was, they've been thrown out of the car."

Jim checked his phone. No service. He keyed the radio and called for any listening station. Nobody answered. The repeater beeped, so he knew he was at least breaking the squelch. It didn't appear anyone was listening. "No luck yet," Jim shouted.

By now, K9 had found the driver of the truck almost 50 yards away. He'd been ejected and was lying in the grass unconscious. He was struggling to breathe and had red foam coming up as he exhaled. One punctured lung at least. Probably both.

K9 tore the trauma kit open to get the shears out and cut away the shirt looking for puncture wounds. There weren't any, but the victim clearly had broken most of his ribs. One or more must have punctured the lungs and collapsed them.

"I'm sure he's got a collapsed lung. Lots of broken bones. You need to go find a cell signal and get help here quick!" K9 shouted to Jim. "I'm going to cath him and see if I can get a lung working again."

"Got it."

K9 rummaged through the kit and pulled out a plastic tube. Opening it to reveal what looked like a large IV needle, he stabbed it into the victim's chest cavity near the collar bone exactly as he had been trained to do prior to each of the last three deployments. It was the first time he'd had to actually use that particular skill, and he was slightly surprised when the air trapped in the victim's chest cavity made a slight whooshing sound as it escaped.

Before K9 had been able to get the chest catheter out of the kit, Jim was back in the car. After making a quick assessment of where they were and where they were most likely to reacquire cell coverage, he turned the car back the direction they had come and headed out as quickly as he could safely navigate the winding road. As he drove, he continued trying to raise someone on the radio.

About five minutes into his search for help, Jim raised a local on the amateur radio repeater who was able to call in the accident. Using the local as a relay, Jim provided the location, a description of what he had seen and what K9 had relayed to him. He was then told that a paramedic team would be inbound from Kerrville and would be on site in about twenty minutes. Also, based on the distance from a trauma center and the description of the accident, they had dispatched a helicopter that would be on-site from San Antonio shortly after the Kerrville medics arrived.

The amateur radio operator promised to stay on frequency and relay information to the emergency dispatcher. So, with help on the way and a communication channel open, Jim turned the car around and headed back to the accident site, hoping they weren't too late.

"He's breathing, but not well," K9 said as Jim approached. "His chest is pretty destroyed, and he's probably got some significant internal bleeding, but there's nothing I can do about that. How far out is help?"

"Probably another ten minutes at best, but they're already prepped to airlift him out. You sure there's nobody else?"

"Didn't see anyone, but wouldn't hurt to double check," K9 said as he turned back to check his patient.

Jim stepped away, circling the accident in a slowly expanding spiral looking for anything significant. He found a hat, random junk that had been thrown from the truck, and not much else. He returned to the inverted truck and double-checked that to make sure there wasn't anyone else. Thank heavens there wasn't. By the time he had finished this exercise he heard sirens approaching and moved to meet the rescue crew.

The first responders on-scene were the paramedics. As they jumped out of the truck, Jim relayed where the victim was and the steps K9 had already taken to stabilize him. Within a few minutes they had a cervical collar on the victim and were loading him onto a backboard, ready for the helicopter.

The county sheriff arrived at the scene, and he and one of the paramedics positioned their vehicles to block traffic for the helicopter landing, apparently just in time. Jim could hear the distant sound of rotors scanned the sky for the helicopter. It rose over a hill and was marshaled in by one of the paramedics, landed, and cut power to idle as the air medics jumped out and moved quickly to the victim.

"Didn't figure we'd be doing this today," K9 said as he leaned against the van next to Jim. He had stepped back to the van in order to get out of the way after relaying what information he could to the paramedics.

"Do you think he'll make it?"

"Maybe. He's pretty screwed up though. And there's more than one way of dying. He could end up like Mutt."

Jim grimaced, then actively tried not to dredge up any more memories as he watched the rescue operation.

"Do you hear that?" Jim said suddenly, looking to the sky.

"Another one?" K9 answered, scanning the sky himself. "You told them there was only one, right?"

"Yeah."

Just then, the Sheriff stepped over to talk to the two of them.

"Which of you called it in?"

"I did," Jim answered, handing his driver's license to the officer who took it and started writing down Jim's information.

"Did either of you actually see the accident?" he asked.

"No. He saw the skid marks and tail lights of the truck and told me to pull over," Jim said pointing at K9.

The officer handed Jim back his license and took K9's.

"Were you the one who did the first aid?"

"Yes sir."

"You didn't happen to find his wallet or any ID in the clothes you cut off, did you?"

"No, I didn't look. But his clothes are still down there," K9 said, pointing to where the medics were beginning to lift the backboard and carry it towards the waiting helicopter. The officer finished writing down K9's info and handed him back his license.

"I scoured the area for other victims, and found a few things that had been thrown from the truck, but I didn't see anything like that," Jim added.

"Do you know who he is?"

Both men shook their heads.

"Where were you headed? This is a pretty out-of-the way place."

"Clovis," Jim answered before adding, "we detoured to 16 when I10 got shut down, and didn't feel like riding with the rest of the detour traffic through to Kerrville."

All conversation paused for a moment as they watched the victim being loaded into the helicopter. Moments later, it powered up and headed straight for San Antonio. However, as it receded out of sight, the sound of rotors didn't fade with it. Both Jim and K9 looked skyward again and saw another helicopter slowly circling the crash site.

"What's with the other one?" K9 asked, pointing at the new arrival.

The trooper glanced skyward before answering, "News. They'll land in a minute now that the medivac is gone. They'll want to shoot some footage and will probably want to talk to both of y'all too. You're the only witnesses."

Jim and K9 looked at each other warily. Neither liked the idea of being on-camera.

"You don't have to talk to them. . . " The officer paused before continuing, "I'd skip talking to them if I could, but I don't really have that option." He paused again, clearly wanting to ask something, but uncertain if he should.

Jim looked at the officer and answered the unasked question, "Yeah, we picked these souvenirs up over there," gesturing towards their prosthetics.

"I was Radio Battalion with the 15th MEU at the tail end of Ramadi. Where'd you serve?"

"We were part of a small unit in that area just before you," Jim said.

"Small unit?" the officer said thoughtfully. "You don't happen to know Cooter, do you?"

K9 smiled, and that was all the acknowledgment that was needed.

"Cooter and I go way back. We worked together before he left the corps and transferred to the Army hoping to join the unit."

"He rotated in just before we went home," Jim said quietly.

"You wouldn't happen to be Shepherd, would you?"

Jim didn't say anything, but K9 smiled again. The trooper nodded acknowledgment with an understanding look on his face, but quickly shifted his attention to K9.

"Kelnhoffer. . . I take it you're K9."

K9 nodded.

"Cooter told me about you guys. . . some crazy shit."

They helicopter that had been hovering overhead moved in to land, and the three of them turned and watched as it gently settled down in the same place the rescue helicopter had been.

"If you don't want cameras in your face, y'alld better be going. If you'll give me your phone numbers, I'll have what I need."

"Thanks," K9 said, writing his and Jim's phone numbers on the back of a business card the officer had handed him. After taking back the card, the officer extended his hand and K9 shook it warmly.

"I get it," the officer said, acknowledging the pair's unspoken desire to get out of there. "Be safe."

Jim shook his hand and started to turn towards the car, but the officer held his grip. "Sir, thanks for what you did over there. It made a real difference. We didn't see it for sure at first, but the more we looked, the clearer it was that al-Zarkawi hated you more than anyone else in the world. I can't come up with a better endorsement. We'd have lost a lot more guys in that town if you hadn't done what you did."

Jim said a quiet thanks, but nothing more.

"One last thing. That guy would have never made it if you two hadn't been here. How many people driving through here would have the training and gear you brought to the fight? He's one lucky bastard."

Jim and K9 climbed in their van and pulled away just as the camera man finished setting up his equipment.

— — — — — — — — — — — — — — — — — —

Doc Chelwood was brushing his teeth with the evening news running in the background.

"Two unnamed Iraq War veterans were credited with saving the life of an unlucky motorist south of Kerrville on Highway 16 this morning."

The doctor stepped out of the bathroom just in time to see aerial footage of what was certainly Jim Harwood and Steve Kelnhoffer talking with a state trooper.

"For unknown reasons the motorist left the roadway at high speed and was subsequently ejected from his vehicle. The veterans, both amputees, didn't let their disabilities slow them down as they put their extensive military training to use. While they didn't wish to be interviewed for this story, emergency personnel on site said the motorist would have definitely died before help arrived if it weren't for the swift actions of these two. Medical personnel declined to comment on the status of the victim."

"Uh oh..." the doctor said to himself before spitting out the toothpaste and rinsing out his mouth. "This could cause problems."

He wiped his mouth on a hand-towel and went to grab his phone.

Who would be calling at 11:30? Jim couldn't help but wonder. Nobody he knew liked to stay up late. He reached over and picked up is phone from where it was charging on the nightstand. Only a few people had this number, and all of them needed to be answered no matter what time it was. That was one of the conditions.

"Hello?"

"Are you guys okay?" It was Doc Chelwood.

"Yeah, Doc, we're fine. You that worried about us already?"

"You made the news. Don't you think I've got reason to be concerned?"

Jim thought about it for a moment, and now that he did, it seemed almost surprising that the wreck and medivac hadn't triggered a relapse or flashback.

"Yeah, I guess you do. But somehow it didn't seem like a big deal at the time."

"What about Kelnhoffer?"

"Him too. I'm not really sure what was different."

"Please check in with me in the morning to make sure it's not just a delayed reaction. Before you start driving."

"Sure thing Doc," Jim promised, "but for now, I think I'm going to take a shower and get some sleep."

Chapter 11

Close Call

Canon Air Force base, just outside Clovis, New Mexico, had little to recommend it other than a place to stay a convenient distance from where they started. The Air Force seemed to like putting bases in the middle of nowhere, and this was a prime example of that principle in action. Maybe, he thought, so the neighbors wouldn't complain about the noise.

"Hey, K9, you up?" Jim said, knocking on K9's room door. There was no answer. They were supposed to meet up about now to head into Farmington where they had a hotel room reserved, but he hadn't heard from K9 yet this morning.

Jim listened carefully at the door for any sign of life in the room. There was none. He knocked again, somewhat louder. Nothing. He dialed K9's cell phone number and could hear it ringing inside the room. There was no answer.

Jim pounded on the door louder and shouted, "Open the door!" Nobody responded. He grabbed the door handle and shook it, trying to force open the locked door. It remained closed.

"Hey, keep it down out there!" another guest growled through a barely cracked door. "Some of us are trying to sleep."

Jim cast a withering stare at the guest, and the door closed with a pronounced snap.

"K9, open the damn door!" Jim shouted, pounding with his fists on the unyielding door. Still, there was no response.

Panic building, Jim turned and moved as quickly as he could to the reception desk in the building across the street. A disinterested clerk stood casually behind the counter watching a television mounted in the lobby.

"I need to get into my friends room," Jim insisted.

"Why?" the attendant asked without looking away from the screen and with little apparent interest.

"He's not answering," Jim answered, his agitation increasing by the second.

The attendant grabbed the remote and turned the volume on the television up before nonchalantly answering, "Maybe he's gone to the gym."

Before Jim could respond, the desk phone rang and the clerk answered it with a casual "front desk."

"What room? Did you say he was threatening you? Well, since it wasn't really a threat, it's after quiet hours and there isn't much I can do about it... I'm sorry, I'll have the manager talk to him... Just a minute, let me see... he checks out today, so you shouldn't have any issues tomorrow... I know you need crew rest... Did you try talking to him yourself? Like I said, I'll have the manager talk to him as soon as she gets in... All right, let me know if there are any further issues."

Throughout this conversation, the clerk stood with his index finger raised as a way of telling Jim to wait his turn. Jim felt an inexpressible desire to break that finger off and shove it down the stupid kid's throat. In the background, a rerun of one of the more popular shock-based talk shows was blaring with a heavily bleeped out cat fight between two large women taking turns beating a man who paternity results had just confirmed had fathered children with both women.

"Now, what did you need again?" the attendant asked.

"My friend isn't answering his phone, and I need to get into his room to make sure he's okay," Jim said as calmly as he could muster.

"Oh... you're the one who was causing the ruckus," the clerk said knowingly, but still looking at the television screen.

"Look, if you don't let me into his room to make sure he's okay, you're going to have a much bigger problem than one intolerant son of a bitch complaining about a little noise."

"Sir, calm down," he said, finally looking at Jim and seeing, but not recognizing, the panic in his eyes. "I can't deal with you when you're acting like this."

"Calm down!" Jim shouted. He reached over the counter and grabbed the young man by the shirt, pulling him up onto the counter in the process. "If you don't give me a key to his room, I'll break the door down and you'll be responsible for the damages."

"Shepherd... what are you doing?" K9 had just walked into the lobby.

Jim released the terrified clerk and dropped to the ground, his back to the counter and his head buried in his hands.

"I thought you'd..."

K9 walked to the television and turned it off.

"Couldn't sleep, so I took a walk."

"I'm in trouble..."

"We could get out of here before anyone comes."

"No."

The clerk looked at the two of them and motioned for K9 to come closer.

"What was that about?" the clerk asked in a subdued whisper.

"We're both pretty broken. I'm almost all he has left, and we've had a few close calls together. He thought I might have killed myself last night."

The clerk walked around from behind the counter and squatted down next to Jim. "I didn't know. Do you need me to call an ambulance?"

Jim just sat with his head in his hands, unresponsive to the clerk's question.

K9 shook his head, "Let me talk to him for a bit and we'll decide together whether or not he needs medical attention."

"I should call this in. . . "

"Do what you have to, but it'd be best to just let me calm him down and get him out of here."

The clerk nodded, then disappeared into one of the back offices.

"Shepherd, let's take a walk. I want to talk for a bit."

Jim stood, and the two of them walked out the door and across the street to the building where their rooms were located. Without saying a word, they loaded their bags into the cars then turned to walk down the street. After a few minutes of quiet, K9 broke the silence.

"You okay?"

Jim just shot a sideways look at K9 with a raised eyebrow.

"I found out last night that that guy died yesterday. Made it to the hospital, but died a few hours later."

Jim nodded, then looked at the ground immediately in front of him.

"The sheriff called me to let me know. The family contacted him to ask him to pass us their gratitude for giving them one last chance to see their dad. I guess he died while they were there. It was all for nothing. . . " K9 said with a heavy sigh at the end.

"No, it wasn't. They got to see him. They got to say goodbye before he was gone. I never had that chance..." his voice breaking up as he forced the last few words out.

"I've been up pacing these streets all night. I keep wondering if there was anything else we could have done."

"And what's your answer?"

"We did everything possible."

"Damn right we did. Nobody else could have done more."

"But I can't quit asking the question."

"The answer's going to be the same every time."

"I know."

They walked on quietly for several more minutes.

"Maybe we should go home," Jim said abruptly.

"Back to the apartments? Why?"

"I just lost it with a guy because he wouldn't give me the key to your room. We'll be lucky if we don't get a ride in the back of one of the security forces' patrol cars before we make it out the gate."

"Nah. I think he understood in the end."

"Probably thinks I'm nuts. I mean, what would you think if some guy tried to beat the crap out of you just because the TV was too loud?"

"We are a little nuts."

"I know, but I can't stand it when that stuff comes out in public. There's a part of me that would like to go back to just drinking myself into oblivion alone every night rather than face the fact that I've become a first class asshole."

"It's a good thing the class six[21] closes after 10:00, I kept walking past it wanting to get drunk again," K9 said knowingly. "I'm surprised the base cops didn't stop me... they kept circling by as I walked, but never stopped."

"Guess they figured you wouldn't be hard to chase down if it came down to that," Jim said with a crooked smile that seemed uncharacteristic under the circumstances.

"Especially if I'd managed to find the means to get drunk. I'm not going to outrun anyone in this rig," K9 laughed. This kind of humor was an agreed upon strategy to bring conversations around to less destructive paths, and each picked up the others cue that it was time to try and start the day over.

"How about we settle for some breakfast and a cup of coffee instead," Jim said, motioning toward the base Burger King a few blocks away.

They walked again in silence and within a few minutes were sitting in a booth at the restaurant staring at uneaten breakfast items.

"I'm not sure I'm ready to do this," Jim said, interrupting a silent streak.

"Which part of it?"

"Seeing where it happened. Meeting Maggie. Facing those demons..."

"Is that what spooked you this morning?"

"I don't think so... but it's hard to say. There were the nightmares, then you didn't answer your phone or knocks on the door. Then that punk kid... and the stuff on the TV in the background..."

"Did you get *any* sleep last night?"

"Nightmares, but no worse than usual."

"I didn't sleep at all. Kept coming back to the night Warlock died. Couldn't shake the look on his face. I saw that same look on the face of the guy from the wreck. I guess I knew he wasn't going to make it."

"If he had any chance, it was thanks to you. And don't discount the importance of his family knowing he got the best help possible. They would have spent the rest of their lives wondering if things could have been different. Believe me."

"I feel so stupid reacting like that," Jim continued after a pause. "I just switch into fight mode so easily anymore. It doesn't take really anything, and I get so wound up I can't contain it anymore."

"Doc Chelwood already explained that," K9 offered.

"It's one thing to have an academic understanding, but I feel like I should be able to control it better. My whole life I've been in control, and now I can't do it anymore. I'm no better than a toddler throwing tantrums. I hate it when I act like that."

"Me too. I lost it with a cashier at the corner store the other day over something stupid. Sent me into a funk for two days."

"Is that what that was all about?"

"Yeah. Nothing more than a damn hot dog."

Jim sighed again. It was becoming the default expression of hopelessness and exasperation that came out when he didn't know what else to do or say. Sometimes it felt like he used that form of expression more than words.

"What are we doing here? This was a bad idea," K9 said to himself so quietly Jim couldn't quite make it out.

"Huh?" Jim said, looking up from the blank space between himself and the table where he had been staring.

"I keep thinking this was a bad idea."

"Me too. Why did we decide to do this?"

"Do you think we should go back to San Antonio?"

"And do what? Sit at home and try to stay sober. What else do we have left to do? We're useless."

"What use are we out here?" K9 asked sadly.

"Well, we gave a family some closure. That's something I guess. I think I'll try and hang onto that thought for a while," Jim said before picking up the breakfast sandwich in front of him and finally biting into it. He chewed and swallowed before asking, "Do you think we ought to stay here another night and try to rest?"

"Nah... you're doing all the driving, I can sleep in the car."

"And when was the last time you were able to fall asleep in a car?"

"I'll be fine. Let me refill my coffee and we can hit the road."

"Not until you've eaten some real food. Finish that," Jim said, pointing to the hash browns and breakfast sandwich in front of K9, "and then we'll go. I don't care about the coffee. I don't really want to stay here and see that poor kid again anyway. He probably thinks I'm nuts."

"I'm pretty sure both of us are nuts."

"Yeah, but I can't stand the idea of facing people who've seen that kind of ugly from me."

"Well, I'll take care of checking us out," K9 offered. "You don't need to see that kid again."

The scenery leaving Clovis left almost everything to the imagination. With no working radio stations, and nothing to look at on the horizon, the two travelers were left alone with their thoughts. For the life of him, Jim couldn't figure out why anyone would settle here – it was such desolate country. He figured it would take over a hundred acres to feed a single cow. There just weren't too many places he knew about that were as empty as what he saw looking out the windshield.

Within a few minutes of leaving the base, K9 had nodded off. Jim was stunned. He'd never known K9 to sleep in any vehicle. Everywhere they had gone he was constantly alert and scanning. Jim supposed in this case there just wasn't enough in the scan to keep him engaged. That and the fact that it had been a few nights since he had gotten any real sleep. There really was nothing to look at except the roadway, and that got almost hypnotic as the dashed line dividing the lanes flashed by at regular intervals.

By the time he reached the small town of Vaughn, he had gone as far as he could without causing an accident so he pulled off to get gas and find a place to nod off for a few minutes.

"What's the matter?" K9 asked, jerking awake in a slight panic as Jim pulled into a gas station.

"I need a few minutes to nap. This drive is killing me."

"You aren't going to park here, are you?" K9 said, looking at the exposed location and the traffic through the parking lot.

"No, but I need to use the head and wouldn't mind picking up a cold Coke. You want anything?"

"No, I'll wait here and keep watch," K9 said, relaxing slightly.

It only took a few minutes before Jim returned with a large bag of Funyuns and a one-liter bottle of Diet Coke.

"High performance fuel," K9 quipped. His version generally included two energy drinks and a can of dip.

"Cut me some slack. It's not like I'm in serious training at the moment anyway. Besides, this was road-trip food back in the day. Don't rob me of a few minutes of nostalgia."

K9 rolled his eyes, but didn't say anything more.

"The lady in the store said there's a city park a few blocks away. I think we can park there for a bit and rest without being bothered any."

"All right. But I'll probably stay up to keep an eye on things anyway. Maybe I'll get more rest when we start driving again. This place seems to put people to sleep," K9 said as he scanned the horizon.

"You might not believe it, but I used to be able to fall asleep anywhere, even standing up," K9 continued. "Was a useful skill when I was kicking doors at all hours of the night..."

"Me too. Learned that trick in training. I'd fall asleep any time someone wasn't looking. I kind of miss those days. Now it takes forever to shut my mind down enough. Started when Leslie got sick, went away for a while, then came back while we were in the sandbox. Now I close my eyes and there are too many things that don't want to leave me alone."

"Mine are usually missions," K9 admitted out loud – almost for the first time. "Ones that went south... there's been a few. Not many where I lost friends, but I still see the faces of so many people we've killed, or some kid who doesn't understand why dad is being taken away with a hood on his head. Sometimes it's hard to remember that they were trying to kill me. What keeps you up?"

"Depends. Sometimes it's memories of the emergency room or radiology department at Brooke. I can't figure those ones out though. Leslie recovered. I should be able to put that one behind me, but I just can't. It's been coming back to haunt me almost every night since that night I ended up back in the hospital after banging my head."

K9 nodded, but he didn't really understand. Jim didn't understand either, so nothing more was said on that topic.

"Sometimes it's missions, but then it's only flashes. Faces of people like that girl on the first night. But I've forgotten a lot of the details... Doc says that's pretty common, and that we'll work through those as time goes on."

K9 nodded again, and this time he clearly understood.

"Then there are times when it's a fat Navajo cackling over the bodies of Leslie and Sammie," Jim said, clipping the words short and trying to stop himself from saying anything more.

Rather than continue the thought, he started the car and drove to the small city park without saying anything more. He spent the next half hour unsuccessfully trying to get some sleep before giving up and resuming the drive.

"Hey, I've got a problem," K9 said as he stood in the doorway of Jim's hotel room propped up on crutches instead of his prosthetic. They had agreed to give each other keys to the other's hotel room in order to avoid another scene like they had created that morning.

"Yeah?"

"I can't stop the bleeding, and it's definitely infected."

"Bleeding?"

"It's not bad, but it keeps weeping. I must have torn it open walking last night without realizing it. It was pretty painful this morning, but it's bad enough now, I think I'd better go into the E.R."

Jim rolled out of bed and reached for his crutches. He had been trying to fall asleep, and had been on the edge of succeeding. The net result was that he was uncharacteristically groggy, and it took a few seconds to get stable.

"The sore on your stump?"

"Yeah."

"What time is it?"

"A little after eleven. Sorry, I should have said something earlier, but I kept hoping it'd go away on it's own."

"Okay. Let's go," Jim said, fumbling on the night-stand for his keys. "The hospital is just down the road a bit."

The two of them stumped out to the car, neither bothering with their prosthetics. It was a new moon, and the street lights only offered a slight glow to break up the inky black of the night. To add to the unusual environment, the roads were abandoned as they drove the few blocks between the hotel and the hospital.

"Remind you of anything?" K9 said, looking out of the window.

"Yeah... any time the streets were this quiet it usually meant a nasty surprise waiting." Jim could feel his hands involuntarily tightening their grip on the steering wheel.

"Hard to shake that feeling, even though I know there's nothing out there to worry about."

As Jim pulled into the ER drop-off, an ambulance turned on its lights and siren and left the parking lot. He watched it as K9 opened the door and started fumbling with his crutches.

"Not sure which is worse," Jim said, motioning towards the ambulance, "that or the quiet."

"Quiet," K9 answered definitively. "When you hear the siren, you know something is going on. With quiet, it's just the unknown staring at you."

"You head in and get checked in. I'll park the car and be there in a bit."

The parking lot was nearly abandoned, and with Jim's handicap placard, it didn't take long to park the car. By the time he hobbled through the doors, K9 was just beginning to talk with the triage nurse. She was unwrapping the dressing K9 had applied and lecturing him on taking better care of himself. Satisfied that the sore was nothing critical, she applied a loose dressing, sat him down in a wheelchair, and sent him to the reception desk so they could get his information.

With nothing else to do, Jim found a seat in the corner of the room where he could watch people coming and going. There was no way he was going to be comfortable enough to nod off... too high a probability of a drug addict causing problems or something of that nature. Then there was the simple fact that this was an emergency room. Damn... he hated emergency rooms. Hopefully this would be over quickly.

Chapter 12

Rage

"Shepherd, they're going to take me straight back. Looks like a quiet night here."

Jim stood and stretched his back before following the aide who was pushing K9's wheelchair. Behind the double doors several nurses, technicians, and residents or junior doctors seemed happy to have something to do. They came over, one after another, and ran through the routine. The same questions over and over again. At this point, Jim could almost sing along to most of them.

From where he was sitting he could watch as one person after another came in, asked their questions, then went out and briefed the next person on the answers they had received. He never could understand why they kept asking given that they'd already been told the answers. Then something changed.

He had heard one of the EMT's radios crackle, but couldn't make out what had been said. A few seconds later the intercom came alive with a call for the trauma team to report to the trauma room. Immediately, the procession stopped and all hands moved to the area immediately adjacent to where he and K9 were. Crash carts were pulled into place, and the ER team shifted into high gear in preparation for the arrival of the ambulance.

Neither Jim nor K9 said anything. They just looked at each other with a shared desire to be far away. The last thing in the world either of them wanted right now was to be anywhere near a trauma patient, but there wasn't anything they could do. Any attempt they could have made to get someone's attention in order to get moved elsewhere would have taken someone away from the preparations that were ongoing.

One of the staff announced a three minute ETA, and Jim could hear someone relaying information to the team from the ambulance crew. Thirty year old male, intoxicated and combative, single vehicle accident into a telephone pole, probable spinal injury. Jim could feel his chest tightening, and his breathing began to be rapid and shallow.

"You okay?" K9 asked.

Jim didn't answer. He sat motionless.

The sound of a siren announced the ambulance's arrival, and doors flew open to give entrance to a gurney pushed by two EMTs.

"Get off me whitey!" the patient shouted. Nobody was on top of him. The staff ignored his complaints and began cutting off his clothes and methodically checking him over.

"Hey, those are my clothes! Get off me bitch!" he continued, slurring every syllable heavily. The staff completely ignored him.

One of the staff asked him how much he had drunk that night.

"I'm not drunk!" he yelled louder, "Why am I being arrested? I didn't do nothing! You can't arrest me for doing nothing!"

"We aren't the police, and we aren't trying to arrest you," one of the staff said, trying to reassure him. "You've been in an accident and we're checking to see where you're hurt."

The exchange went on like this for quite a while as the trauma team tried to get information from him. He refused to give them even his name.

"If I tell you who I am, you're just going to arrest me," he bellowed. "Get off my feet!" he continued, "Why won't you let me use my legs? Get me off of this damn board, it hurts!"

Jim, watching this, started rocking back and forth in his chair with a growing look of despair in his eyes, but he said nothing.

"Lets go ahead and sedate him," Jim heard a doctor say, "we won't be able to stabilize his back with him fighting us like this."

"Why are you poking me!" the patient whined. "Just let me go home. I want to go home. I didn't do nothing!"

After a few minutes of fighting and yelling the doctors managed to sedate the patient, and they were prepping him for x-rays and emergency surgery. They had forgotten K9 for the time being.

Jim remained in his corner, rocking forward and backward, but was otherwise motionless and expressionless.

"Shepherd," K9 whispered.

Jim didn't respond. K9 shifted in the hospital bed so he could nudge Jim with one of his crutches. He didn't move.

"Hey man, snap out of it," K9 said a little louder. It had no effect.

A trickle of blood was oozing from the corner of Jim's mouth, and the muscles in his face and head rippled as he repeatedly clenched and relaxed his jaw. His hands clenched into tight fists, and his forearms trembled.

"Shepherd!" K9 shouted, pushing him with a crutch hard enough to almost knock him over. Jim didn't respond.

Hearing K9's cry, a nurse poked his head around the curtain to ask if everything was alright.

"My friend..." K9 said, pointing at Jim.

The nurse turned to Jim and looked him over. "Has he ever had a seizure before?"

"No, I don't think that's it."

"What's his name?"

"Jim."

"Jim, can you look at me?" Jim's eyes darted to the nurse, then back out into the bay.

"He's not diabetic, is he?"

"No. He has problems with hospitals though... Big ones."

"Jim, I need you to focus on me," the nurse said, positioning himself between Jim and where he was looking. "You're going to be okay, nobody here is going to hurt you. Can you relax your hands?"

"We've both had some bad experiences," K9 continued almost to himself. Nobody was listening.

"Jim, I need you to focus. Focus on relaxing your right hand," the nurse continued, taking hold of Jim's right hand in the process. "It's okay. You're okay. Focus on me."

"It's NOT okay," Jim shouted, ripping his hand free of the nurse's grip. "I'm not okay. It's not going to be okay, and if you don't let me alone to fight this out inside my head, that drunken bastard they just brought in won't be okay. Someone like him killed my wife and kid. They stole my future and all my hope. It's all I can do to fight the urge to go over there and choke the life out of him before he makes anyone else suffer like I have."

"Jim, I need you to focus on me," the nurse said, taking hold of both of Jim's hands as he spoke, and this time holding fast. The commotion had brought two additional nurses who were positioning themselves to help.

"I've been sitting here calm," Jim screamed, trying to wrench his hands away from the nurse. "I haven't done anything to anyone. It's bastards like THAT that have do real damage."

"Jim..." the nurse tried again as a few more aides came into the small space.

"I've been sitting here using every bit of strength I have to keep from ripping the heart out of him. I lost my family to a dirt bag like that, and you dare to tell ME to calm down!"

"Shepherd, it wasn't him," K9 said softly.

By this point, four of the hospital staff were restraining Jim, who was thrashing in attempts to free himself from them. Several more had come near in an attempt to help, and the room was getting crowded.

"They killed my kid! They killed my wife! Let me go!" Jim continued to scream.

"Shepherd..." K9 pleaded.

Jim was still thrashing and resisting as the staff struggled to move him to a gurney and restrain him with something other than raw muscle. The attending physician came into the room and almost immediately understood that all the people and chaos were feeding the problem. The moment Jim was restrained to the point he couldn't hurt himself or anyone else, the doctor ordered everyone out.

"Everyone out! Now! Close the curtains, kill the lights, and find me a quiet room where he can be isolated."

The staff dispersed and did as they were told, and within a minute or two, Jim had been wheeled into a small examination room and left to shout and cry his lungs out for a few minutes with only the original nurse left to watch and make sure nothing bad happened. This complete, the doctor returned to K9.

"What's his back story?" the doctor asked.

K9 related some of their story. A vague reference to combat, the convoy and IED attack, and a quick description of the circumstances behind Leslie's and Sammie's deaths.

"When was this?"

"About a year ago," K9 said, shifting uncomfortably.

The doctor nodded. "We need to admit him, I think. Do you know enough to feed the paperwork Nazis?"

"Yeah," K9 replied, beginning to breathe deliberately in his nose and out his mouth.

"What about his regular doctors? Do you know who they are?"

"Yeah. I can give you all that," K9 said, looking at the door and fidgeting with hands.

"Okay, I'll send someone in to get the information from you in a bit."

"What about this?" K9 asked, pointing at the sore on his stump.

"We'll keep you here tonight. At least long enough for a round of IV antibiotics. The infection is pretty bad, and you run the risk of it getting into the bloodstream. No more walking on it for a while too."

"Uh... doc... I'm not feeling so well myself. All this is a little much..."

"We'll get the two of you admitted as quickly as we can and move you to a quiet room. That's the best I can do for now."

"Hi Maggie," one of the nurses said as a short native woman came into the emergency room.

"Is he still in surgery?" she asked. Apparently, she had already been apprised of the circumstances surrounding the patient's arrival.

"Yeah. They're immobilizing his spine, and once he's out of recovery, it's pretty likely they'll transport him down to UNM. Looks like it's completely disrupted. He's not going to walk again."

"Looks like it's been a busy night," Maggie said. "Anyone else here from my part of town that I can help with while I wait?"

"Couple of bumps and bruises. There's a woman who is having issues with COPD and not breathing very well, Agnes – they moved her upstairs."

"Okay, I'll go check on her. Anything else to keep you busy tonight?" Maggie asked.

"Had a guy go into a pretty extreme panic attack."

"That's not all that unusual."

"It is when they're not from around here and are missing part of a leg. Strangest part is that it was his friend who came in to get help. He was an amputee too, and had an infected pressure sore. They moved both of them upstairs for the night."

"Oh?" Maggie said with a surprised look on her face. "They were both amputees?"

"Yeah, why?"

"Never mind... I'm going to go upstairs and check in on Agnes."

Maggie stepped away from the nursing station and headed upstairs. Agnes was sleeping, so Maggie turned and headed back to the emergency department. The same nurse was there, and it didn't look like anything had changed.

"That panic attack. His name wasn't Jim Harwood, was it?"

"I don't know. His friend is Steve Kelnhoffer though," she said, looking at a chart, "if that means anything to you."

A shadow fell across Maggie's normally happy face that was impossible to miss. She sighed deeply and shook her head slightly.

. "That's Jim for sure. Was he in here when they brought my guy in?"

"Yeah. How do you know them? I didn't think they were locals."

"Never mind. Tell me about what happened."

The nurse then relayed the facts, Maggie growing more concerned at every detail.

"So he saw and heard the whole thing?"

"Yeah."

"What about the other one? How did he react?"

"He got quiet. Other than that, not much."

"Did Jim hurt himself at all?"

"Bit through the inside of his cheek, but that's it."

"Do you remember the night they brought my son in here after he'd killed that woman and little girl?"

"Yeah, why?"

"The woman and child were his family."

"What?"

"And those two men came to town to see me..."

"Whoa..."

- - - - - - - - - - - - - - - - - - -

"Mr. Kelnhoffer..." an aide said, sticking his head just into the room. He and Jim had been moved together into a shared room in the main hospital about an hour ago.

"Yeah?"

"There's someone here who wants to talk to you, can I send her in?"

Jim still wasn't responding, but he had been quiet for a while so K9 nodded his ascent.

Maggie stepped through the door, briefly illuminating her face enough for K9 to recognize her from their brief encounter at the cemetery in Idaho. She pulled the door closed behind her, returning the room to darkness except for the glow from various medical instruments. She pulled a chair close to where K9 was seated and sat down next to him. Jim was lying down with his back to the both of them.

"This wasn't how we were supposed to meet again," K9 said sadly.

"No. It wasn't."

"How'd you find out we were here?"

"I come in when one of our people is in trouble to help them navigate the system. They called me when that man was brought in," she said, referring to the drunk man. "I was talking to the nurse, waiting for the patient to get out of surgery, and he described the two of you to me. There can't be too many people like you."

K9 didn't answer. They were definitely an uncommon pair, especially in a relatively small place like Farmington.

"Jim," Maggie said, gently placing a hand on his shoulder, "are you awake?"

Jim just jerked his shoulder to throw her hand off of him.

"I'm sorry we met this way," she said, pulling back from him a little and sitting back down next to K9. Jim didn't acknowledge her.

"It must have been awful sitting there watching that man," Maggie said to K9.

K9 just sighed heavily. He didn't know what to say. Jim didn't move.

After a minute, K9 spoke again, "I'm not sure which is harder, watching someone bleed out in my arms, or watching someone slowly die on the inside."

"I think the latter," Maggie answered. She pushed herself upright from the chair as she said, "the first is over fairly quickly, and the suffering is done."

She extended her hand to K9 in parting and turned towards Jim. "Jim, I think I understand why you feel the way you do.

I know it's not okay now, but you're not done fighting. I'll come back in the morning and see you again."

————————————————

"Doc?" K9 said uncertainly into the phone. He hadn't been able to sleep at all, and had taken to pacing the hallways on his crutches. When the dull gray light of early morning turned to a blue and showed through the windows, he stopped at the nursing station and asked to use the phone to call Doc Chelwood.

"Yes?"

"It's Steve Kelnhoffer. We've run into some trouble."

"What happened?"

"Jim freaked out when we went to the ER to take care of my leg. They brought in a drunk guy who'd crashed his car, and Jim just lost it."

"Did anyone get hurt or the police get involved?"

"No. The ER doc seemed to recognize at least some of what was going on. I'm worried though."

"Oh?"

"He's still checked out. He won't even answer me."

"Did they sedate him?"

"No. Just put him in a quiet dark room."

"Make sure they keep an eye on him, and call me back if he hasn't started to come out of it in the next few hours."

"Okay. What if he doesn't?"

"We'll cross that bridge later."

Chapter 13

Released

"Mr. Harwood," the doctor said, stepping into the room where Jim was sitting propped mostly upright and motionless on the hospital bed, "I just spoke with Doctor Chelwood."

Jim nodded, but didn't say anything.

"He thinks you should call your parents to come take you back home."

"No," Jim said sadly, but with finality, "I came here to get some closure, and I can't come this far and not do that."

"After what happened last night, he and I are both worried about how you'll take it."

Jim's head sagged, and tears welled up in his eyes. His throat tightened up to the point that he couldn't really talk either. After a moment that felt like forever, he was able to squeak out a broken, "I need to do this."

"Tell me what happened last night."

"Didn't all the mini-me's out there fill you in already?" Jim said bitterly.

"Yes, but I want to hear it from you."

"I've got issues with hospitals in the first place," Jim said, working hard to stabilize his voice. "But I can do what needs doing. My friend needed some help, so we came here."

Jim then visibly shifted gears and related the highlights of
his wife's death as if he were reading from a script – mechanically, and without emotion. He had learned to switch all that
off and tell the story as if it were a plot line in a bad movie he
had seen a few years ago. It was the only safe way.

"Do you blame that man who came in here last night for
your wife's death?"

"Do you really think I'm that dumb?" Jim answered, the
emotions turning back on in an instant.

The doctor didn't respond to the jab, and waited for what
Jim had to say next.

"No, it's not that simple, and you know it. However,
among other things I blame the culture that seems to think
it's okay to drink yourself into oblivion and drive."

"Is that why you tried to hurt that man?"

"I never made a move to hurt anyone!" Jim yelled in response.

"You were trying to break free and were talking about hurting him."

"I was trying to get out of this goddamn place. The walls
here make me crazy. I needed to get away, and you geniuses
strapped me to a gurney and wouldn't let me go."

"So you don't think you would have hurt him?"

"HELL NO!," Jim said angrily, "I've seen too many people
destroyed. I've already helped too many people destroy themselves. Why would I damage someone else like that now? How
could I live with myself if I took some little girl's father away
because I was too weak to control myself? What good would
it do to further hurt someone who's already hurt themselves
like that? How could that ever make anything better?"

"Why were you threatening people then?"

"You've never said anything irrational when you were angry or panicked?" Jim countered acidly. "Think about it. I

wanted nothing in life more than to be out of that emergency room, but I couldn't leave. Then everyone crowded around me and added to the chaos I was fighting against. I was drowning. Don't you think you would be a little irrational if you were drowning?"

"What would you have done if you had been able to leave?"

"I don't know."

"Do you think you would have hurt yourself?"

"Probably not," Jim said, trying to reassure himself.

"Where would you have gone?"

"Anywhere my leg and crutches would take me. I usually just walk it off when stuff gets too heavy. I wouldn't have left my friend here abandoned."

"All right, I'll call Doctor Chelwood and discuss this with him. I'll be back in a while to talk to you about options for moving forward."

"Steve?" Maggie said, knocking on the hotel room door. He had been released earlier in the day, and had already returned to the hotel by the time Maggie came through the hospital on her regular rounds mid-morning. One of the hospital staff had told her that Jim was still upstairs, and would be for at least the rest of the day. After learning where K9 had gone, she immediately left the hospital and went to find him. There was no answer to her knock, and she couldn't hear any movement inside.

"He left about fifteen minutes ago," the desk clerk said when Maggie returned to the lobby and asked. "He said he'd be staying a few extra nights, extended the stay for two rooms, then went out the door."

"Didn't say where he was going or when he'd be back, did he?"

"Nope."

Maggie thanked the clerk and decided to sit in one of the chairs in the lobby and wait for a while in the off chance that it was a short errand that had taken K9 out the door. Waiting didn't bother her, she was well practiced at it. After about another ten minutes, the sliding door opened and the click-click of crutches heralded K9's return. Maggie stood and moved to meet him.

"Maggie," K9 said somewhat surprised.

"Hi Steve." She reached out and took the bag K9 had been trying to carry with a hand that was also occupied with a crutch. Inside was a glass bottle – some kind of alcohol for sure. She decided not to bring it up.

"I wasn't expecting..." K9 started to shift a bit and looked past her to where his room was.

"I know. Can I come talk to you for a minute?"

"Uh... sure," he replied before heading the few feet down the hallway to his ground-floor room. Maggie followed him silently. Rather than fumble with his crutches, he handed the key card to Maggie, who opened the door for him and followed him into the room.

"You hear anything about how long they're going to keep him there?"

"No," Maggie admitted. "Last I heard they were trying to get him to call someone to come pick him up and take him home."

"He won't do it," K9 said with a sense of finality. "He's made his mind up to meet you and see where it happened. He won't leave here until that happens."

While he was speaking, K9 kept looking furtively at the brown paper bag Maggie was still holding and wishing she would just leave him there with it.

"He didn't seem too interested in meeting me last night," Maggie said, walking over to the mini fridge and opening the door.

"He'll get over that soon enough. He's really good at doing things he doesn't like when he thinks it's the right thing to do."

"Do you want me to go get some ice? There isn't any in here."

"Doesn't really matter to me, but it does make it go down easier."

Maggie picked up the ice bucket and disappeared out the door, leaving it propped just open enough so the door wouldn't lock. A few minutes later, she came back in the room with the ice and a couple of plastic cups she must have taken from the water cooler in the exercise room. Without saying anything, she put a few cubes of ice in one of the cups and poured the amber liquid over it, then handed the cup to K9.

"What are you celebrating?" Maggie asked. "I don't drink, otherwise I'd join you."

"It's my fault he's in there," K9 said, looking at the glass in his hand without drinking from it.

"How do you mean?"

"We went there because of this stupid sore," he said gesturing angrily with his hand. "If I hadn't aggravated it walking around so much, we wouldn't have been there...." K9 started lifting the glass slowly to his lips.

"If my son hadn't gotten himself drunk every night instead of dealing with his problems, Jim wouldn't have been there," Maggie said kindly, but the rebuke stung.

K9 paused the progress he was making towards taking a drink and lowered the glass back into his lap.

"Sometimes it feels like this is all I have left," he said, raising the glass almost like for a toast before lowering it back into his lap. "Everything else I touch, I destroy. This, at least, only destroys me."

"Your last letter sounded pretty upbeat. What happened to change that?"

"Nothing and a whole bunch of stuff at the same time. . . It's hard to explain."

"I'm ready to listen. Tell me about the sore."

"It's from spending too much time walking on my prosthetic. But sometimes I just have to go. I can't sit still. It's like I'll go crazy if I can't just get up and move. That happens a lot, and I've spent way too much time with weight on my feet."

"Do you feel like you're trying to run away from something when you have to walk?"

"Yes and no," K9 said. He'd forgotten about the drink. "Mostly I feel like fighting, and that if I don't walk away and keep going, I'll give in. Killing people isn't exactly an option anymore."

"How long do you end up walking when that happens?"

"Depends. The other night it was all night. Probably six or seven hours."

"Is it normally like that?"

"No, that one was kinda bad. Usually an hour or two is enough to wear me out."

K9 then told Maggie about the accident and his role in saving the man's life, only to find out he died a few hours later at the hospital. Initially the adrenaline and sense of success had made him feel a little euphoric. He felt relevant and useful. Like he mattered again. He hadn't felt that way since he had left Iraq the last time, and it felt good. Then he got that phone call from the Sheriff. After that, it all went to hell in a moment.

"You feel like you're the reason that man died?"

"No, but for a minute I felt needed and useful. Then that was taken away."

"Maybe you need to take a different look at how you've been useful."

"I know... but it's the kind of thing that's a lot easier to say than to do."

K9 was fidgeting with nervous energy as he sat in the chair talking, with the result that he spilled the contents of the glass in his lap. Instantly K9 let loose a string of violent profanity, completely losing control of himself. Rather than react, Maggie calmly stood, retrieved a hand-towel from the bathroom, handed it to K9, then filled a second glass like the first and silently offered it to him. After a brief minute, K9 calmed down enough to wipe himself off, then took the proffered cup.

"Sorry," he said quietly while looking at the plastic cup in his hands. He couldn't look Maggie in the face now. He was too ashamed of what he had just done.

"I bet you'd rather be out walking now," Maggie said calmly.

K9 just nodded without looking up.

"Did you bring a wheelchair with you?"

"Yeah. It's in the van," he said, gesturing to a small table where his set of keys were.

"Well, let's go for a walk together. It'll get you out of here, and with me pushing, you won't aggravate your sore."

K9 sat the untouched drink down, and the two of them left the room. Maggie wrestled the wheelchair out of the van, tossed the crutches into the space where the wheelchair had been, and off they went.

"If you insist on staying in the area, Doctor Chelwood wants you out of the hospital as soon as possible. He thinks you'll better off without all the reminders of what happened. In fact, he says that if either you or Mr. Kelnhoffer need medical treatment, you should go to an urgent care unless someone is about to bleed out."

"About time," Jim said with a deep sense of relief. "How long do you think it'll take?"

"Probably about an hour, maybe two."

The doctor left the room, and Jim tried calling K9 to come pick him up. K9 had taken the van when he checked out, even though he still wasn't supposed to be driving, so he was stuck here until K9 came back to get him. There was no answer. Slightly irritated, Jim sat the phone back down and resigned himself to a few more hours of waiting. He'd try calling again later.

"Why don't we head back over to the hospital and check on Jim?" Maggie offered. The hospital was less than a mile from the hotel, and only a short way from where they were at the moment. K9 nodded in agreement.

"I didn't know you worked at the hospital here."

"I don't really, I work over at the Native Health center... the hospital on the Res. But I come over here to try and help Diné who end up in this hospital. Trying to sort out the paperwork between the hospital here and the Indian Health Service can be confusing. A lot of times, I end up being a go-between between the police and the patient too."

"Doesn't it get kinda old seeing the same stupid stuff over and over again? I think I'd get worn out and give up."

"Sometimes, but I try to spend my memories on the successes. If I let the failures get to me I'd have to quit, and then there would be nobody to help."

K9 just grunted in acknowledgment. He didn't like being pushed in the wheelchair, but Maggie insisted that it wouldn't do to have him get sores on his hands to match the one on his stump. She was right. He hadn't used the wheelchair much so he didn't have callouses, and he didn't have a pair of gloves to protect his softening hands. Reluctantly he sat there watching the scenery slowly pass by.

"Tell me about how you met Jim."

"My unit was headed to Iraq, and some general got the bright idea to embed an intel analyst with us to try and roll up the major players in our area. Jim was the analyst."

"Is that normal?"

"Not in my experience. We were usually given an objective, and we figured out how to tackle it. We had a lot of latitude to do what we needed to do without high-level intervention," K9 explained. "Having an outsider tell us what to do wasn't a popular idea with the guys in the unit. Everyone was pretty sure he'd get us all killed."

"I take it things didn't turn out quite that way?"

"Nope. He showed up looking scared out of his mind, but he didn't really try to change the way we did things. He mostly worked with Warlock – the warrant who ran our shop – to identify new objectives, then we did our normal thing. It actually seemed to work really well... at least at first."

"Why do you say 'at first'? Did he change things for the worse later?"

"No, he got really good and just became part of the team. From what I've been told, we were the most feared men in Iraq. What I meant was that it didn't seem to matter all that much. The whole idea was that we would be able to put an end to the insurgency – you know, cut off the head, kill the body kind of thing. Not long after we left that whole area exploded. It didn't seem to matter how many leaders we rolled up, how many weapons caches we destroyed, or anything."

"As time went on, Shepherd started to spiral. Things weren't going well at home, and we all ended up in a bunch of tight spots that can be really hard on people. Then we lost Warlock and a few others..." K9 trailed off, not wanting to explore that part of history.

Maggie seemed to pick up on his reluctance, and decided to shift the topic of discussion. "Why do you call him Shepherd?"

K9 laughed. "His dog. Every week for the first month or two his daughter would send him stick-figure pictures of his German Shepherd, and he would hang them on the wall of his hooch. They were supposed to protect him from the 'bad guys.' That's how it started anyways... Over time it kinda morphed though. He really cared about everyone on the team, and was always working tightly with Warlock to make sure we all made it back. I'm not sure when he ever slept. He took the loss of Warlock really hard. Anyway, he was a real shepherd for our team of independent operators – if that makes any sense."

"Does he still have the dog?"

"Lola? She's with his parents in Idaho. He keeps talking about bringing her back, but hasn't managed to talk himself into it yet. Too many memories."

––––––––––––––––––––

"Here's your copy of the discharge paperwork. Sign here," the nurse said, pointing to the bottom of one paper, "and here," pointing to another, "and you'll be free to go."

"I still can't get a hold of my ride," Jim said with a worried voice.

"No hurry. You can stay here, or you can go down and wait in the lobby or cafeteria if that's more comfortable for you."

Jim looked sideways at the nurse. A crowded cafeteria was never high on his list of places to sit, and one in a hospital was orders of magnitude worse. The smell alone was enough to give him a panic attack. "I'll wait here if that's okay."

"No problem."

––––––––––––––––––––

"I've never liked elevators," K9 grumbled, "I always figured they were for lazy people."

"Now you know different. They're for guys like you who need them. The fact that lazy people like me use them is beside the point," Maggie teased. "You're welcome to take the stairs if you can haul yourself up them."

The elevator door opened and K9 wheeled himself inside, followed by Maggie. A moment later they walked into the room where Jim was sitting and looking out the window.

"When are they going to let you out of here?" K9 asked.

Jim started and turned to face K9. "I've been trying to call you for at least an hour and a half."

K9 patted his pockets, "I must have forgotten it," he said apologetically. "I was in a hurry to leave the room."

"I can go any time. I was just waiting for you so we could get out of here."

"I didn't think you were going to be released today, so I didn't bring the car. Are you up to walking back to the hotel?"

"Anything to get me out of here. They don't need to know that we're on foot."

Jim didn't even acknowledge Maggie. Nor did he look directly at K9. He mechanically grabbed the backpack with his things, slung it over his shoulders, and propped himself up on his crutches. "Let's go," was all he said.

The trio left the hospital without a word. K9 recognized the strain in Jim's face caused by clenching his teeth. He was clearly trying not to say anything he'd regret. However, as the got further from the hospital, he slowly began to relax. By the time they were within sight of the hotel he was ready to talk.

"I take it you're Maggie," Jim said.

"Yes," was all she said.

"I'm sorry about how I reacted last night."

"I understand."

"How did you know we were here?"

"I help the natives navigate the health system. I was called in for that crash victim, and the nurse told me about you."

"Oh. . ." He was the subject of stories. Why couldn't the world just forget about him. He didn't want to be remembered as the crazy guy who lost his mind and was trying to kill a crash victim he didn't know.

"He told me two visitors with amputations came in from out of town, that one of them had an infection, and that the other had a panic attack when my guy was brought in. About the only really remarkable thing for him was that you weren't locals. He thought this was a strange place to come visit for two guys like you."

"I'm supposed to believe that someone freaking out in the emergency room is an every day occurrence?"

"It's not uncommon. Some of the stuff that comes in those doors is pretty wild. After a while, you just get used to it and nothing surprises you anymore. The hardest ones are the little kids. Sometimes those stick with you, but you forget most the rest of them as soon as the next one comes in the door."

Jim wasn't sure if she was telling the truth or just trying to make him feel better, but he didn't really care. Maybe he would believe that his outburst was just another day in the office for the people who had to deal with it.

They had reached the hotel, but rather than head for the doors, Maggie pushed K9's wheelchair towards the parking lot. "I think we all could use some real food. Do you want me to drive your car, or do you want to follow me? We can come back for my truck later."

Jim just nodded, and K9 tossed the keys to Maggie.

Chapter 14

Maggie's House

Jim couldn't remember the last time he'd willingly sat in the back seat of a passenger car. In fact, he didn't think he'd ever been a passenger in his van. He'd always preferred to be in control of the car, and Leslie never really liked driving – especially on long drives. He was used to being in control, and usually had a minor sense of anxiety when someone else was driving. However, now he was feeling a deeper sense of anxiety. He could feel himself pushing is foot into the floor onto an imaginary brake, tensing up the muscles in his back, neck, and shoulders, and clenching his teeth every time Maggie did anything. Finally, he decided to just close his eyes and try to pretend they weren't moving until they got where they were going.

They'd been driving for several hours, and had left Disney World far behind. Sammie was asleep, and Jim believed Leslie had been asleep too. The quiet was refreshing after the loud crowds and chaos at the park.

"Honey," Leslie said, breaking the silence.

"Yeah?"

"What would you do if my cancer came back and I didn't make it?"

This question came out of nowhere. Jim was unprepared, and stumbled with unintelligible single syllable sounds for a minute or two before collecting himself enough to put together a coherent but non-committal answer.

"What makes you ask that?"

"Nothing in particular," Leslie answered, sensing fear in Jim's response. "It's just been on my mind a lot lately. I can't explain why, and I want to talk about it."

"I've been trying to forget those kind of thoughts."

"I know," Leslie said, pausing for several minutes as they continued the drive up I95 in silence. "Do you worry about that sometimes?"

"Any time I let myself," Jim said sadly. "That fear never really has left me."

Leslie sat quiet again, trying to put what was on her mind into words. Several times in a row she opened her mouth to say something, then stopped before a sound came out. Finally, she collected enough words to begin.

"I'm not sure what was harder for me: coping with my own mortality, or watching you try so hard to keep going in spite of your fears. It felt like my illness was slowly crushing the life out of you."

"There's nothing I fear more than life without you, especially with Sammie."

"If I get sick again..."

"I'm not ready to think about that."

"Jim," Leslie said slowly and with a quiet calm that spoke to her deadly seriousness, "If that happens, I need to know that you'll be okay. I need to know that you'll find a way to move on. I need you to know that it's okay to move on -- to find things and people that make you happy. I need to know that you'll find a place in your heart to keep me, but open it up to share with others rather than closing it up and letting it die."

"Honey, everything's always come back clean..."

"I know."

They drove quietly again.

"Jim," Leslie pleaded through tears, "promise me that if I go, you won't let it destroy you."

"I promise."

Jim started awake as the car came to a halt in a gravel driveway. He couldn't believe he'd actually fallen asleep, but then again, he hadn't exactly slept well last night. Looking around, it was clear that they were nowhere near a restaurant. There was a small house, a hogan nearby, and a few rickety structures that probably housed animals of some sort in a few-acre irrigated pasture behind the house.

"Where are we?" Jim asked.

"My house."

"I thought we were going to go get some food."

"I've got better food here than you'll get in town. Come on in. Don't mind Maki, he'll come over to say hello, but he'll leave you alone if you tell him to go away."

Opening his door, Jim found a medium-sized border collie sitting and looking at him with his tail wagging. Jim ignored the dog and followed Maggie. The dog followed a few paces behind, but stopped at the threshold to the house.

Maggie motioned for them to sit down at the kitchen table. They sat down and leaned their crutches against the nearby wall. Meanwhile, Maggie opened the refrigerator and pulled out a dish of something and began serving up plates for all three of them.

"Sweet potato pie," she said handing plates to both men. "I made this the other day, but haven't had time to sit down and eat it. It'll tide us over until dinner."

"It's good," K9 said before putting a second heaping forkfull in his mouth. Jim ate mostly in silence.

While they ate, Maggie gave them a virtual tour of her place. As she spoke she pointed to various corners of the room – presumably to where outside the thing she was talking about was. She told them about her goats, the dog, rabbits, and how she used to keep a horse but couldn't ride anymore because of her arthritis so she found him another home. The entire conversation (though one-sided) felt oddly normal. Like they were old friends from high school who had just reconnected and were catching up on the last twenty years.

Her house was small and rather old, but tidy. As she talked she moved throughout the kitchen gathering various things from the cupboards as she went and piling them on the kitchen table.

"Can you start peeling those potatoes?" she asked, gesturing towards a ten pound bag she had just flopped in front of K9.

"Uh, okay," he answered, picking up the peeler she had placed on the table just a minute earlier. "How many do you want?"

"The whole bag."

K9 looked puzzled. There was no way the three of them would be able to eat a ten pound bag, and the idea of a large dinner with strangers made his skin crawl.

"Don't worry. We won't be having a feast," Maggie said reassuringly. "Once or twice a week I take dinner to a few people who have a hard time getting out. You don't mind helping me, do you?"

K9 looked at Jim, who just shrugged and picked up a peeler and a potato.

"No, we don't mind. Do you deliver them?"

"Yes, they're all pretty close by. Mostly older folks who don't have family here on the Res anymore. Sometimes I stay and visit with them for a bit. Other times I just drop it off, say hello, and head on my way. Today, I think we'll just be dropping stuff off."

They spent the next hour preparing food and loading up platefuls for delivery. The whole time Maggie alternated between quiet and casual small talk. She didn't seem bothered by the fact that she did most of the talking, and the quiet spells didn't seem to bother any of them.

When all was said and done, they had a stack of sixteen heavy-duty paper plates wrapped in plastic wrap and neatly stacked in a large cooler with a few hot water bottles in it to keep them warm. They hadn't eaten yet, and it didn't appear they would before they had finished the deliveries.

"I'm afraid we're not going to be much use with the deliveries," Jim said. It was the first he had spoken since they had arrived.

"You can drive. I'll just give you directions as we go." Jim nodded. His weak excuse for getting out of the deliveries had been swatted down, and he didn't feel like it would be worth another attempt. He would drive.

"We'll be gone about an hour, maybe two. If you're hungry at all, you should eat something now," Maggie said as she heaved the bin up off of the table and went out the door to load it into Jim's van. "We can go pick up my truck after we're done."

Maggie's version of "close by" was nothing like Jim's. They had driven all over creation delivering the plates of food. As they pulled into one driveway after another, Maggie would step out, grab a plate or two, let both K9 and Jim know they were welcome to join her, then disappear into the home alone. Sometimes it was a quick hand-off at the door, but more often she would be inside and out of sight for several minutes.

"Last one," she said as she climbed into the back seat of the van. She had just spent the last twenty minutes in a small worn-out trailer, presumably talking with whoever was inside. "Let's go get my truck and I'll introduce you to my animals."

"I'm not sure which way to go," Jim admitted. They had taken so many twists and turns down often unmarked back-roads that he had become completely disoriented. It didn't help that the sun was behind a gray sky and he didn't have anything on which to orient himself.

"Don't worry, soon enough you'll know this area like the back of your hand."

"How long have you lived out here?" Jim asked.

"Most of my life. I was born here, but went down to Albuquerque for college and stayed there for a while. I came back here after my husband died so my mom could help out. By the time I was ready to leave again, my mom got sick and I stayed to help her. Now it's home, and I don't think I'll ever leave."

"I've never managed to stay anywhere very long," K9 interjected. "Even when I was a kid we moved around a lot trying to get away from my dad. Then I joined the Army and nowhere has felt like home ever since. Right now, I guess I'm trying to find a place to call home."

"What about you, Jim?" Maggie asked. "What feels like home for you?"

Jim half grimaced, but not in anger or frustration. It was a look that he tended to make when he didn't have a ready answer. It was a look of uncertainty and deep thought. After a few moments of unsuccessfully trying to come up with a good answer he replied, "I don't really know anymore. It used to be Idaho, but I don't think I can go back there... Then it was wherever Leslie was..."

"I'm sorry," Maggie apologized, "I didn't mean for that to be a tough question."

"No, don't worry about that," Jim said. "A lot of things that should have easy answers seem out of reach at the moment. In this case, I haven't actually thought about it before now."

Where was home? He had always felt tied to where he grew up, but there were too many people there who knew him before all this. People who would recognize that the person they had known before was gone and all that remained was a shell that resembled him on the outside. How would he deal with the constant reminders of who he used to be and what he used to have? There were too many people who would pity him. He couldn't stand the pity. . . it reminded him too much of what he had already lost.

"I've been thinking about moving to somewhere in the mountains of Colorado, Utah, Montana or Idaho," K9 admitted. "Somewhere with a relatively low cost of living so I can make it on my retirement, and that doesn't have loads of people who feel the need to notice my missing leg."

"Could be worse, they could be staring at your face," Jim countered jokingly. Joking about it was a coping mechanism. In truth, Jim had been having difficulty with this aspect of his recovery. The scars had mostly faded, but anything more than a casual glance would be enough to notice the damage, and people would almost invariably focus on the scarring instead of him. There was something about looking into the eyes of someone who was looking at you, but not focused on you. Something about someone being distracted by the scars before they saw you. Something that really bothered him. He had tried growing a beard to hide the scars, but the scars themselves prevented it being thick enough to do anything but accentuate the damage.

"Well," Maggie answered, "if you're thinking about a rural life, this is a great place to get a taste of what you're in for. Why don't you check out of the hotel and stay with me for a while? I could use some help around the place, and I think you should learn a little about small town life before you jump off that bridge."

K9's version of a small town was something along the lines of the tightly knit community on Fort Bragg or other installations. He'd never really lived in the country before. He looked at Maggie slightly concerned, but didn't say anything.

"I've done the rural thing," Jim said. "My dad used to say that the neighbors were too close if you couldn't pee of the back porch without someone complaining. The space and the quiet are two of the things I miss the most."

"What kind of quiet are you talking about?" Maggie asked. "My animals make so much noise it drives me crazy sometimes. Especially when they think it's time to eat."

"Exactly," Jim answered. "That kind of noise is quiet to me. I'd rather hear a donkey braying because he's bored or lonely than the sound of tires on a freeway or the neighbors TV blaring some stupid show."

"I thought your family was in Boise," K9 said in surprise.

"They moved there after I left. The home I grew up in belongs to someone else now."

Maggie seemed to understand, and smiled compassionately. "Well, you'll get plenty of that kind of quiet at my place. What kind of animals did you raise?"

"We usually raised a couple of pigs each year, had a bunch of chickens and rabbits, sometimes goats, we did turkeys once, half a dozen dogs, and we usually had a small flock of sheep in the back pasture. The neighbors had horses and usually had a few steers around."

"Wait," K9 said, roaring with laughter, "you mean you actually were a shepherd?"

Jim tried to deflect by talking about the difference between the real shepherds and his family who only raised a handful of butcher lambs each year as a hobby. K9 was having none of it. If there was ever a chance to lose the call sign, it had gone forever.

"Yeah, Dad didn't think it was a good idea to let young boys have any free time. Back then I hated it most of the time, but I miss it now."

"So, should we go get your stuff and bring it to my place?" Maggie said, bringing the conversation back around to her original point.

K9 and Jim looked at each other and each shrugged a silent "why not?" Maggie took that as a yes, and the decision was made.

"You've milked goats before?" Maggie asked Jim as the three of them walked towards the barn. She assumed he had based on the earlier conversation. She had left the house with two milk pails slung over her left arm, but handed one to each of them now. She left it to them to figure out how to carry them with their crutches.

"Yeah. Twice a day for most of three years."

"Good. I'll introduce you to the girls then, and you can teach Steve how to do it while I go take care of the rabbits," Maggie said as she picked handfuls of a tall grass that grew along the path. "It's a kind of sorghum... the goats love it. Here," she said, motioning to K9, "pick a couple of handfuls and you'll be their best friend in the whole world."

K9 complied with a slightly worried look on his face. "I've never dealt with animals that walked on more than two legs."

"Goats are a lot like happy stupid dogs. You'll be fine," Jim reassured him after letting out a slight laugh. The thought of K9 being worried about handling anything, especially a goofy little nanny goat, was irresistibly funny. "Worst case, they head-butt you. But that's usually the males."

"My girls would never do that," Maggie said reproachfully. "They're absolute sweethearts."

"How do you make them hold still?" K9 asked, still worried.

"Don't worry about that. They know more about this than you do. Just follow their lead."

As soon as they walked up to the pen, three goats with stubby little ears trotted to the gate waiting excitedly for them to enter.

"Careful," Maggie cautioned, "they'll try to get out and eat my fruit trees. They're slippery little buggers sometimes."

She slipped through the gate, using the sweet grass as a lure to draw the animals away from the exit. Jim and K9 both followed closely behind, pulling the gate closed to prevent an escape.

"What happened to their ears?" K9 asked. "Do you dock them like a dog's?"

"They're LaMancha goats. They come that way," Jim answered. "The ones we raised were alpine goats with long floppy ears. LaManchas are kind of ugly, I admit, but they're pretty nice animals. But if you think that's weird, check out their mouths. Goats don't have front teeth on the top."

K9 just shook his head and stood stiffly as one of the goats came up and started nibbling and tugging on the tuft of grass he'd picked and was holding tightly against the handle of his left crutch.

"That's Annie. She likes to be scratched on her head. Give her a scratch and just grab her collar and walk her into the barn. That one," she said, pointing to one near Jim, "is Annabell, and this one is Lulu. Why don't you grab Annabell. I've got two milking stanchions. Lulu will have to wait her turn."

Watching Jim and K9 try to balance their crutches, the animals, the handfuls of grass, and the milk pails must have been quite entertaining, but Maggie just went along about her business. In the barn, Maggie showed Jim where she kept the brush, feed, and other necessities, then left him and K9 to make peace with the increasingly impatient goats who were expecting their feed and some pressure relief.

Jim showed K9 how to load the feed tray, lock the bar on the stanchion to hold the goats head in, brush it down, clean the teats and bag, and strip the first few squirts of milk into a dish for the barn cat who was waiting patiently for her share. K9 cautiously approached his goat (who was standing in the stanchion looking expectantly for her food) and dumped a measure of feed into the trough, locked the head-bar, and moved to begin brushing her. He looked like he was trying to defuse a roadside bomb, and Jim couldn't help but be amused.

As K9 started to brush the dirt and leaves from the goat, its skin shuddered, and K9 jumped backwards with a "Whoa, what's that?"

Jim broke down laughing, and took a few minutes to collect himself. "Here, come work on finishing off milking this one. I'll take care of it."

They traded places, but the result wasn't much better. K9 was struggling to get more than a few drips per squeeze, and was getting increasingly frustrated. By the time he had more than a few cups in his pail, Jim had finished off Annie and gone out to get Lola. Instead of starting right on Lola, Jim came over to offer a few more tips and demonstrate again. With this help, K9 was able to get a reasonable stream of milk and he settled into a rhythm.

"You did this twice a day, every day?"

"Yeah. It gets easier, and I learned to like it. The critters are always happy to see you and don't care if you've had a rough day or hard night."

The sound of Jim's rhythmic squirts into the pail countered the irregular pace of K9's.

"I used to be able to watch the sunrise through the door of the shed we used for milking, and it was a nice quiet few minutes every day to myself."

"I'll take your word for it." K9 was still uncertain about the animals. "You actually drink this stuff?"

"Yeah."

"Doesn't it taste funny?"

"Not if you cool it off quick and drink it fresh."

"Aren't there germs in it? Don't you have to pasteurize it?"

"This from the guy who ate all kinds of random slimy things in the field?"

"That was different."

"Yeah, that stuff wasn't intended to be food. This is. Trust me, you'll be fine." It was funny to see K9 reacting like this. Blood and guts? No problem. Eating grubs and slugs? No problem. Wading through a chest-deep cesspool of a swamp? No problem. Touching a silly looking goat and drinking raw goat's milk? Problem. Wow. Just Wow.

They finished the milking, put the goats back into their pen, and headed back towards the house with almost two gallons of fresh milk dangling from their crutches and sloshing perilously back and forth with every step.

Chapter 15

Amy

"Oh good, you finished." Maggie was cleaning up what remained of the mess they had made preparing the dinners as the two entered the kitchen through the back door of the house.

"Fearless here doesn't know what to make of your critters," Jim teased. He seemed almost relaxed – a marked change. "Just about jumped out of his skin when one of your girls twitched."

"Hey, I've never been around farm animals before," K9 said defensively as he plopped his milk pail on the counter.

Maggie came over and immediately began straining the milk through a filter and into large mason jars. As each one filled, she put it in the fridge where there were half a dozen already there.

"What do you do with all that milk?" K9 asked. "A gallon a day seems like a lot for one person."

"It's more like three a day," Maggie answered. "I take some to my neighbors. Some to the people I visit. Sometimes I make cheese. Some just gets fed to the animals. Just depends."

"What do you think of my girls?" Maggie asked Jim.

"Perfect ladies. Didn't even try to step in the pail. You know, it's been probably fifteen years since I milked a goat. I forgot how much I love doing that."

"Well, they'll be ready for you in the morning if you're up to it."

She moved to the stove, pulled out a sauce pan, and poured a quart of the fresh milk into it. K9 watched curiously as she sprinkled some cinnamon, ginger, and cardamom into the milk, then added a bit of sugar as it warmed up.

"What's that for?" he asked.

"You've never had a glass of warm milk to send you off to bed?"

"Can't say I have."

"Well, I often get woken up in the middle of the night for work, so I like to fall asleep fast. This helps me calm down and get to sleep quick. Besides, it tastes delicious."

The concoction had reached a low simmer, so she pulled it off of the burner and poured it into three mugs. "This needs to cool a bit, so we'll go get your stuff and get you set up for the night. Then we can enjoy this before calling it a night."

They went out to the van and retrieved a few essentials, leaving the bulk of the stuff for the morning, and followed Maggie as she led them to two small bedrooms at the back of the house.

"These were Amy's and Raymond's rooms. Jim, you take Amy's."

Both Jim and K9 dropped the backpacks containing their things in their respective rooms, then returned to the kitchen and sat down at the table.

"Here," Maggie said, handing a still steaming mug to K9.

Jim picked his up and cradled it in his hands smelling the sweet spices and feeling the warmth. His mom had made something similar but without the cardamom and with a raw egg blended in. He slowly sipped on the warmth without saying anything.

K9 looked doubtfully at the mug, but raised it to his lips and took a small sip.

"This is really good."

"You don't have to act so surprised," Jim laughed. "It's just milk, and fresher than any you've ever had before."

Maggie let out a brief giggle, and the three of them finished their drinks in silence.

"Well, good night," Maggie said as she got up and started towards her bedroom. "I often have to leave in the middle of the night. If that happens, don't worry. I'll be back before breakfast, but if I get caught up, Amy will come by to make sure the animals are okay. She knows you're here."

"Thanks for this," Jim said, holding up his almost empty mug.

"Night," K9 replied.

Jim finished off the warm milk, said good night to K9, and went to lay down. Thinking about the sense of peace he had while sitting next to a goat milking, his mind began to wander in other happy memories.

"Come on, you can help me with the animals."

"She didn't come up here to do chores Jim," his mother said disapprovingly. "She can stay in here while you go take care of the animals."

"Oh, I don't mind. Anyway, I've heard so many stories I'd actually like to see how many of them could possibly be true."

They had arrived that morning. It was the first time Jim had taken anyone home to meet his family, and so far it had gone pretty well. Leslie followed him to the back porch where he handed her a pair of rubber boots to slip on.

"You'll want these. I'd hate for you to ruin your shoes or pants."

"You can really see the stars out here, can't you?" Leslie said as she kicked off her sandals and slid her feet into the boots. "I remember nights when I was a kid when it looked like this... back before they put street lights in our neighborhood. But that was a long time ago."

"Kinda makes school feel pretty crowded, doesn't it?" Leslie just nodded, and they walked hand in hand out to the barn listening to crickets and other random bug noises.

Leslie leaned on the stall door and watched as Jim went through the evening routine. "It must be hard to leave this behind and go back to school," she said.

"I miss it, but then again, when I'm here I miss you."

"Must be a tough decision choosing between the two," Leslie teased.

"Nope," he said as he began milking one of the goats. "You win easily. But at the moment I get the best of both worlds."

"What if you could have both?"

"Not any time soon. Mom and Dad are selling this place. This is probably the last time I'll be here. In the best of cases, I get one of the two."

"Oh?" Leslie smiled.

Jim didn't take the bait. He finished milking the goat, retrieved and prepped the other, and began milking again.

"They're moving to Boise. With me gone it's getting harder to keep up with. It'd be nice if I could come back here, but that's not going to happen."

"Must be hard to see it go."

"Yeah. But things change." Jim paused a second, then asked, "do you want to give it a try? She's pretty patient."

Leslie came over, sat where Jim had been, and he showed her how to get a stream of milk going.

Jim was awake well before sunrise and didn't feel like laying in bed any longer. He got up, went out to the car to get his prosthetic and a flashlight, and wandered out to where the animals were. The rooster was crowing, but otherwise the only sounds were the crickets. However, as he approached the shed where they had milked the goats the night before, he noticed a light was on inside. Curious, he headed that direction.

"You must be Amy," Jim said as he came through the door and found a woman preparing one of the goats for milking.

She started a little and looked up at Jim. "Yep. And you're either Jim or Steve."

"Jim," he answered. "Mind if I help?"

"Do you know what you're doing?" she asked doubtfully.

"Yeah. We had goats for several years when I was a kid."

Jim moved to get one of the other goats without waiting for an answer.

"You're Maggie's daughter?" he asked as he began milking.

"Yep."

"I take it you live nearby."

"Next door. I bought my grandma's place when she died a few years ago. I come over and help Mom most mornings, and sometimes in the evening. She sent me a text saying she got called into work real early this morning, so I figured I'd come take care of this for her today."

"She seems pretty busy."

"Yeah. She's been that way my whole life. Always bustling here and there to take care of people. I think that's how she coped with my dad dying, and she just never got out of the habit."

"You're pretty good," Amy said changing the subject with obvious surprise in her voice.

"It's been a few years, but yeah, I've done this a few times."

"Well, I'll let you get Annie, and I'll go take care of the chickens if that's okay," Amy said as she sent the goat she had been milking back to its pen.

"No problem."

Jim finished milking in the quiet of the morning, made sure the goats had plenty of fresh hay and water, then grabbed the pail of milk and headed back to the house. When he got there, K9 was sitting on the back porch watching the sky turning gray in preparation for sunrise.

"Twenty years of getting up before the sun... I haven't yet been able to break that habit," K9 said both by way of greeting and explanation.

"How'd you sleep otherwise?"

"Not bad."

"Had a decent dream last night. Must be something in the air."

"Who's she?" K9 said, gesturing towards the goat shed.

"Amy."

"The Daughter?"

"Yeah. Lives next door."

Jim took the milk inside, strained it, and added it to the collection of milk in the fridge. This done, he returned to the back porch and sat down in one of the two available chairs.

"I suppose you get used to the smell?"

"Huh?" Jim hadn't noticed any unpleasant smells. He took a deep breath and realized K9 was smelling the mixture of fresh cut hay and the morning dew. "I love that smell. I guess I associate it with good memories."

"I grew up smelling the dumpster in the alley."

"Did you get used to it?"

"Not really, but I think I could get used to this."

Amy was walking towards the house with a coffee can in her hands containing two dozen eggs she had collected.

"I take it you're Steve," Amy said while extending her hand.

K9 shook her hand and answered with a simple, "I am."

"I'm Amy, Maggie's daughter. I live over there," she said, pointing to the nearest house. "From what my mom told me, you're supposed to help with the chores."

"I don't remember that being part of the bargain."

"That's the way Mom works. She'll rope you in before you know what you've signed yourself up for."

K9 chuckled. "You mean like delivering a van full of dinners all over the reservation?"

"Yeah, something like that. Jim, will you take these inside?" she said, handing the coffee can to him. He took the eggs and disappeared into the house.

"Your friend there is a fair farm hand."

"He's pretty good at a lot of things. That one surprised me though."

"Well, come on. Lets go take care of Maki, then you can come help me with my animals."

"I hope you're not in a hurry. It took me forever to milk one silly goat last night."

"She made you milk?"

K9 shrugged.

"Well, I've got a couple hours before work, so no hurry. Pet food is in the bin behind you. Grab a cup-full for Maki, and a tuna-can full of cat-food for thimble. You fill them, and I'll carry them since you're on crutches."

By the time Jim returned to the porch, K9 and Amy had already left. He sat back down and watched as the sun turned the gray sky a bright orange. He loved watching sunrises, and they were particularly brilliant where the air was clear. This one didn't disappoint.

204 CHAPTER 15. AMY

"So where are you from?" Amy asked innocently.

"I don't really know how to answer that," K9 answered honestly.

"What do you mean?"

"We moved a lot when I was a kid. Then I joined the Army. The longest I lived anywhere was in North Carolina, but I spent most of my time there deployed or getting ready to deploy."

"I grew up here. I moved away to go to school, but this has always been home."

They entered the goat shed to find a large tabby cat meowing expectantly over a now empty bowl that had contained goat milk.

"I think Mom should feed her less so she'll spend more time hunting, but she's such a softy." Amy sat the can of cat food down and they stepped back outside. Maki had appeared at the door and was anxiously awaiting his breakfast.

"Maki. Kind of an odd name. What does it mean?"

"Who knows? Mom cooked it up," Amy laughed. "She comes up with some strange names for her animals." She paused, then shifted subjects. "So Maki has to work for everything he gets. Before you can give him his food he needs to do at least one puppy push-up."

"Huh?"

"Make him sit, lay down, then sit up again." Amy demonstrated, and Maki eagerly complied hoping to get his food.

"Before you give him the food, give him a good scratch behind the ears too."

K9 did as he was told. So did Maki, who was rewarded accordingly.

"So, the dog gets rewards for working. What's mine?" K9 teased.

"Same as his. Breakfast. After we take care of my sheep, I'll cook for the both of you today. Mom's probably not going to be up for a while."

They walked across the field to where Amy's sheep were on a section of irrigated pasture behind her house.

"I like to give them some grain so they'll come when I call. Can you manage to carry a bucket and still use your crutches?"

"It'd be a hell of a lot easier if I had my leg on, but I managed with a bucket of milk last night. I should be okay."

"She made you carry the milk too? I should have known. I bet she never even asked," she laughed.

K9 chuckled too. It was funny the way she just expected him to do things and he complied.

Amy scooped some grain into a metal pail and handed it to K9. She filled a coffee can with some more, and the two of them went to the pasture gate.

"Shake the bucket while I call them. They'll come running. Feed a few of them by hand, then dump the rest of the grain in the trough."

K9 squirmed a little, but put his reservations behind him and did as he was told. The sheep came running, and one of the biggest stuck her head through the gate to nibble the grain he had in his hand. It tickled a little, but the sheep was amazingly gentle. He scooped another handful and fed another, then another.

"That's enough," Amy said. "Dump the rest in the trough and we'll head in for breakfast."

When they returned to the porch, Jim was sitting on the bottom step, petting Maki who was mostly curled up at Jim's feet.

"I see you made a friend," Amy said as she stepped around Jim and up the stairs. "Any requests for breakfast?"

Jim just shook his head. K9 wanted to request nothing with goat milk in it, but decided against it and gave the same response as Jim.

"Alright. I guess you get a surprise." She stepped inside and could be heard banging cupboards and opening and closing the fridge.

"You know K9, I think it might be time for me to go get Lola. I forgot how much I like something as simple as petting a dog."

"You're already halfway there," K9 offered. "You could go see your parents and pick her up when we leave here."

"Maybe," Jim conceded. He still wasn't ready to face the full range of family up there. The last time he'd seen any of them was at the funeral, and he wasn't exactly in his best form then. How much pity would he see on their faces if he went back? He hated that. He hated the pity. He hated that nobody treated him like they used to. They treated him like a china doll or something else equally fragile.

Jim knew it wasn't their fault. He was fragile. He knew it. Stupid little things would get him spun up, then the worst parts of him would come to the surface. But knowing that didn't change the fact that he didn't want to face the pity and the kid glove tactics. There were other reasons to avoid Idaho too... two of them carved in a granite monument.

"What'd you think about the sheep?"

"Kinda neat. They ate right out of my hand."

"They were always some of my favorites. Stupid, but easy to take care of."

"So is she like her mom?" Jim asked a few minutes later.

"I don't know. She sure likes to laugh about some of the things her mom does, but not in a mean way."

"Like what?"

"Like convincing us to carry the milk pails while we were stumbling along on crutches," K9 answered.

"She acts like she doesn't see what's wrong with us. Do you think that's deliberate, or is she just kinda oblivious?"

"She's anything but oblivious as far as I can tell, and that's the impression I got from Amy."

"That's what I think too. It's nice to have someone just look at me and not focus on things like the missing leg and scaring on my face. If she notices it, she's careful not to show it. Almost makes me feel a little normal. Must take a lot of practice."

Jim sat caressing and scratching the dog who was thoroughly enjoying the attention. He felt like he could sit here forever. K9, however, was restless.

"I think I'll go down and see the goats again," K9 said as he stood up from the chair he'd been sitting in and leaned on his crutches. "They can't be as bad as I remember."

"I'll come with you," Jim said. Instead of crutches, this time he had his running leg on. He stuck the blade of the 'foot' in one of the muck boots that had been on the back porch. It'd didn't fit anything like a regular boot so he had to walk funny to keep the boot on, almost dragging the boot along as he went. It was awkward, but he didn't want to have to clean manure and mud off of his leg before going back inside.

"Don't go too far," Amy called from inside the kitchen. "Breakfast is almost ready. In fact, why don't you come wash up?"

They immediately turned around and followed the suggestion. Going inside was still going somewhere, and that was all K9 really needed.

"So Steve, why don't you use a prosthetic?" Amy asked.

"I usually do. I wore a hole in my leg, and I need to keep the pressure off so it can heal."

"Well, crutches aren't the best option for around here. Would you let me look at it after breakfast? We might be able to work something out that would work better."

K9 looked doubtful. The last thing he wanted now was for the sore to get worse or the infection to spread.

"Don't worry so much. I'm a wound care nurse... that's what I do for a living. Usually it's diabetics who haven't taken care of themselves. I'd actually really like to work with an athlete for once who hasn't totally ruined his vascular system."

K9 agreed to let her look at it after breakfast, and the three sat down to eat together.

Chapter 16

The Code Talker

"All right, let me look at it," Amy said.

K9 hesitated.

"It'll be easier if you just drop your pants."

Jim chuckled. For all the times he'd seen K9 and the other team members nonchalantly walking from the showers to their hooches stark naked, it was funny to see him like this. He was clearly out of his element. After a brief pause, K9 stood on his good leg and dropped his pants to expose the stump then sat back down.

Amy quickly but carefully unwrapped the dressing to expose the sore. "You must spend a lot of time on your feet to get a sore like this."

"It's how I cope sometimes."

"Well," she said thoughtfully, "you definitely need to keep the pressure off so circulation doesn't get compromised any further. I'd hoped it was pretty minor and that I could rig up a pad to keep pressure off of the sore part."

"How long do you think it'll take to get back in my leg?"

"Depends if you actually let it heal. Looks to me like you don't do that as a general rule."

Jim laughed again.

"Like you're any better Shepherd," K9 growled.

"Yeah, I guess you're right. We're not the most compliant patients."

"I think the best bet for now is to put a boot on your crutch so you don't sink into the mud. You're going to be stuck with them for a while, and post-holing into the mud every step isn't a long-term strategy. In the mean time, someone else will need to do most of the hauling."

Amy re-wrapped the bandage, then walked out of the room and came back in with a pair of worn out hiking boots and an extra pair of crutches in her hands.

"You can leave these by the door outside and trade out with the other pair when you go inside so you don't track mud all through the house. Do you want a worn-out backpack to carry stuff in?"

"If you have one. All I've got here is the one I use for clothes and such. I don't really want it dragged through the dirt."

Amy tied the boots tightly around the crutches, using the laces to lash them in place. She then disappeared again and came back with an old ALICE pack that looked older than she was.

"This was my dad's. You can use it."

"Thanks." K9 said. He'd already put his pants back on and was reaching for the newly modified crutches. "I'm getting a little stir crazy, think I'll go try out the new innovation. I can't imagine the techs at Brooke coming up with a low-tech solution like this."

"You go ahead," said Jim as he stood and stretched his back out. "I think I'll take a nap while the task-master isn't looking."

"Sometimes low-tech works best," Amy laughed. "Why don't you come with me," she offered, "I can show you around the neighborhood. More to see out there than just pacing back and forth here. I just need to be back by eight so I can get ready for work."

K9 agreed, and he and Amy wandered away towards the street. Jim was left alone with nothing but the sounds of morning to keep him company. He sat quietly with the dog, barely moving, for half an hour before he heard stirring inside the house. A few minutes later Maggie stepped outside and sat down in the chair next to Jim.

"Sorry I wasn't up. I got called in late last night."

"Happen often?"

"A couple times a week."

"Must be tough."

"I'm used to it. It's easier now that Amy is nearby and can help in the mornings."

Jim just nodded.

"I see you've made friends with Maki."

"Seems like he'll suck up to anyone who gives him attention."

"I think you've got him pegged," Maggie agreed. Maki would take attention from anyone. "Where's Steve?"

"Went for a walk with Amy. She offered to show him around the neighborhood before she left for work."

"Oh," Maggie said with a hint of surprise. "She's usually gone already."

"I expect they'll be back soon," was all Jim said in response.

"Steve never talks about family in his letters," Maggie said unexpectedly.

"He doesn't really have any. The Army was his family, and that's mostly gone now. I think that's why he puts up with me."

"Well, anyway..." Maggie said as a way to shift gears, "what do you plan on doing all day while I'm at work?"

"I think I'd be good just sitting here hanging out with Maki, but K9'd go crazy. He was restless before sunup. I don't think he's gotten used to the quiet yet."

"You know, the hospital can always use volunteers..."

Jim just looked sideways at her with a raised eyebrow.

"Yeah, you're right. Probably not a great idea at the moment." She scratched her head and screwed her face up into a look of deep thought. "Is he a decent mechanic?"

"I'm the better mechanic, but he's not bad. Why?"

"I've got a friend down the way who's truck is on the fritz, and she can't afford a real mechanic. She could use the help. Her dad used to take care of stuff like that, but the poor old guy's getting to where he has a hard time doing much at all."

"What's wrong with it?" Jim said, his interest piqued.

"You'd have to ask him that. I'd get it all wrong. You can ask him tomorrow though. He's on the dinner route."

With this, she stood up, stretched, and turned back to go inside. "I've got to head in to work. I'll be back in the early afternoon though. You and Steve'll be okay here alone for the day?"

"Yeah."

"Help yourself to anything in the house. Make yourself at home."

- - - - - - - - - - - - - - - - - -

"Did you get your wiggles out?" Jim chuckled as K9 came up the driveway.

"Huh?"

"It's what I used to ask Sammie after she'd gone on a walk or anything like that."

"Oh. Yeah, I guess so."

"Well, we're here on our own for a while at least. Maggie left for work a while ago. What are we going to do with the day."

"Doesn't seem right to just sit around and watch TV, does it?" K9 asked rhetorically. "Wouldn't feel right."

"Funny, because that's pretty much what we've been doing for almost a year. You're right though. It just seems like that wouldn't be right here."

"You been sitting here the whole time I was gone?"

"Yeah. Just listening to the quiet. Where'd *you* go?"

"Amy showed me how to get to the top of that ridge," K9 said as he pointed, "then turned back to go to work. I got to the top and decided to just sit and look down at the river and farms down here."

"So what are we going to do?"

"We could go out to four-corners."

"Been there, done that. I'll take you if you really want to go, but there's not much there worth seeing."

K9 shrugged. "Do you think we could find some tools around here? The shed for Amy's sheep looks like it's about to fall over."

"Now there's an idea I can get behind. Take a look in the garage. I'll see what I can find in the house."

After scavenging around the property, they had tools and a few other things they thought they would need, but still needed some lumber and a few fixtures if they were going to do things right. They emptied the rest of the contents of the van (including the back seats) into one or the other of their two rooms and drove into Farmington.

"Any standard project of mine takes at least three trips," Jim said as they pulled into the hardware store parking lot.

214 CHAPTER 16. THE CODE TALKER

"I don't think we can afford more than one trip a day though. That's quite a drive."

"Why don't we just load up on stuff to do projects in general, and save ourselves the trip back?"

Jim didn't honestly believe that buying extra stuff would cut down on trips to the store. He had far too much experience with running short of some application-specific thing to believe it was possible to buy everything in advance. However, he went along with the suggestion and the two of them piled a selection of lumber, tools, and other odds and ends onto the cart Jim was pushing slowly through the store. Any time they needed to move something large, a store employee was standing by to give them a hand.

After checking out, the clerk asked Jim to go move his vehicle into the loading zone, and two employees quickly loaded the contents of the cart into the van.

"I would've never believed you could fit a full sheet of plywood inside this thing," K9 said with wonderment. "I figured we'd have to load it onto the roof."

"Yeah. I learned that several years ago. Leslie used it as an argument for why I didn't need a truck."

After a quick stop for lunch, they headed west again.

— — — — — — — — — — — — — — — — — — —

As Maggie pulled into the driveway she noticed the back door of Jim's van was open and nobody was in sight. After parking her truck, she walked over to the van and found it with several sheets of plywood and other lumber inside.

"Jim, Steve?" she called out. Nobody answered.

She walked over to the house and found the back door slightly open. Concerned, she entered the house calling out for them again. Still no answer. Amy's room. Empty. Ray's...

"Steve?"

K9 was sitting on the floor with his back against the walls in the corner, sitting with his head slumped forward in his hands. He didn't move.

"Steve," Maggie said again, but softly, "where's Jim?"

K9 just shook his head.

"What happened?"

"He left."

"Why?"

"Me."

K9 started rocking slightly forward and back. Maggie sat patiently waiting for him to tell her more.

"All I wanted to do was to help." He started pulling at the hair on the sides of his head.

"I believe you."

"I ruin everything." At this point he let go of the hair and started slowly and deliberately knocking the back of his head against the wall.

"Tell me about what you were doing to help."

"We were going to fix Amy's sheep shed." He still wouldn't look at Maggie.

"Is that what the lumber is for?"

K9 didn't answer.

"What happened with Jim?"

"I dropped it."

"Dropped what?"

"The board. It fell and knocked him over."

"Was he hurt?"

"No. He just swore and called me useless."

Maggie again sat and waited for more.

"We got in a fight, then he took off running. I couldn't even follow him. He was right, I'm useless."

"How long ago did he leave?"

"An hour, maybe two. I don't know."

"Does he often run that far?"

"Sometimes. Why did I do that?"

"Are you going to be okay here for a few minutes?"

K9 just nodded without saying anything and went back to rocking back and forth.

Maggie stepped outside and began dialing a phone number when Jim stepped into the driveway. He was soaked in sweat. She canceled the call and put her phone away. When Jim saw Maggie, he just shook his head and turned to go back the way he came.

"Jim," Maggie called out, "let me walk with you?"

Jim shrugged and turned back towards the house. He walked silently past Maggie and plopped himself in one of the chairs on the porch. Maggie followed him and sat down next to him.

"All we wanted to do was be helpful," Jim said bitterly.

"You don't think you can do that now?"

"We can't even move a damn board without ending up trying to kill each other."

"Do you feel that way because you couldn't unload the van?"

"No. You don't understand."

"You're right. I don't. Help me."

"It's the anger. Stupid little things make me so damn angry I can't contain it. Even *I* don't like being around me, why would anyone else."

"What made you angry?"

"Everything and nothing. I don't have a good excuse."

"I didn't ask if it was good or not."

Jim sighed. "I was embarrassed when I got knocked over. Frustrated that we couldn't do simple things. Then it felt like the hope that I got from having a project to do was taken away."

"I just wanted to be useful again," Jim repeated with an air of desperation.

"Did the run help?"

"Yeah."

"Good. Then I need your help with Steve. He's not doing too well. Get him in the kitchen and you two can help me prep dinner."

It took a while for Jim to get K9 up and in the kitchen. By the time he got there, Maggie had placed a large pile of vegetables on a cutting board for them to chop up and assemble into a salad. She acted like nothing had happened. Jim didn't know how she did it, and wasn't sure how he felt about it.

"We're having dinner with my cousin and her dad at her place."

K9 silently began deliberately cutting up vegetables, but didn't say anything in response. Jim did the same.

"It's just the two of them. Uncle Saul doesn't like too many visitors, but I think he'd like to meet the two of you."

Jim nodded.

"Steve, where did Amy take you on your walk this morning?"

"She showed me the trail to the top of the hill, then she had to head into work."

"Did you like it up there?"

"It was beautiful. I stayed for an hour or more just looking down here at the farms and the river."

"How about you Jim, where did your run take you?"

"Upriver. I wasn't paying too much attention, but I figured if I kept close to it I'd be able to find my way back here eventually."

Maggie kept up a slow stream of small talk while they finished preparing the food, and in the process both Jim and K9 had an opportunity to unwind and settle back into a more normal frame of mind. By the time they were ready to deliver the meals both were feeling the effects of a shame hangover, but both were ready to reengage. As they moved to take the meals out to the car, though, K9 froze in his tracks.

"The car..."

Jim stopped in his tracks too. Both were tensing up again.

"We'll take my truck, and you two can finish unloading that tomorrow," Maggie said matter-of-factly, opening the door of her truck and climbing in. "It'll be a little crowded, but we'll manage."

K9 sagged a little, but moved around to the passenger side and climbed in, handing his crutches to Jim who tossed them in the bed before climbing in next to him and closing the door. The crap in the van would wait. Neither was sure how they would do it, but they would find a way to unload it in the morning.

"Uncle Saul, these are my friends Jim and Steve. I told you about them last time I came over."

"Oh. I didn't know you were bringing company," the old man said, extending a thin hand in greeting. "I would have cleaned up."

"No sir, please don't feel like you need to put yourself out for us," Jim said as he shook the proffered hand. "We're more worried that we're inconveniencing you."

K9 greeted the daughter and asked if he could help get things set up for dinner. He followed her into the kitchen as Maggie motioned for Jim to sit down across from Uncle Saul.

"Maggie tells me you're quite the war hero," Saul said loudly.

"His hearing aids don't work very well, so you'll have to either talk very loudly or sit very close," Maggie explained. "Sometimes you have to do both."

"I did some things," Jim answered, "but I'm not quite sure what a war hero really is."

A broad smile spread across Saul's face and he relaxed back into his plush recliner. "Then you understand. Good. Maybe tonight will be okay after all."

Jim looked around the room, and saw a small and simple shadow box on a bookshelf containing a tattered flag. "Where did the flag come from."

"Iwo Jima."

Jim let a look of disbelief briefly cross his face before containing it.

"No, not that flag," Saul explained. "I was on the island, but not that part. One of my squad gave it to me before he died. He'd been carrying it since he left basic, and I carried it until I came back home after the war."

"I didn't bring any souvenirs back from my war," Jim said.

"Really," Saul said disbelievingly. "Most of my souvenirs aren't really visible."

"In that case," Jim conceded, "I suppose mine are similar. I wish I could unload some of them and leave them behind."

"I used to feel the same way. For a long time I after I got back I was so angry," Saul said.

"I'm pretty tired of being angry," Jim admitted. "But I haven't figured out how to give it up."

Saul nodded in understanding. "I lost my mom, dad, and sister while I was gone, then the tribe took my land because I had been gone too long," Saul said without a hint of anger or resentment. "My girlfriend left too. Married a factory worker. I really had nothing. Not too far from your experience from what Maggie tells me."

Jim just nodded. Coming here was a bad idea if it was going to turn into a griping session. There were few things more effective at dredging up bad memories and feelings than war stories.

"The government sent me to school to beat the Indian out of me and teach me to be a white man, then sent me to war and asked me to use the same language they were trying to kill off. And what did I get in return? I got to start over with nothing, and nobody really cared. I was just another useless vet." Even now, Saul's delivery was with a sense of resignation, but completely free of anger.

Jim wasn't sure he could spend much more time commiserating with what he feared would be an older version of his angry self. It certainly wasn't helping him feel better at the moment.

"But do you know what I did?" Saul asked with a smile on his face.

Jim shook his head 'no' without saying anything.

"I proved that they couldn't break me. I started over with nothing," he said with a solid single nod to punctuate the point. "I proved that I wasn't just a number. I proved I was stronger than that. They stole the future I had planned on, so I built a new one."

Jim was watching closely as emotion slowly built up from the polite but flat and emotionless start of the conversation, ending with a look of triumph.

"Everybody who comes here wants to talk about the war and what I did there. That's why I don't let too many people come over here. I'd rather talk about my wife, daughters, and grand kids. I'd rather talk about the people I've helped since then. That's what I'm most proud of."

"What did you do after the war to start over?" K9 asked from the doorway to the kitchen where he had been standing and listening.

"I went to school on the GI bill. Then I came back here and taught high school. My second year back I met my bride."

"Must be tough teaching," Jim said, "I think I'd rather be back in Ramadi than work with teenagers."

Saul laughed. "There were times when I felt the same way. But I had to find a way to help people, and out here there's always a need for teachers who care about and understand the kids."

"He taught me," Maggie interjected. "Best teacher I ever had. He's the one who convinced me to take the route I did. And, he took care of me when my Aaron died too. My second Dad," she said, speaking the last part very loudly, putting her arm around his shoulders, and leaning in to give him a kiss on the cheek.

Saul smiled with a look of contentment. "Thank you dear."

"How long did it take before you could talk about what happened that way?" K9 asked.

"What way?"

"Without getting angry," Jim answered before K9 could clarify.

"Years. It got a little easier every year that I focused on helping others, until one day I realized I was done being angry."

"Wouldn't that be nice," K9 said in a whisper low enough that Saul didn't hear it, but Maggie did.

Just then the door opened and Amy came in.

"Sorry I'm late Uncle Saul," she said, giving him a kiss on the cheek. "I brought you a birthday cupcake so we can celebrate in style."

Chapter 17

Crash

"Hi Mom, it's Jim."

There was a short silence on the other end of the line that Jim interpreted as a stunned pause.

"Is everything okay?"

"Yeah, I'm just checking in. I figured it'd been a while."

"It has. Are you still in New Mexico?"

"Yeah."

"What've you been doing to keep busy? You've been there a while now?"

"We help make and deliver meals to some of the folks who are mostly shut in, and K9 and I have been keeping busy during the day working on stuff."

"Like what?"

"We've built a few shelters for animals, fixed a handful of trucks and such, and generally acted like the neighborhood handymen. That and we usually take a long walk along the ridge or the river in the mornings."

"Does it help to keep busy like that?"

"Yeah. A lot. I think sitting in that apartment doing nothing was eating away at my soul."

"How much longer are you going to stay there?"

"I don't know. I still haven't been out to the crash site, and that's what I came here to do."

"Have you thought any more about our offer for you to come up here with us?"

"Yeah, all the time. I'm just not ready to be around the family."

"We all love you."

"And you all knew me before. Things have changed, and I don't want to see the disappointment or pity in everyone's faces."

"It won't be like that."

"It's like that here, and they didn't know me before. I'm just not ready to face that."

"What if you were to move out towards where our old place was? That's far enough out you wouldn't need to see anyone if you didn't want to, but still be close enough we could be part of your life."

"I'll think about that."

Jim hadn't really decided where he wanted to go next. At this point, all he was sure of was that he wasn't going back to Texas. There was nothing there for him anymore except a storage unit full of stuff he didn't want to face. Once he decided where to go, he'd have that stuff shipped there. He wasn't going back.

"Would it help if we came down to be with you when you go out to the crash site?"

"Maybe. I'll let you know."

K9 was over at Amy's house patching a hole in the wall where he and Jim had redone some wiring earlier, leaving Jim and Maggie alone to prepare dinner.

"Maggie," Jim said as he pulled a pan out of a cupboard, "you never talk about the accident or ask me about it. Why?"

"I figured you'd bring it up when you were ready."

"I'm not sure I'll ever be ready."

"Well, I'm not sure I'm really ready either. But, I doubt you intend to stay here forever, you won't go until you've been there, and we need to talk about it before going out there."

"You're right," Jim Jim sighed. "I suppose I'm about as ready as I'm going to be any time soon."

"Well..." Maggie started, "when Ray was little he was my cuddle kid, but he would always go to his dad when he needed anything. Always a daddy's boy. He took it real hard when his dad died. I think that's what started all of it. I was so busy trying to stay afloat I don't think I realized he was drinking to deal with it. I just thought he was spending time with friends."

Jim paused what he was doing and sat down. He knew he needed to hear this, but he also knew it would be hard to hear.

"By the time I realized he was having problems, I couldn't do anything to help him. He wouldn't let me. He was just so hard headed."

Jim nodded, but didn't say anything.

"After I forced him into an in-residence rehab he just left. I didn't know where he was for a couple of years. Then he'd only resurface when he was out of money or needed to be bailed out. Nothing I did seemed to make any difference."

At this point, Maggie sat down across the table from Jim.

"I've spent most of the last ten years questioning what else I could have done. Wondering how I screwed it up so bad. Sometimes I'm angry. Sometimes I'm sad. Sometimes I just accept it. But none of that ever changes him. It makes me feel like a failure."

"What about Amy?" Jim asked. "She lived through the same times, and came out quite differently."

"Yes," she said sadly, then paused for several seconds. "Yes, she's my comfort. But that doesn't erase the failure and pain. Anyway, about two years ago Ray disappeared. Last word I had, he was living in Arizona somewhere. He cut off all communications with me, Amy, and anyone else who could tell me where to find him. I watched the newspapers and evening news hoping that I would see something about him, and at the same time dreading that I *would* find something."

"The night your Leslie died, he had been at the Ute Mountain Casino north of here on the other side of the Colorado border. Nobody seems to know where he had been before that. He was there for several hours when he left. The staff called a cab for him, but he wandered off before it arrived. The next anybody saw of him was when they pulled him out of the mangled truck he had stolen."

Tears were streaming down Maggie's face, and she was choking on some of the words as they came out.

"Witnesses say he had been weaving back and forth in the lane, ran out of the lane on the right side, over-corrected into oncoming traffic and hit your family. They never saw it coming. The car right behind your wife's had an EMT in it, but it didn't matter. Your wife died instantly. Your daughter died before they could get her out of the car seat."

"They had to cut the car apart to try to get to her. It didn't even look like it had ever been a car in the first place, it was smashed so bad. Ray only survived because the passenger side of the truck he was driving took the brunt of the impact."

Maggie paused for a minute to catch her breath and collect herself. Jim was sitting and staring blankly through her.

"I was at the hospital when they brought him in, but he wouldn't talk to me or let me see him. I could hear him cursing out the doctors, claiming that someone else had been driving, and shouting that the other car had crossed into his lane. I could smell the mixture of alcohol and urine coming off of him. But that was all I got from my own son. When I tried to go see him a few months ago he wouldn't come. He stayed in his cell rather than see his own mother."

––––––––––––––––––

"Hey," K9 almost shouted to get Jim's attention, "what's eating you? You haven't been like this since the fight."

He didn't know anything about the conversation Jim and Maggie had earlier. All he knew was that his friend was checked out again.

"Sorry. That bad, eh?"

"You've been staring at that blank TV screen since I came in here. At least 20 minutes."

"That long?"

"At least."

"Oh." Jim's face fell further, though it didn't have far it could go. He turned and looked directly at K9, "I don't feel good. Maybe it was a bad idea to come here."

"You didn't think that yesterday after you'd manged to get that old truck up and running for the guy down the road."

"Sometimes its hard to remember that kind of stuff. You know that," Jim said reproachfully.

K9 nodded, but didn't say anything. He turned back to the kitchen and picked up where he had left off – the work Jim had started. Maggie had excused herself when he had arrived and hurried into her room without explanation, so he was left to himself to get food ready. He inferred that something had happened between the two of them, and was uncertain if either of them would be eating. He prepared three plates none the less. Twenty minutes later he ate alone. Two hours later, he stuck his head into the living room to tell Jim good night and shut himself into his room.

––––––––––––––––––

"K9..." Jim said hesitantly as he stuck his head through K9's door.

"Huh?"

"You've got to take me to the ER."

"You hurt?"

"No."

"Oh."

They had agreed to this. They had talked about this. But neither of them believed they'd ever have to do it. They'd both been so close to the line so many times before, and managed to step back from the abyss each time, that they didn't honestly believe it would ever get to this point.

"Let me get my leg on. What time is it?"

"Four."

"Where's your handgun?"

"In the car. I put it out there like we agreed."

"You have anything else?"

"No," Jim said sadly.

"Did you call anybody?"

"No," with the same tone.

"I'll take care of that later."

K9 kept asking Jim questions to keep him talking as he pulled on his leg, then a pair of pants and a shirt. Within a minute or two, K9 had Jim by the arm and was walking him out to the van. The questioning continued as K9 drove towards the hospital. Neither the questions nor the answers mattered. It was just a tool to keep Jim focused. K9 knew it must have been hard for Jim to come get him. He knew it would have been easier to just walk outside and find a quiet place to die. They'd both been there before, but they had made a promise to each other that they'd stick it out.

"Doc?"

"Yes?"

"It's Steve Kelnhoffer. Jim's in the hospital."

"What happened?"

"I don't really know, but near as I can tell he heard Maggie's side of the story. He was near comatose at dinner, and came to get me early this morning."

"Did he try to follow through?"

"No. He kept his promise."

"Good. How are you taking it?"

"I ain't gonna lie Doc. It's a little rough."

"Do you need to check yourself in too?"

"Not yet," K9 said heavily, "but I might." The admission stung.

"Who is there to hold you accountable?"

"Amy, Maggie's daughter. I've told her almost everything, and she's willing to be my backup."

"Good. I'll get a hold of the docs there and give them what they need to know. What are the odds Jim'll agree to come back here."

"Zero from what I can tell. If that's going to happen it'll take a court order."

"Okay." Doctor Chelwood was clearly disappointed, but not surprised. "I'll see what I can do on my end to keep it from getting to that."

"Mom?" Amy had just finished taking care of the animals by herself for the first time in weeks, and had stepped into Maggie's kitchen to find out what was going on.

"Mom, are you in here?"

There was no answer. She stepped back outside. Both her mom's truck and Jim's van were gone.

She called her mom's phone, but could hear it ringing from where it lay on the kitchen counter. Evidently Maggie had left without it. That was very unusual. She called Jim's. It rang from her old bedroom. She stepped through the door to look. It was unoccupied.

Almost panicked, she went outside again scanning the horizon and wondering what she should do. In the distance she could hear the distinctive sound of her mother's truck rattling down the dirt road. Not long afterward, the gray morning light showed she was right. Her mom was coming home. Breathing a sigh of relief, she waited for the truck to pull into the driveway.

"Mom, you had me worried."

"Not as much as I've been," Maggie said as she stepped from her truck.

Amy's puzzled and concerned look said all that needed saying.

"I heard the boys leaving early this morning. I was worried, so I followed them. I left my phone home in my hurry."

"And?"

"Let's go have some coffee and I'll tell you what I know – it isn't much."

Maggie walked wearily into the kitchen and began preparing a pot of coffee. It needed to be strong. She hadn't managed to fall asleep at all last night, and was almost to the point of dozing off when she heard Jim and K9 leave.

After a few more minutes, she handed a cup to Amy and poured herself one, then sat down and began to tell Amy what had happened earlier. Amy's concern returned as she heard her mom's side of the story.

"Jim's been doing so well lately. How could he have collapsed so quickly?" Amy asked.

"It doesn't take much to shatter a fragile piece of crystal, does it?"

"No."

"I told him about the accident before dinner last night. I'm pretty sure that's what triggered it."

"Oh..." Amy paused for a minute and sipped at her coffee. "Do you think you should have waited longer to talk about that?"

"I've been asking myself that all night. But like you said... he seemed to be doing so well. Imagine if he'd followed through instead of waking up Steve."

"Is he staying at the hospital?"

"Yes, they've admitted him."

"Sorry, I meant Steve."

"He said he had some phone calls to make, and that he'd be back here when he was sure Jim was taken care of."

"Is he okay?"

"Better than Jim, but worse than me."

Amy stood up and started making some breakfast while Maggie sipped her coffee in silence. She didn't know what to say, and apparently the feeling was mutual. A few minutes later she put two plates of scrambled eggs and toast on the table and they ate in silence. Once the plates were cleared, Maggie stood and disappeared into her room with a weak, "I'm going to go lay down for a minute. Will you make sure Steve gets back here okay?" She didn't wait for the answer.

Amy immediately reached for her phone and dialed K9's number.

"Steve, are you alright?" Amy asked as soon as K9 answered his phone.

"Not really."

"Do you need me to come get you?"

"No. I'm on my way back to your mom's now. Are you at home?"

"No, I'm at Mom's helping her."

"She was pretty shook up when she left here."

"Is Jim going to be okay?"

"He's safe for now." He paused for what felt like forever before adding, "I don't think I should be alone though."

"I'll be here."

"Okay."

K9 hung up. What was she supposed to do now? All she knew was that K9 had taken Jim to the hospital early that morning, and that her mom had told him about the accident. They had only been here a few weeks, but it seemed longer than that, and the thought of anything bad happening to them really bothered her. She spent the next hour cleaning and re-cleaning the counter tops and other things in the kitchen - pacing back and forth to pass the time. By the time K9 stumped in, she was as worked up as she'd been since her dad had died.

"What took you so long. I've been worried sick."

"I had to call a few people."

By the look on Amy's face, it was clear she didn't understand why he would need to do that.

"Before we left to come out here, Jim and I made a pact that we would take care of certain things if it ever got bad. Last night, it got bad for Jim. Real bad. He was ready to do it. I promised him I would get him to the hospital, make sure the docs there were connected with the folks in Texas, and let his family know what was going on."

"What happened?"

"He heard your mom's story."

"He was doing so well. I wouldn't think that would be enough to send him over the edge like that."

"It's a funny thing. When you're as screwed up as the two of us, you can go from feeling pretty normal to homicidal or suicidal in a flash. Stupid little things can set it off. Sometimes the same thing can make you feel great at first, only to bring you to a crash later."

"Like that car crash you helped in on the way here?"

"Yeah... like that."

"How are you doing now?"

"Not good," K9 said before pausing to gather his thoughts, "but not as bad as Jim. If he hadn't come to get me, I'd be a lot worse off."

"How much worse?"

K9 just looked at the wall behind her. He couldn't say it out loud. Losing Jim at this point would be devastating. Other than the friendships he had developed with Maggie and Amy, Jim was just about all he had left.

"Do you want to go for a walk, or do you need to sleep first?"

"No way I'm going to be able to get to sleep any time soon. Where's your mom? Is she okay?"

"She went to bed. I think she'll be fine after some sleep and a little time. She's a tough old lady."

"What time do you need to leave for work?"

"I can call off..."

"Could I just come with you? Movement and doing stuff helps, and I don't want to try to do that around here today."

"Yeah. Get some real food with that coffee, take a shower, and we'll head out. I'm gonna run home and clean up while you do that. Will that be okay?"

K9 nodded, "I've gotta make one more phone call first." He didn't feel like eating, but that wasn't particularly uncommon. He really didn't feel like calling Jim's parents either. He would do both. After all, he had spent most of the last twenty years making himself do things he didn't want to do. It was one of the things he was really good at, and he would need that skill to get through the next few days.

Chapter 18

Decision

"Doc Chelwood called again. He wants me to go to some in-residence treatment center."

Jim was clearly on some kind of anti-anxiety medication or a heavy sedative. His speech was slurred and slow, and he was having trouble focusing on K9.

"You gonna go?"

"Can't stay here like this. . . "

The Psych ward at the hospital wasn't really designed for providing the kind of environment needed to bring someone like Jim back from the brink. It was just there to stabilize people who were critically ill – enough so they would survive the trip to somewhere more effective. It was about like comparing the trauma section of an inner-city emergency department with a high-end children's hospital. It was sterile, and full of people who were in crisis – most of whom were completely out of touch with reality. The only advantage to being at the hospital was that they could take away most of the means of suicide and keep a close eye on him.

"Where is it?"

"Texas somewhere. Doesn't matter though. . . I get taken there. . . Then taken somewhere else. . . Seems I've don't have any choice." Jim spit this out, though slowly, as if it had a strongly bitter taste that remained in his mouth for a while afterward. "I swore I'd never go back there."

"You've been to that treatment center before?" K9 asked confused.

"Texas. Damn the place."

K9 grunted in acknowledgment but didn't otherwise answer, meanwhile nervously scanning his field of view repeatedly. He was clearly uncomfortable here. Even in his drugged state Jim noticed.

"It's the smell..." Jim said, "and the sounds... I hate hospitals... But the drugs help... I'm so high I can't stand up long enough to piss... Guess it makes it harder to run away."

"It's the people for me," K9 replied. "That, and the floors. There's something about the floors and doors that I can't explain."

"You should go. They'll add you to the collection."

"Where am I supposed to go?" K9 asked nervously. "I don't think I can come with you."

"Stay with Maggie and Amy?"

"I don't know..."

"Go to my parent's house..."

"Maybe."

"Back to the apartments?"

"No."

"When I get out, let's go find a place up in the mountains..."

"Yeah."

"Tell Maggie I'm sorry. I didn't mean for it to be like this."

"She knows."

"I'm kinda dizzy. I think I'm gonna nap for a while."

"Okay. I'll see you tomorrow when your parents get here."

_ _ _ _ _ _ _ _ _ _ _ _ _ _ _ _ _ _

Amy was waiting outside the psych ward when K9 came through the door on his crutches. He'd reopened the sore on his stump while pacing and walking constantly since Jim was taken to the hospital two days ago.

"They've got him pretty tanked up," K9 said, answering the questioning look on Amy's face.

"It's only temporary," she said reassuringly.

"I know."

He moved towards the elevators, Amy walking by his side.

"They want him to go to an in-residence treatment center."

"Where?"

"Back in Texas somewhere. He wasn't sure."

"Are you thinking of going with him?"

"To the treatment facility?"

Amy nodded.

"No. They probably wouldn't take me anyway."

"What makes you say that?"

"I haven't been suicidal in a while."

"Do you have to be?"

"I don't know... maybe... I guess it depends on what they treat there."

"You could stay here. Mom and I can help keep you on track while Jim's gone."

"You hardly know me. Why would you waste your time on me?"

"You told me yourself that you don't have any family. Where else are you going to go? The worst thing you could do now is be alone all the time."

"I don't know what to do without him. The night I stopped him from shooting himself back in Iraq, I had decided *I* would be the next one to go. I was never going to let anyone else be the first in on a raid. I wasn't going to lose anyone else. I didn't care if I lived or died, but I wasn't going to send another friend home in a box. Stopping him was the first step in that mission. Now it feels like I'm failing."

"You're the reason he's still alive in there, instead of dead out in the desert somewhere. And, he won't be there forever. You can stay with us until he's back."

"Amy," K9 said seriously, pausing in the parking lot and turning to look at her, "I like you more than anyone else who hasn't been one of my brothers in arms, maybe more than that. I can't ask you to do that. I can't risk ruining that."

Amy turned to face him and blinked. She was a little stunned at his admission, but not disturbed. She didn't understand what it was he was afraid of though.

"Jim and I learned to put up with each other because we've both been there," K9 explained. "He's a jerk sometimes, but so am I. He's broken, and so am I. We understand each other, so we put up with each other. I don't mind when he has to deal with me because I know I'm going to have to return the favor. With you, it's different. I can't ask you and your mom to put up with the stupid shit that happens when little things go sideways. It's not fair to you to ask you to put up with the kind of reactions I can't always control. And most of all, I couldn't live with myself if I hurt you or your mom."

K9 recoiled instantly. He was horrified that she might think he was talking about physical injury. That wasn't what he had meant.

"I didn't mean that the way it sounded," he said quickly. "I meant that I couldn't stand watching you suffer because of my mental illness. I'm still too screwed up to be out in the general public most of the time."

"Steve," Amy said reaching her hand up and placing it on his upper arm, "trust me a little. This isn't my first rodeo, and

Mom and I aren't the general public. I know you're broken, but I've already seen some of what that broken body and mind can do. Stay with us, at least until you are really ready to leave. Don't go just because Jim has to leave."

K9 nodded, but was supremely unsure if he could stay. At the same time, he was completely out of options for places to go. He could go back to San Antonio, but he was sure the result of that would be drinking himself to death. Finding his dad was an even worse option – they'd both be on the streets even if his dad had found a way to be stable for now. Everyone he considered friends was either here or at Bragg – and going back to Bragg was out of the question. He'd be dead faster there than if he went back to the apartment – too many reminders of what he had lost.

He thought about starting over on his own. Doing like he'd talked about and finding a cabin in Montana. But without Jim or someone else to go with him the loneliness and isolation would almost certainly ruin any hope of a brighter future.

He thought again about staying here. He had been as happy here as anywhere else he'd been in years, maybe ever. Maggie and Amy both seemed to care and weren't outwardly troubled by what they had seen. He'd been able to find ways to contribute. He had things to do that seemed to matter to at least a few people. He didn't feel alone here. He didn't feel pitied. He didn't feel ashamed – at least not very often.

Then again, he had been ashamed of himself. He had been ashamed of the way he and Jim had lost it with each other several times over the last several weeks. Maggie and Amy had been mostly unflappable, but how much longer could they maintain that act? Already, Maggie had seemed to take Jim's crash very hard. How long would it take for him to wear out his welcome? How much more could they put up with? Why would they waste that kind of energy on a worthless broken down soul like him?

There didn't seem to be an answer. Every thought circled back to the same result. Every option seemed a bad one.

Every hope seemed out of reach. There had to be an answer that didn't involve losing his friend or starting over... he just couldn't find it yet.

The drive back to Maggie's house was filled with silence as his mind raced back and forth between the various non-options. He was looking for a loophole or a way to make it turn out okay, and in the process became completely absorbed in his own thoughts. It didn't really matter though. The results always came out the same. He had nowhere he could go without ruining something.

He had to stop thinking about that. All the options were bad. All would make things worse for the people around him. He could see no way out. There was no way out. There was one way out... There was always that way... But he had promised Jim... But he couldn't bear the thought of going where Jim was headed... He had to stop thinking about that.

The thoughts raced through his head over, and over, and over. Telling him he was a burden. Telling him everyone would be fine without him, and that nobody would miss him for long. Telling him that there wasn't any other way. He fought with himself the entire ride back to Maggie's house.

When they finally got back to Maggie's house, K9 was desperate for something to distract himself. He couldn't walk it off. Not with the open sore. Maybe he'd spend some time with Maki... And, there was the food prep and delivery... But he couldn't remember if this was the big delivery night. He was in a fog, and couldn't remember much of anything really. Besides, 10:00 was a little early to focus on preparing dinner. He needed something to focus on. The internal debate raged on right until he stepped through the door into Maggie's house.

"Who are we cooking for tonight?"

"Karen's bringing over Uncle Saul, but other than that it's just us," Maggie answered. "I thought it would be a little easier than driving all over creation today. Someone else is taking care of the route this week, and we'll trade them another night next week to make it even."

"I really need something to do."

"Have you ever butchered a lamb?"

"No," K9 said doubtfully. "That's a little outside my realm of expertise."

"Amy can teach you. She's been doing it since she was a teenager. If you start within the next hour or so, you'll be done just in time to help roast some of it for dinner."

"I don't know... I'm not sure I'm up to seeing something die right now."

"You've seen some awful stuff. This isn't like that. And you've fed and cared for those animals. I get it. But think about it for a minute. If we don't start butchering lambs, they'll go to waste, or we'll have to auction them off. If we do that, who knows how they'll be treated. Butcher them here, they live a happy life right up to the point where they fulfill their reason for being on this farm, and we can use the results to keep feeding people who need it."

K9 did think it over. Academically, he had no problems with animals being butchered for meat. It was the way of life, and had been as long as there were predators and prey. But he'd seen so many people die that he was afraid it would spark flashbacks. At the same time, however, it would give him something to do for the next several hours. And he knew that the way it was done the lamb wouldn't feel anything.

How would he react to the blood? To watching the animal die? Four or five years ago he would have done the deed without even a passing thought. What had changed? He wasn't sure. He wasn't really all that sure that things had actually changed. He was more afraid that things had changed, and he didn't want that confirmation. Not now. But then again, maybe it would reassure him that some things hadn't changed.

"Okay, I'll do it." He was resolved.

"Well, head on over to Amy's then. She'll be starting soon."

"But I'm stuck on crutches again."

"Since when did that stop you? You'll figure it out."

K9 shrugged and headed heavily for the doorway. By the time he'd crossed over to Amy's house, she had already begun preparations. She had a gambrel hooked to the bucket of the tractor, had a folding table set up with butchering knives and cutting boards, and was wearing a heavy apron and rubber boots.

"Mom talk you into coming over here?"

"Yeah."

"Good, I can use the help. Ray used to help, but that's been a while."

"What do you need me to do?"

"Jump up on the tractor, and follow me over to the pen."

"Talk me though it, so I don't get surprised. I'm really anxious that I'll react badly, and the less surprising it is the better."

"Well, I separated the lamb into a pen already. We're going to head over there, I'll stun it with the 22, then hook it on the gambrel. We'll bleed it, wash it down, and gut it over the compost heap, then take the carcass over to the processing area. There, we'll skin it, quarter it, then cut the quarters up into stuff like you see at the grocery store. Mom wants one of the legs tonight. The rest of it we'll wrap and pack in the freezer."

She said this with a resounding tone of clinical sterility. All matter of fact. As if it were an every day occurrence. What could be more normal than processing animals in your back yard. He found that tone slightly reassuring, but also a little disconcerting.

Trusting her, and overcoming his reservations, K9 climbed onto the tractor and wedged his crutches between the seat and wheel well. He'd learned to run it last week, but that was when he had the use of his prosthetic.

"You don't happen to have a stick I could use to run the foot-controls do you?"

The tractor had a hydrostatic transmission, which made it easier to manage, but the controls were right where his missing leg belonged. He'd managed to run it roughly before in a low gear by hoisting his prosthetic up and down on the pedals. That wasn't an option now, and this seemed to call for more careful work than lugging around hay bails like he had done previously.

"Way ahead of you," Amy smiled, handing him a cane she had brought out for just this purpose.

As they worked, K9 found the gunshot startling, but with the warning that it was coming it wasn't too bad. The rest of the process was mechanical, just the way Amy had described it. It was reassuring. Being with someone who treated him like he was almost normal was reassuring too.

"By the time we're done with this year's flock, you'll be a pro," Amy said as they finished wrapping the last cuts.

"How many are you going to do?"

"All of the young ones. I can't afford to let the flock get much bigger than it already is, and my ewes are all pretty young still."

"What'll you do with all that meat?"

"Black market."

"No, really, how do you eat all that?"

"Black market. I'm a low-life criminal," Amy laughed. "I can't legally sell it once it's been processed, but the people who want to buy it don't want it to still be alive. So I trade it to folks around here. I give them lamb meat, they give me something I need. Besides, Mom uses a lot of it on her meal route."

"A criminal, I never would have guessed." K9 still wasn't sure how he felt about eating the work they had just completed, but the time with Amy had been important to resetting his thought patterns.

Amy cleaned up the table and hauled all the butchering equipment into her house. She'd wash them up after dinner. Meanwhile, K9 jumped back on the tractor and parked it under the carport where Amy kept it. This done, Amy grabbed the leg of lamb she'd reserved for tonight's dinner and the two of them headed back over to Maggie's house.

"Well... how'd he do?" Maggie asked as they came into the kitchen.

"He only fainted once," Amy teased. K9 laughed in response. It was the first time he'd done that since Jim had gone into the hospital. "What can I do to help?"

"I've got it," Maggie said as she shooed them out of the way. "All I need to do is dress that leg and get it in the roaster." She took the roast from Amy, and returned to the counter where she was working.

K9 shrugged and headed back outside where he sat down on the porch. Maki came over and sat his head in K9's lap, and the two of them sat quietly for several minutes just watching the afternoon. Amy came outside a few minutes later and sat down in the other chair.

"What are you thinking about?" Amy asked.

"Nothing," K9 answered, almost surprised at the answer. "If anything, I was thinking how soft Maki's fur is. That and how calm he can be when he wants to."

"Another one of Mom's rescues. He was skin and bones and afraid of everyone when she picked him up on the side of the road."

"She seems to have a thing for strays."

"You mean like you and Jim?"

"Something like that."

"No, you two are a first. She usually goes to visit the strays, not bring them home with her. You know, when she told me you were coming here I was worried about it. I'm sorry about that."

"Two dysfunctional veterans with severe PTSD and missing limbs visiting the family of a man who killed the family of one of them... what could possibly go wrong?"

"Yeah, that's pretty much what I was thinking."

"Sounds like a valid concern to me. I'm sorry things turned out like you thought they would."

"What? No. You didn't turn out anything like I was afraid of."

"Sometimes I feel like I'm living my own nightmare."

"You've had what, a hand-full of bad days since you've been here? What about the rest of the time? You've seemed to do pretty well, I thought."

K9 thought for a second. He knew she was right, but it was hard to remember or focus on the good times. For years, the bad stuff seemed to float to the top no matter what else was going on.

"They've been some of the best days I can remember."

"Like what?"

"Feeling useful again."

"And?"

"Feeling safe. Hearing quiet. People treating me like a normal human being. It's stupid, but your mom's insistence on ignoring the fact that I'm missing a leg has meant a lot to me."

"You know why she invited Uncle Saul over for dinner tonight?"

"No."

"She wants him to convince you to stay. She's afraid you'll leave before you're ready."

"Well, I'll hear what he has to say, I guess."

"Don't tell her I told you. She thinks she's being sneaky."

"She really wants me to stay longer?"

"Yes. She does."

"Maggie tells me your friend has to leave for a while," Saul said as soon as he came into the house. It didn't look like he was going to waste any time getting to the point. The women had left the two of them alone in the living room with the nominal excuse of getting dinner on the table.

"He has to leave, but I don't think he'll ever come back," K9 answered.

Saul shook his head, "that's too bad. You two have done a lot of good around here."

"People keep telling me that. Mostly I think we just messed things up."

"No, you're messed up, but that doesn't mean that's what you've done."

K9 looked a little stunned.

"You two are two of the most screwed up people I've met in years," Saul continued.

K9's face began to twist in disbelief. Was this conversation supposed to convince him to stay?

"Probably since my neighbor's kid came back from Vietnam. He left to the city, and never came back. Got caught up in drugs and overdosed. He never was a very strong kid."

K9 continued to listen, partly to try and figure out what the point was, but mostly just to try and be polite to someone who meant so much to Maggie. It was hard. Very hard.

"I think you're stronger than that."

K9 grimaced doubtfully.

"I think you're more like me. I think you can do what needs doing. Maggie's told me about how you two have picked yourself up over and over again and kept moving."

"This time seems different. Jim's gone."

"He gave you a reason to keep going. I know. But now you need to find a new reason. What options do you have?"

Saul knew the answer just as well as K9 did, but he didn't really expect K9 to say it out loud.

"Look around here... This is where I found my reason. You can find yours too. Think about the people you've helped in just the last few weeks. Think about the support you have here."

"When I first got back from the war, I was so angry. If it were nowadays, they would have said I had PTSD or some other fancy name, back then they just discharged me and wrote me off. I didn't have any hope, and was ready to be done with the world. My sister took hold of me and kept me going. She brought me back here and helped me find a way to matter again. Serving the people here taught me to trust again, and made me feel like a human again."

"Yeah, but this is your home, and these are your people..."

"You think that means you don't belong here?" Saul said with a slight shake of the head.

K9 didn't have an answer.

"You and Jim had each other, and were keeping each other going. How are you going to keep going now that he has to go?"

Again, K9 didn't have an answer.

"You need to stay here!" Saul said forcefully. "You aren't ready to be on your own. You aren't ready to leave. It would break my Maggie's heart to see you leave knowing you were on the road to a crash. It's hard enough for her to know that Jim has to go, and he has family who will take care of him. Why can't you just accept the family you are being offered here?"

K9 had felt almost like family here, but hearing someone use that term was shocking. Amy was standing in the doorway to the kitchen, a tear moving slowly down her cheek.

"Do you really want me to stay?" K9 asked looking up at her, his voice unstable and quiet.

Chapter 19

Trial

"The food here kinda sucks, but it's no worse than the dog food they put in MREs," Jim said, trying to lighten the mood. K9 looked super stressed when he came into the common area to visit with him.

K9 coughed out a short laugh, but didn't say anything else. He had flown out here from New Mexico by himself to visit with Jim. It'd been almost two months since Jim's parents had brought him to this treatment facility.

"The first few days were the hardest," Jim sighed, "but it's not quite like I thought it would be. They keep me pretty busy between therapy and more therapy. Even down-time is purposed therapy around here." Jim sighed again. "I'm starting to get used to it, which is good, because it looks like I've got a few more weeks before they'll let me out unsupervised."

Looking around the room, it would be hard to distinguish K9 from any of the patients. There was a look in the eyes that seemed to be etched into everyone's countenance. The look, to those who knew to look for it, said that everyone here was a veteran, that they had all suffered, and that they all wondered if it would have been better if they'd been sent home in a box. K9 shared the look, and seeing himself surrounded by shadows of himself made him worry that he belonged here instead of back in New Mexico.

If truth were to be told, K9 probably should have been a
patient here too, but his hand hadn't been forced like Jim's.
He hadn't quite crossed that threshold, but he was starting to
doubt how long it would be before he followed in Jim's shoes.

"Does it help?" K9 asked. Jim understood.

"Yeah, but not as much as being around Maggie. She almost made me feel normal."

K9 just nodded.

"My problem, they tell me, is that I haven't dealt with
things. I've had to tell almost all the stories, and sometimes
over and over again. It's supposed to get easier. . ."

"Does it?"

"I guess. . . I can make it to the end of most of them without
blacking out now, but they still won't let me be alone with
anyone during the sessions. They keep a nurse or something
nearby in case I lose it. I don't think they understand that
I'm not violent."

"It's hard to tell sometimes when you get worked up."

"I know."

The two of them sat quietly for a while after this. When
K9 had bought the ticket to come here, it was part of a plan to
pick Jim up and bring him back to New Mexico at the end of
his treatment. However, progress had been slower than hoped,
and Jim wasn't ready to leave yet. What K9 had hoped would
be a happy trip was quickly devolving.

"How's Saul?" Jim asked, breaking the silence after several
minutes of tension-relieving silence where they both collected
their thoughts and took several slow, controlled, breaths.

"Tired, but just as quick in the mind as when you left. He
convinced me to stay there when you had to leave. I was ready
to take off to who knows where, but he kinda forced me to see
the truth. I think he knew I wouldn't make it on my own."

"Do you think Maggie put him up to it?"

"Her and Amy both, I think."

"What I don't get is why they chose to adopt two broken screw-ups like us. It's got to be easier to pet a cobra than get emotionally invested in us."

"They sure put a lot of work into trying to help..." Jim mused. "I keep coming back to that thought every time I talk about it in my 'sessions.' I kind of wonder if it's therapy for Maggie at least."

"Maybe..." K9 trailed off. There wasn't much more to say on that front. The mystery of why Maggie did what she did was too deep for either of them.

"What are you doing to keep busy," Jim asked, "now that you don't have me to babysit?"

K9 looked sideways at Jim to punctuate the absurdity of that question. They had never lacked for things to do while with Maggie. She thrived on activity, and spilled it over to almost everyone in her orbit – at least that's what it felt like to both of them.

"I've been going along with Amy on her rounds," K9 added to the unspoken answer. "She's a lot like her mom... almost kills herself to take care of others. I've been volunteering to do small stuff for the people she visits. Gives me something to do while I wait for her to finish her work. I didn't think it would be a good idea to sit at home all day alone."

Home. He called Maggie's place home. It was a word Jim had hardly ever heard K9 use. He always used terms like "the apartment," or other less emotionally charged words. But now he called Maggie's house home without even thinking about it.

"Do you think you'll ever be fixed enough to marry her?" Jim asked suddenly.

"Amy?"

"No, dumb shit, Maggie," Jim said sarcastically.

"No," K9 said sadly. "I wouldn't want to tie her down to my broken ass. One of these days, she and her mom are going to wise up to what a jerk I am and kick me to the curb."

"Don't sell yourself short," Jim countered. "You've been my savior more than once."

"And you mine."

They sat quietly for a few moments looking out the window at the grounds.

"Do you think she would have me?"

"Yeah. I think so."

They lapsed into silence, punctuated only by quiet sighs.

"You know I'm not going back there, right?" Jim asked.

K9 had known, but hadn't admitted it to himself. He had harbored hope that they could go back to the way things were just before Jim's crash. It was as happy as he'd been in a very long time. All he could do was nod his head in response.

"I needed my time there. You and Maggie are probably the only people in the world I trust to understand anything about me. But going back now would just reopen wounds that I can't handle."

K9 sagged a little and let out a heavy sigh.

"I don't know how to live without you at this point," Jim continued, "but we're going to have to figure that out. You can't leave there, and I can't go back."

"We could go north, up to Montana or something," K9 countered.

"I can. You need to stay where you are, and you know it."

K9 nodded, took a deep breath, then offered his last resistance. "You should at least be there for the trial."

"You're right, but that's as far as I can go."

"Where are you going to go until then?"

"My parent's until I can find a quieter place. They're adamant that I need to be within an hour drive of them."

"Do you think Amy would come to Idaho?"

"I don't think you would ask her to do that."

K9 knew Jim was right. He would never try to take Amy from the life she had built. If there was any chance for a life with her, it would have to be in New Mexico unless she decided to go somewhere else of her own accord.

"We could come visit you."

"That would be nice."

_ _ _ _ _ _ _ _ _ _ _ _ _ _ _ _ _ _

"Shepherd, do you think you could come down a few days early?"

Jim was finalizing plans to drive with his father down to Farmington for the trial, and he had called K9 to get his input. He'd been in Idaho for almost six months.

"Yeah, I think so. Do I need to bring a tux?" It had become increasingly clear to Jim that K9 was getting close to developing the courage to ask Amy to marry him. Perhaps he had finally pulled the trigger.

"We might not make it that big a deal. Amy's trying to accommodate me and keep it informal, but I don't think I'm going to let her trade away her wedding day just because I don't like pomp and circumstance."

"When did you propose?"

"Last night."

"That's awesome. I take it she said yes?"

"Yeah."

"I wouldn't miss it. Is Maggie going to be okay with doing a wedding right before her son's trial?"

254 CHAPTER 19. TRIAL

"She says it'll give her something positive to focus on."

"It's not a very long engagement..."

"No, but I don't see the point in one."

The trial was scheduled to last two weeks. Why it needed to take that long, Jim couldn't say. The whole court system seemed opaque to him. It was pretty open-and-shut as far as he could tell. Then again, Ray had hired a notorious ambulance chaser of a lawyer who was trying every trick in the books. It would be a tough two weeks.

Jim and his father had arrived the night before K9 and Amy's wedding, and were installed in the two rooms he and K9 had occupied when they first arrived. He and his father spent the next day helping prepare the lamb that would feed the "small" wedding party which consisted of about a hundred of Amy's closest relatives and friends, augmented by about half a dozen men from K9's old unit.

"I didn't mean to put you to work Mr. Harwood," Maggie apologized.

Jim just laughed. "See dad, I warned you."

"Please, call me Ethan," Jim's dad laughed. "You did warn me," he said to Jim, "and I came just the same, so I guess it's fair game."

"You're pretty good with a butcher knife. Jim told me you raised animals."

"Yep. I've always loved working with livestock. Leaving the farm was a tough decision, but I just couldn't keep up with all of it much longer."

"Well, I'm going to go take care of some decorating," Maggie laughed as she turned to head towards Amy's house. She was smiling ear-to-ear and singing as she walked away.

"Do you think she planned on us doing this, or did she just underestimate the work she would have to do herself?" Ethan asked Jim.

"She planned on it. I don't think she believes in accidents or coincidence. Besides, she did that kind of stuff to me all the time when I was here."

"Where's Steve," Ethan asked. "I haven't seen him all morning."

"He went over to get Amy's great uncle Saul. He's going to walk Amy down the isle."

"I feel like I should be planning egress routes and briefing the breaching team," K9 said as Jim helped him get dressed for the ceremony. "I don't think I've been this scared since my first mission outside the wire."

"No egress routes. You missed that opportunity."

"I keep thinking she's going to change her mind. . ."

"She would have done that a long time ago. You're the one that took forever to make up your mind."

Jim straightened and smoothed the bow tie around K9's neck.

"Were you nervous when you married Leslie?"

"I don't really remember."

K9 looked a little worried, "you mean it's something that you've repressed?"

"No," Jim reassured him, "it was just such a blur. Everything happened so fast, and then we were married and it felt like it had always been that way. It was like that when Sammie was born too."

"Well, what do you say we get this show on the road?" K9 said as he looked himself over in the mirror. This was one uniform he hadn't thought he would ever wear.

"Let's."

With that, the two of them stepped out of Maggie's house and made their way to the small arbor where the officiator was waiting. All the guests had already assembled and were sitting and chatting quietly on rows of folding chairs arranged on Maggie's back lawn.

"You know, I never would have thought she would be my type," K9 mused. "Shows how much I knew."

"She's pretty amazing," Jim agreed as Amy and Saul appeared.

All present fell silent as they watched the bowed but very proud Saul take his grand-niece by the arm and walk her through the happy crowd. A short ceremony later, and the everyone rose and shifted to Amy's house where the food was waiting. Jim placed himself in a corner that quickly filled with the men from the unit. They told a few stories, laughed and joked at the things they could, and mostly just sat quietly happy for their friend. Most were leaving tomorrow, but a few had decided to stay with Jim for the trial, and would be here until it was over. This was the easy part.

Four days after the wedding, the trial began. Jim sat in the gallery, flanked by men from the unit. They took turns, only filling two of the limited number of seats at a time, but always making sure Jim wasn't alone. Some were men who had been in Iraq with him. Some were strangers who had served with K9 or who had just volunteered to come down. It didn't matter. They were brothers, and they were there to help their brother. He wasn't going to go through this alone.

Maggie was there too, with her cousin at her side for support, but they sat quietly a few rows back from where Jim was. Amy and K9 both decided it would be best if they didn't come in person. At the end of each session, Amy, K9, Maggie,

Jim and Jim's father gathered exhausted in Maggie's kitchen for a meal and a silent prayer for strength before retiring for the night to start again the next morning.

On the fourth day of the trial, the venue was moved to the crash site, and Jim finally saw what he had come to New Mexico to see. There was no evidence on that bleak stretch of road to indicate anything had ever happened here. Time, wind, and sun had erased all traces. Ray's lawyer tried to use the accident reports, aided by a scene recreation, to explain how it could have been possible that Leslie had drifted into oncoming traffic. It was a pointless exercise, as the state produced multiple witnesses who had seen the crash as it happened. The trial wrapped up several days early when the judge threatened to sanction the defense lawyer if he continued to waste everyone's time.

As expected, the jury handed down a conviction for aggravated vehicular manslaughter along with a raft of other lesser charges. He was convicted on all counts. When the judge offered Jim the opportunity to make a statement addressing the impact of his loss, he politely declined. He was having a hard enough time as it was without talking about how his life had been changed.

The sentencing concluded rapidly with Ray given a 30 year sentence. He wouldn't be eligible for parole for at least fifteen years. Maggie sobbed softly. Jim just sagged. He couldn't bring himself to feel any kind of triumph or joy at this outcome. Another life destroyed. That's all it was. It almost didn't matter that Ray's life had been basically destroyed before the accident even happened. This outcome would have sealed the fate of almost anyone. There was nothing to celebrate.

Before the court adjourned, the judge offered Ray an opportunity to say something to Jim. Ray nodded and took the stand.

"I didn't hurt nobody," he began with acid resentment in his voice. "That crazy bitch came into my lane and hit me. She sent me to the hospital when I wasn't doing anything."

The judge moved to cut him off, but Ray ignored her.

"It's your fault I'm here," Ray screamed at Jim. "If you hadn't left her she would never have hit me. You ruined my life. If you were a real man, she would still be alive and I'd be free."

The judge was doing all she could to get Ray to stop, and the bailiff was moving in on Ray to restrain him.

Jim launched himself from his chair and at the witness stand. He was going to kill Ray, even if it meant going to jail himself. He was going to choke the life out of that remorseless piece of trash if it was the last thing he ever did.

As soon as Jim was out of his seat, two sets of very strong hands simultaneously restrained him, one wrapping him in an inescapable bear hug. "Shepherd, this isn't your fight right now," his guardian whispered as he held Jim fast. There was nothing Jim could do to overpower him. Jim was helpless again.

"Let him go, I'll beat his crippled ass," Ray shouted as the bailiff cuffed him and dragged him out of the room. As he was hauled down the hall, he could be heard yelling, "you ruined my life whitey, I'll get you for this!"

Maggie, completely overcome and dealing with an involuntary flood of tears, ran from the courtroom.

"Mr. Harwood, are you okay," the Judge asked when Jim had calmed enough for his companions to release him.

"Not really, I don't think I'll ever really will be," Jim answered, clearly straining to control his reactions. He took as deep a breath as his tense chest would allow, then left the courtroom. His father followed close behind without saying anything. They would leave New Mexico that evening, and Jim would never return.

Chapter 20

End

"Are you sure you want to be this far out of town? Wouldn't it be better to have a few more neighbors?" Jim's mother wasn't thrilled with his choice of locations to set up house. The nearest police station was twenty minutes away, as were the nearest ambulance and fire department. If the truth were to be told, there were probably three bears for every human within a few mile radius.

"I need the quiet," was Jim's only answer. It was precisely this kind of isolation, coupled with easy access to the mountain behind the small cabin, that had brought him here in the first place.

"What are you going to do? Where will you work?"

"My retirement and disability are plenty. Besides, there are things to do around here. I'll find something."

"What if you get hurt?"

"I've been hurt before. That's not something I'm worried about anymore."

She was having a hard time accepting that Jim was leaving them. He had done well in the months since he returned from Texas, and she had hoped she could keep him close by for good. But now, he was determined to be independent.

"It's not like I'm moving to the dark side of the moon. It's only an hour from town. You can come up and visit any time you like," Jim offered in a conciliatory tone.

"I'm worried about you being alone."

"That's what I'm coming up here for. Nobody here knows how I got so screwed up. Nobody here pities me yet. Nobody here expects anything from me. Nobody will be offended if I don't come to random social functions."

Jim stretched his back and looked up at the mountain. "Besides, I've got Lola to keep me company. She and I can leave the front door and go straight up the trail any time we want."

This wasn't a fight she could win.

"You're kinda overqualified," the short mustachioed man said from under his hard hat.

"Not much call for the kind of things I'm best qualified for around here," Jim answered.

"But hauling road-base and pushing snow?"

"It's not about that."

"You want the graveyard shifts?"

The foreman was struggling to understand.

"Yes."

"You know it gets pretty lonely out on those roads in a snow storm. You okay with being gone all night every time it snows?"

"The only one who would miss me is my dog, and she can ride with me."

"We don't allow pets..." the foreman started to say, then stopped himself. "But I suppose yours isn't..."

"No, she isn't."

"Well, if that's what you want. It's on-call work, so you won't know more than a few days in advance for roadwork, and snow is just unpredictable."

"That's fine," Jim reassured him. He needed something to get him out of the house when he couldn't be on the trails or working outside. He could only split and stack so much firewood before he ran out of space to put it. Hauling for the Transportation Department when they needed extra help would be just right. The first night pushing snow proved he was right. The world was quiet when the inky night and white snow closed in around him.

- - - - - - - - - - - - - - - - - -

"Jim?" His dad sounded like he doubted he'd dialed the right number.

"Yeah?"

"Uh, mom and I have been talking..."

"You worried about me being alone this week?" Later in the week would be three years since the accident.

"Yeah," Jim's dad was relieved not to have to explain. "What are your plans? Mom and I could come out there and stay with you."

"K9 and Amy are coming up. Maggie might be coming too."

"Oh." His dad was obviously deflated.

"You and mom could use my room and I can sleep in the loft. They'll take the spare room. It might be good to have all of you around."

"Oh?"

"I'm going to the grave site. Then I'm going home to talk about it. I'm not sure I'll talk about it after that again, so you should be here."

"What about Leslie's parents?"

Jim didn't want to face this. They had realized how hard it was for him to see them not long after he returned to Idaho, and they had given him space, but it was wrong to keep them in the dark indefinitely.

"Can they come with you?"

"We can meet you at the cemetery, and follow you to your place if that's what you want. We don't need to spend the night unless you really want us to."

"Nobody else, okay? You can tell my story to the rest of the family later when I'm not around."

"Okay."

"I'll let you know what time to meet me later."

"Mom and I love you."

"Night Dad."

Three years. Or, it would be in a few days. Sammie would be almost ten... He'd be a year or two from regular retirement. How different his life could have been right now... He sagged and sighed, but Lola nudged him and pulled him back to the present. She hadn't been trained to do that, she just somehow seemed to know. It was her full time job now.

Jim flipped through the few contacts on his phone and dialed K9.

"Hey, your plans firm up yet?"

"Yeah. A few small details to work out, but nothing big."

"Is Amy okay to travel?"

"Yeah, the baby isn't due for a while yet. She'll be fine. Besides, she wouldn't let me come up there without her. She wants to see you as much as I do. Same thing for Maggie."

"How's your walking leg?"

"Perfect. You still hiking all the time?"

"Do you think they will let you break off for a few hours and go out with me and Lola? There are a few special places I want to show you."

"I'm sure we can make that happen."

"When are you getting in?"

"We're stopping in Salt Lake for the night. Amy doesn't think she can manage the whole trip in one shot. We should be there by noon, day after tomorrow."

"How long do you want to stay?"

"Until you're ready to start again. A couple days, or a couple weeks. Whatever it takes."

"Thanks. Tell the ladies I can't wait to see them."

The next two days disappeared in a blur. Jim wasn't conscious of them as his anxiety about revisiting the past climbed to a fever pitch. He stayed ferociously active to maintain some sense of control; cleaning and re-cleaning the house, making sure everything was ready for the guests, and hours walking the trails with Lola.

K9, Amy, and Maggie arrived as planned, and were installed in the guest bedroom where Jim had set up two air mattresses. It was a bit of a tight fit, but Maggie had expressly forbidden him giving up his room to her. Given that restriction, it was the best he could manage. His parents had opted to make the drive home rather than spend the night, and would meet him at the cemetery with Leslie's parents the following afternoon.

That evening Jim listened happily as K9, Amy, and Maggie updated Jim on all that had happened in Shiprock since he had left, and they talked until about midnight when Amy announced that she needed to get some sleep. Jim gave Amy and Maggie a hug, then left them to settle in for the night.

K9 awoke early in the morning to try and beat Jim out of bed. It didn't work. Jim was already up and had a cup of hot coffee ready for him.

"Got your walking leg on?"

"Yeah."

"We'll hit the trail as soon as you're ready," Jim said as he handed the coffee to K9. "I want to show you something."

K9 took the coffee and just nodded.

Jim whistled for Lola, who jumped out of the bed she was curled up in and hurried to the door where she waited impatiently for Jim. Clearly she knew the routine. They stepped outside, closing the door carefully behind them to avoid waking anyone up.

"Where you taking me?" K9 asked, shaking off a yawn.

"Jump in," Jim said as he opened the door of his truck and Lola jumped into the back seat, "the trail-head is just up the road a bit. Normally I walk there, but we don't have any time today."

K9 climbed into the passenger seat, and they drove half a mile up the road to a small pull-out. Without a word, Jim stepped out of the truck and Lola eagerly waited for Jim to let her lead off. He gave the signal, and she led the way up the well used trail for a mile or two before abruptly leaving the trail to cross a small creek.

"Where's she going?" K9 asked.

"To our favorite spot. It's a little off the beaten path, and I have to limit how often I go there so I don't make it too obvious to passers by."

Jim stepped across the trickle of a stream and followed Lola, walking mostly on rocks that poked out of the turf. K9 followed, but couldn't manage the light tread that Jim could. His prosthetic simply wasn't as nimble.

"There are several routes in here," Jim explained, "I try to rotate between them so they don't look like more than a game trail. The most direct route is straight up the hill behind the house. Sometimes I come in from the west. Today, we're taking the scenic route."

"You don't think I could manage the direct route?" K9 said accusingly.

"Nah, it's not that. This route is just prettier."

They cut sideways across the slope for several minutes, then turned downhill through the trees. Jim stopped just short of a small clearing and motioned for K9 to do the same. Lola had stopped a hundred yards back and was laying down watching Jim.

"About half the time I come up here," Jim whispered while pointing across the clearing, "there's a black bear eating over there. Looks like she's not here today though." Jim waived his hand, and Lola bounded forward into the clearing.

K9 stepped into the clearing and the sun. He could understand how this could become Jim's favorite place. It was peaceful, beautiful, and solitary. The only noise came from the wind rustling the trees and grass. Turning in a slow circle to take it in, he saw that Jim had hung a hammock and built a well concealed blind a few feet from where they stood.

"Sometimes I'll stay up here all day," Jim said, breaking the silence.

"I can see why, but we need to leave pretty soon if we're going to make it back in time."

"Yeah. I know." Jim admitted. The best part of the day was already over, and it wasn't even seven o'clock. "Next time, we'll make plans to stay up here for a while. But for today, you're right. We need to head back."

They hadn't stayed at the cemetery long. When Jim and his friends arrived, Leslie's parents were there and had already placed a bouquet of flowers and a stuffed animal by the head-stone. They were holding each other and crying quietly a few feet away. At Jim's request, he went to the grave alone. They watched from the truck as he knelt down and cried. Then, Jim picked up the bouquet and teddy bear, motioned for his parents and in-laws to follow, and headed for home. The drive was uneventful, and the small group filed through Jim's front door to take seats in his living room.

"You know," Jim said, finally breaking the silence that had reigned since they entered his cabin, "Leslie wouldn't approve of me crying over her headstone like that. She always said that graves were just warehouses. She would have wanted me to remember her somewhere else," Jim said slowly, motioning to the flowers and teddy bear he had placed on the mantelpiece. "You can take these back there after tonight if you want."

"What's your plan?" K9 asked.

"I'm gonna tell it all, but it'll take a while. We ought to eat something first."

Nobody moved. Both Jim's and Leslie's parents sat in si-lence, frightened of what was to come and looking at Jim in almost horrified anticipation. Amy was in tears just think-ing about it. Maggie was fidgeting in her seat, trying to find something to do to with nervous energy. They all knew the big parts of the story, but they had never heard the whole thing. K9, on the other hand, sat quietly stoic. He knew what was coming. He'd either lived it or already heard it before.

Jim walked into the kitchen, grabbed water and a sand-wich, then came back into the living room and sat them on an end-table. Everyone expected him to sit down in the armchair, but he just began pacing across the room as he began to talk.

"A lot of what I have to say is horrible. I don't know how to talk about it using polite words," he said, looking at his parents. They had never approved of profanity. "And even if I did," he continued, "the reality is so awful that it is likely to mess with you at least a little. If you're not ready to hear this,

I understand. Just get up and leave the room if you need to. It won't bother me, but I can't promise I'll ever talk about it again."

He paused to see if anyone was going to take him up on the offer. Nobody did, so he began. Diving right in as he paced back and forth, he talked about how he had planned to leave the Air Force before Sammie was born. He talked about Leslie getting sick. About the hospital nightmares. He told about the missions, the failures, the losses. He told about his suicide attempt K9 had stopped. He talked about the death, destruction, and decay that surrounded him in Iraq. He talked about the team. He told as much as he knew about the IED and his time in the hospital. For the first time, he told his parents about the drinking. He let it all out, but with intensely focused self control that held out for four hours.

When Jim finished talking, the weight of what he had shared filled the room. Jim collapsed into his arm chair and buried his face in his hands. The water and sandwich were untouched.

Leslie's mother stood and moved towards the kitchen, motioning towards Maggie and Jim's mother as she went. "Why don't we work on some dinner. . . make sure everyone has something to eat before some of us have to head back into town." Everyone understood she was mostly concerned about Jim, and the three ladies left the room. The sound of food preparation was all that disturbed the prevailing silence. Half an hour later nobody felt like eating, but they gathered around the table none the less and dutifully ate what was prepared. Shortly after the dishes were cleared from the table, Jim's parents and in-laws left to make their way home.

Jim and the rest returned to the living room. Nobody seemed to know what to say though. . . the ladies were still in something of a state of shock, and K9 had fallen into a funk almost as deep as Jim's.

"Tell me how you met her," Maggie asked, breaking a silence that had reigned for several minutes.

Jim looked up, but hesitated a moment. He wasn't sure he could talk anymore. He chewed on the thought for what felt like an eternity, but ultimately decided to follow Maggie's lead. Answering that question broke the ice, and a flood of stories and memories that K9 had never heard came out. They listened as Jim talked about his lost family well into the night. Along with the pain and loss, buried joy and memories of hope came to the surface – the joy and hope that had been so difficult to find. Shortly before two in the morning, Jim finished the last story of the night.

"You know I'm going to be a wreck for a few days, right?" Jim asked with a trembling voice.

They all nodded.

"I haven't talked about any of that stuff in a long time. I don't think I'll be okay tomorrow."

"We'll be here to help you," Amy reassured him.

"I probably won't be able to talk much."

"I know," K9 answered. He thoroughly understood.

"I might be a real asshole and try to kick you out."

"We'll stay until you're ready," Maggie promised.

Jim nodded, and managed a faint, "thanks," before standing and turning towards his bedroom. "I couldn't do this without you."

They all stood, and one-by-one they embraced him before letting him escape to the solitude of his bedroom where he cried himself to sleep.

They repeated this same process every year, the only variation being that Jim's parents and in-laws stayed for the happier memories. Jim would start the day with K9 and a hike up the mountain, followed by a visit to the graves and a long evening of listening to Jim say things he couldn't say to anyone else or at any other time of year. Then, K9, Amy, and Maggie would spend the next few days helping him back on his feet again before heading back home.

A little over eight years after he initially left for Iraq, and a month before the planned visit to the grave site, Jim's parents found his phone had been disconnected. Expecting the worst, they went to his house where they found it unoccupied. Everything inside had been boxed up neatly. The carpets had been freshly cleaned. The kitchen and bathroom were spotless. Most disturbing for them were two hand-written notes left on the Kitchen table. The first wasn't addressed and explained that Jim wished for the contents of his home be donated to the local VFW, and the home and truck sold with the proceeds going to a nearby program that helped veterans with PTSD.

The second note was addressed to "Mom, Dad, K9, Maggie, and Amy." It read:

> *I know you will grieve at seeing this. I'm sorry I couldn't help it. Please understand that this is a long hoped for release, and I am happier now than I have been in years. You are the totality of what I regret leaving behind.*
>
> *Four days ago, I lost the last connection I had with my former self. Lola passed away, and I buried her in a clearing up the trail we hiked so often. I can't think of a better place for my guardian who so loved these mountains to rest. I'm up there with her now. K9 knows the place, but please don't come to find me yourselves. I want you to remember me as you last saw me if you can't remember what I was before. Send someone else to collect what remains.*
>
> *I love each of you dearly, and am grateful for every day I had with you. Please don't mourn me, and don't believe you could have changed this. Please try to remember the good times occasionally, smile at the memories, and continue to serve and teach*

the way you have for so long. I was blessed to have such friends and family.

Please tell Doc Chelwood he did all he could. Tell him I said thanks.

My last request is to be buried simply next to Leslie and Sammie.

Jim

The local search and rescue team recovered Jim's body later that afternoon.

Per his request, the funeral was simple. It wasn't, however, small. That would have been impossible. As alone as Jim had felt, he had made a big impact in the lives of a lot of people. They came out of the woodwork to say goodbye. The chapel was full to overflowing. Family had come in from across the mountain west, and they filled well over half the available space on their own. Neighbors came with stories of work Jim had done for them in quiet. Coworkers filled several pews. And several friends who had been left behind when Jim's life fell apart after the accident made their way up from Texas and Virginia to share memories. Nobody realized just how wide his influence had been until they saw the grieving crowd.

Among those attending were all but eight of Jim's team from Anbar. None of the eight who were missing could possibly have come. They had gone ahead of Jim and already completed their journey. Four had been killed in action. The other four had died after coming home. Jim was the fifth. He almost certainly wouldn't be the last.

Of those who remained, there were three still on active duty and staring imminent retirement in the face with a sense of dread and foreboding that surpassed their worst days downrange. The rest had already retired, left, or been forced out and were struggling in their own ways to find a path in a world that felt intensely alien. The world would never understand them. They understood each other. That's all they could hope for.

As they sat in the chapel, several were suffering from the shakes because they had chosen to come to the funeral sober and were dealing with withdrawal. They needed to be sober for this. Others had shaved and cleaned up for the first time in years. Some were unable to speak without breaking up, so they stood mute and stony. Some openly cried. All were devastated. All hoped they wouldn't need to do this again. Above all else, they all wondered if they would be next.

As the funeral procession moved to the graveside, only Jim's parents, siblings, in-laws, Maggie, K9, Amy, and members of his team remained. The pallbearers, all from Jim's team, solemnly lifted the casket from the caisson and carried it to the grave site. The Honor Guard (composed of junior Air Force members from the base nearby) ceremonially draped the coffin in a flag and the rifle team fired a series of three volleys as a final salute. The chaplain dedicated the grave, the honor guard folded the flag and presented it to Jim's mother, then everyone slowly filed past the coffin to offer a last goodbye or render a final salute. A lone airman was all that remained, standing guard over Jim's remains until the groundsmen came back to lower the casket into the ground next to Leslie and Sammie.

Jim's family all left immediately, but K9 and the rest of the team gathered just a few yards from the grave to say goodbye to each other. Who knew when they would next be together. Hopefully never. At least, not like this.

"Gomer," K9 said quietly, "do you mind?"

CW02 Turner, standing stiffly in his dress uniform, nodded slightly, and everyone circled up. Together they bowed their heads and silently repeated the words of the brief prayer: "Lord, take care of Shepherd; and please, don't let the old'un laugh at us anymore."

Epilogue

Uncle Saul died peacefully in his sleep three days after K9 and Amy's wedding. His last words were to thank his daughter Karen for taking such good care of him for so long, and to breathe a sigh of relief. He'd been waiting for this for decades.

With Doc Chelwood's help, K9 found a local therapist who he continues to see weekly. He spends time volunteering in the community and taking care of his small family and farm. Even years later he still has good days and bad, but the bad days are fewer and farther between than they once were. Within a year of his arriving in Shiprock, the bad days had gotten infrequent enough that he was able to take a job as a teacher's aide in the local high school where he still works three days a week during the school year. The kids there call him "lha-cha-eh tsoh."

Amy continues to work as a nurse in the community. She gave birth to a healthy baby boy named Jim a year after she and K9 married. 18 months later, they had a little girl they named Leslie. While she never understood why her mom had done it in the first place, Amy never regretted her mom's decision to invite two very broken men to come stay. She regularly attempts to convince K9 to start a program to bring veterans struggling with PTSD out to the farm to experience a little peace and quiet, but K9 hasn't been ready. Maybe next year.

Maggie continued to make the drive every month – first to Albuquerque, and then Grants – to try and see Ray. It took years before he would see her at all, but it has never been any better than even odds that he'll come out to the visitation area when she's there. She is a fixture in her community, and still takes meals to people who have a hard time getting out. Shortly after Amy and K9 had young Jim, Maggie retired from her job with the Indian Health Service to become a full-time grandmother and community volunteer – both are jobs she thoroughly enjoys.

Doc Chelwood retired from active duty the summer after Jim left San Antonio. He became a vocal critic of the way both the Department of Defense and the Veterans Administration were caring for victims of PTSD. In his efforts to improve the situation, he ended up playing a key role lobbying for Congressionaly mandated reform and investment in health care for wounded veterans. He was offered a high-level position at the VA, but he declined it. He'd had enough of working for the Government. Instead, he opened a very busy private practice outside Atlanta where he continues to treat veterans. Business is sadly good, with the constant supply of new patients vastly outstripping the capacity of the providers.

The team got together several more times over the following years, but the hardest was for Gomer who died at the hands of an Afghan soldier he was training. To the end, he could never quite shake off the harsh cackling that seemed to follow him everywhere he deployed. Now, unlike those few who remain, he doesn't hear it anymore.

Notes

1. SSgt: Staff Sergeant

2. CENTCOM J3: US Central Command has responsibility for operations in the middle east. The J3 is the portion of the staff responsible for current operations. Generally, when someone references "The J3" they are referring to the senior officer in charge of that staff element. The J-prefix indicates the staff is "joint."

3. DoD: Department of Defense

4. DLI: Defense Language Institute - the DoD school where military members are taught foreign languages

5. SERE: Survive, Evade, Resist, Escape

6. ROTC: Reserve Officer Training Corps - One of three officer commissioning programs where cadets attend military courses and training. ROTC training is incorporated as part of the cadet's education at colleges and universities across the nation. The other two commissioning programs are the Service Academies and Officer Training/Candidate School.

7. Reclama: Request reconsideration. Commanders can reclama deployment taskings based on local mission needs, but the practice is discouraged and infrequently exercised.

8. COP: Combat Outpost - a small forward-deployed outpost, typically supporting only a small number of military personnel.

9. CW2: Chief Warrant Officer 2 - Warrant officers serve in positions that require both the authority of a commissioned officer and the kind of technical expertise regular commissioned officers at that level would not have had the opportunity to achieve due to their generalist career development path.

10. Battle rattle: A colloquial term for the individual equipment each soldier carries into combat.

11. Plate carrier: The vest that holds ceramic armor plates and has various attachment points for adding pouches and other gear.

12. NVGs: Night Vision Goggles

13. IED: Improvised Explosive Device - any configuration of explosive weapon not designed by the military for its intended purpose. IEDs can be made from anything from artillery shells and shaped charges to piles of fertilizer and diesel fuel.

14. RPG: Rocket Propelled Grenade - a shoulder fired anti-armor weapon favored by insurgents for its low cost, low complexity, and ability to penetrate substantial armor. Often mistaken for a bazooka (the US WWII equivalent).

15. S3: The current operations division of an army staff. Similar to the J3 previously mentioned.

16. Rotator: A regularly scheduled flight used to take people in or out of country.

17. QRF: Quick Reaction Force – a combat force held on standby to respond to emerging crises.

18. AWOL: Absent Without Leave

19. RON: Remain Overnight

20. S2: Head of the brigade's intelligence division

21. Class six: Class six is a logistics designation for consumable liquids. As a result, the class six is the name given to the base liquor store.

Peter Johnson is the owner of Curious Minds Classroom and an author, educator, and poet. After 20 years of active duty service in the United States Air Force, he worked briefly in the aerospace industry before stepping away from the government to found Curious Minds Classroom. When he's not developing STEM, economics, history, or other curricula, he spends his time with his family, writing, turning wrenches, or working with his livestock. He has a PhD in Laser Physics and Image Processing, a Masters of Science in Electro-Optics, a Bachelor of Science in Electrical Engineering, and is fully aware that these degrees are useless when it comes to writing fiction.

Made in the USA
Columbia, SC
29 July 2024

39234704R00169